Praise for *Three Card Murder*

'A real puzzle box of a story! I especially loved the strident, salty, can't-live-with-can't-live-without relationship between the two sisters. More Tess and Sarah please!'
J. M. Hall

'J.L. Blackhurst brings a fresh, modern twist to the classic locked-room mystery. Three deviously clever impossible crimes propelled me to keep reading late into the night to finish *Three Card Murder*.'
Gigi Pandian

'I was gripped by this clever, intricate murder mystery.'
Louise Jensen

'A clever modern interpretation of a classic locked-room mystery, with two engaging protagonists and an ending I never saw coming. What more could you ask for in a mystery?'
Faith Martin

'Slick and sparkling, a brilliant premise executed with such panache. Twisty, tricksy and whip smart, *Three Card Murder* is huge fun and a cracking read.'
Marion Todd

'Ingenious, fun and very different from so many of the crime books out there
Ajay Chowdhury

'I loved this book! It's delicious
I turned the last page and wa
Imogen Clark

'The perfect summer holiday read. Filled with murders, twists, feuding sisters and a real heart.'
Derek Farrell

'What a joyous ride *Three Card Murder* is!'
T. Orr Munro

J.L. Blackhurst is a pseudonym for Jenny Blackhurst who was born and grew up in Shropshire, where she still lives with her husband, two boys and two beagles. She has written eight psychological thrillers including *How I Lost You*, which won a Silver Nielsen award and became a Kindle number one bestseller in the UK and a *Spiegel* Bestseller in Germany. She can solve a Rubik's Cube in three minutes.

Also by J.L. Blackhurst

Writing as Jenny Blackhurst

How I Lost You
Before I Let You In
The Foster Child
The Night She Died
The Perfect Guests
The Girl Who Left
The Hiking Trip
The Summer Girl

Three Card
MURDER

J.L. BLACKHURST

ONE PLACE. MANY STORIES

HQ
An imprint of HarperCollins*Publishers* Ltd
1 London Bridge Street
London SE1 9GF

www.harpercollins.co.uk

HarperCollins*Publishers*
Macken House, 39/40 Mayor Street Upper,
Dublin 1, D01 C9W8, Ireland

This edition 2023
4
First published in Great Britain by
HQ, an imprint of HarperCollins*Publishers* Ltd 2023

Copyright © Jenny Blackhurst 2023

Jenny Blackhurst asserts the moral right to be
identified as the author of this work.
A catalogue record for this book is
available from the British Library.

ISBN: 9780008567248

This book is produced from independently certified FSC™ paper
to ensure responsible forest management.

For more information visit: www.harpercollins.co.uk/green

This book is set in 10.7/15.5 pt. Sabon by Type-it AS, Norway

Printed and Bound in the UK using 100% Renewable Electricity at
CPI Group (UK) Ltd, Croydon, CR0 4YY

To Grandad Len,
we miss your smile and your mischief.

Prologue

*T*IN *CAN ALLEY*, the bright green sign at the entrance to Brighton Palace Pier declared. *THREE THROWS FOR £2. TRY YOUR LUCK*. The delighted shrieks of children playing on the sand below and the sweet smell of fried dough, spun sugar and salty sea air made the declaration seem like a promise – *today is your lucky day*.

Giant multi-coloured soft toys lined the top of the stall, framing the girl with the dark dreadlocks who was restacking shiny tins with a practised flick of the hand. She wore light denim daisy dukes and a red vest top emblazoned with the moniker *Ginny* in swirly lettering. Ginny's skin was tanned and smelled of coconut.

'Come on lads, how about a free practice shot?' she called, directing the full beam of her charm onto a group of three teenage boys. Polo shirts buttoned up to the top, knee-length rolled-up shorts, hair slick with gel, the lads stepped up to the challenge.

'What do I want with a giant teddy bear?' the first lad asked in a thick South London accent.

The girl leaned forwards onto her arms, the swell of her breasts exaggerated by the movement. 'You could give it to your girlfriend,' she suggested, the grin still dancing on her lips. She blew the gum in her mouth into a pink bubble then let it pop.

'I ain't got a girlfriend.'

'Boyfriend then,' she said, quick as you like. She had replaced her usual soft tones for a cheekier *Carry On* style of banter and the other two boys laughed.

'I ain't got one of those neither,' he grumbled, his cheeks colouring.

'Good-lookin' bloke like you? Must be beating them away.' She knew the patter and the boys knew it too. It was a sweltering summer afternoon at the coast and this was what they were here for, what they were all here for, the dozens of tourists milling around on the pier with their candy floss and ice creams. The authentic British seaside experience. They had money to burn, every one of them. She'd take thirty quid off this group alone, easy. She might even let the quiet one on the end win something. 'You gonna have a go then? I'll give you a practice go for free.'

The boy looked at his friends, who nodded and shoved him forwards encouragingly. Another couple of tourists stopped to watch – she would definitely let one of them win now.

She handed him three beanbags, one yellow, one red and one blue. Stood back and gestured to the cans. 'Go for it, tiger.'

He stretched out his shoulder as though limbering up for the Olympics. Then he pulled his arm back and hurled the first beanbag at the tins.

He didn't need the other two bags. The tins clattered to

the ground with a satisfying crash and the watching crowd whooped. Ginny jumped up and down, cheering and clapping.

'Woohoo!' she said, restacking. 'You made that look easy. Told you it weren't hard, if you've got the skill.'

As the boy handed over his money for another go, she noticed a young woman with dark blonde hair join the crowd at the end of the stall, head down, eyes glued to her phone, but there was no doubt she was watching. Twelve months, the woman had been away. Why was she here?

The lad hurled the beanbags again, as straight and true as the first time, but on this try only the top three tins crashed to the ground. The crowd groaned as the second bag shifted the remaining three cans along the shelf but none of them fell. Before the lad could take his final swing, the woman with the dark blonde hair looked up from her phone, took the lad's arm and whispered something in his ear. The girl behind the stall gritted her teeth.

'What did she say to you?' she demanded, her cheerful *Carry On* lilt dropping away.

The boy frowned. 'Here, swap those tins with the ones on the floor,' he said, pointing at the three left on the shelf.

The girl shook her head. 'That's not the game. Why don't you just take your last shot? You'll probably get them with this one.'

She'd lost and she knew it.

The boy shook his head. 'Swap them or I'll tell this lot what she said. Maybe I'll tell the police too.'

With a scowl, she swapped the tins for the three on the floor. The boy took aim and knocked all three tins off with his last shot. The crowd cheered and he grinned.

'I'll have that one, cheers,' he said, pointing at a giant green lion. Ginny pulled it down and handed it over, furious. He turned to the woman who had given him his lucky tip-off and, with a flourish of a bow, presented her with the lion. 'For you.'

The woman grinned and took the soft toy, raising her eyebrows at Ginny. The crowd dispersed, not entirely knowing what had just happened but knowing well enough the show was over. All except the dark blonde woman, who stood surveying the Tin Can Alley stall with her lion clasped in her arms.

'Thanks a bunch,' Ginny said, climbing over the stall to sit on a stool out front. 'I had them on the hook then. What are you doing here, anyway? You're lucky Dad's not here to see you narc on your little sister.'

The woman shrugged. 'I came to show you this.' She pulled something out of her pocket and showed it to the girl, whose face darkened.

'So the rumours are true. Why bother coming back then?'

'I wanted to be the one to tell you, but I should have guessed you'd already know. What does Dad think?'

'What do you think he thinks?' the girl said, hopping down and pulling the shutter closed. 'You've made your choice. Now we all get to live with it.' She put her hand to her eyes to shield the sun. 'Shame. We liked having you around.'

'I'm sorry, for what it's worth.'

'I know.'

The woman gestured to the closed-up Tin Can Alley. 'Seems a bit small fry for your tastes.'

'Ginny' shook her head. 'It's not even my stand. The owner was on his break and I was just having a bit of fun.' She raised her eyebrows at the giant green lion. 'So technically you've stolen that toy. *Officer.*'

4

Chapter One

The first body fell from the sky at 16.05 p.m. on Tuesday 5 February, landing seconds later at the feet of a woman waiting for the number 7 bus on Grove Hill. The woman, who gave her name to the 999 operator as Emilie Jasper, was so distraught that she spent the emergency call alternating between sobs and rapid half-sentences in French, and consequently, paramedics and police were sent in the first instance to a suicide. It was not their first at this particular row of Brighton flats, marked with the graffitied evidence of despair and drug overdose. But what was a surprise was the discovery by paramedics that the dead man's hands were bound loosely with rope and his throat so viciously slashed that it was almost sliced clean through. That was when the paramedics rapidly progressed the call to a murder, and it was put through to the spotless desk of Acting Detective Inspector Tess Fox of Sussex Major Crimes Team. Special emphasis on the *Acting*.

DI Fox was on her feet before the call ended, waving a piece of paper in the face of Jerome Morgan, her detective sergeant.

'Incident in Grove Hill, Brighton. Suspected homicide.' Tess lifted her jacket from the hook – February evenings were bitter the closer you got to the sea. She shrugged it on and twisted her long blonde ponytail into a bun, wondered if that possibly looked too harsh, and let it back down into a ponytail. Jerome, who had already decided the last hour of his shift was not going to be a productive one, hadn't moved. He was holding his phone at arm's length, then bringing it up close to his face, squinting at the screen as though trying to figure out something significantly more important than Tess's first murder as an acting DI.

'Can you ever see these hidden picture things? I couldn't see a bloody giraffe when I was a kid and I still can't see one now. Do you think that means I'm colour-blind?'

'Get. Up.' Tess prodded him in the shoulder with her pen. 'Is Oswald still in his office?'

'Gone home,' Jerome replied of their DCI. 'Janice wants a new car. He's had to go with her to stop her buying the most expensive thing on the forecourt.'

Tess circled the room, silently thanking her boss's wife as she calculated her next move. With Oswald gone, she would be the first detective on the scene, an opportunity she'd been waiting for since her temporary promotion three months ago, a chance to show that she deserved for the job to be permanent. If she called him now, he might call someone else in to cover it – someone with more experience. She made her decision.

'We'll call him from the car. When we're almost there. On your feet, Morgan.'

Jerome raised his eyebrows and pushed himself away from his desk. 'Whatever you say, boss. Time to make a coffee first?'

'No, we bloody haven't.' Tess twisted her ponytail back into a bun and headed for the door. Motivating Jerome was like trying to get a child ready for school. 'Get a move on.'

Jerome let out an exaggerated sigh. 'He's not getting any less dead if I have some caffeine.'

'Tell you what, I'll let you drive. Fast as you like. If you just get a move on.'

Jerome grinned and pretended to roll up his sleeves. 'Not one of the shit cars then.'

Tess smiled back. 'Whatever you can get your hands on. Your choice.'

Twenty minutes later, high-rise flats and Victorian houses began to spring up between the trees, Lewes retreating as every turn of the wheel took them further into urban Brighton. Tess's head had begun to pound, her stomach churning as if she was on a Palace Pier rollercoaster. Was she nervous? Bloody hell, that was a new one on her. Tess Fox did not do nerves. Although her queasiness could equally have been due to the speed they were going – driving fast was one of Jerome's favourite things in life. Tess was half convinced that he had joined the police in the first place because his driving was too shitty for a Formula One racer.

'"White male, early forties, wound to the throat believed to be fatal. The police sergeant at the scene has the building locked down and is awaiting your arrival for further instructions. Crime scene manager on route."' She read the note from Control out loud and looked for Jerome's reaction. 'Does that sound like a domestic to you?'

Jerome raised an eyebrow, keeping his eyes on the road. Which, given the speed he was driving at, was a godsend. 'Unlikely,' he said. 'When was the last time you had a domestic where the wife slits her husband's throat and shoves him from a window? Sounds more like—'

'Don't say it.' Tess pointed her biro at him. 'Don't say organized crime. I am not handing over my first case as acting DI to SOCU.'

He shrugged, and a brooding silence descended on their unmarked police car. To have her first murder turn out to be just a domestic, or – at the other end of the spectrum – serious organized crime, would be a major disappointment, if not a disaster.

'If it's not a domestic, Walker is going to be furious he missed out on it,' Jerome said.

'I know.' Tess grinned. 'Shame. It would have really helped his chances of getting the promotion.'

'I've never heard anyone sound so gleeful at the news of a gruesome murder.'

Tess cringed. 'Shit, I know. I'm a terrible person. I've just worked so hard for this, Jerome.'

'Don't sweat it,' he said, and Tess wondered if one day she might walk in and he'd have those words tattooed on his face. Jerome was the most sweatless person she knew. 'We all know that promotion is yours, boss.'

She didn't answer. If she was completely honest, she agreed with Jerome's estimate of her, but she wasn't going to tempt fate by saying it out loud. Instead she gave him a small smile. 'From your lips to the DCI's ears.' She glanced out of the window at the terraces filled with pizza places, convenience stores and gateless, gardenless houses that had probably once been beautifully rendered pure white but now looked like a row of greying, time-worn sentries.

'God, I hate this place. It's like an arthritic, ageing ballerina who can't let go of the fact that she used to be someone.'

'Nah, I love it,' Jerome disagreed, one finger tapping the wheel as he took another corner at the speed of light. 'Mum and Dad used to bring us here every weekend in the summer – my aunty had one of those houses in Hanover and I spent half my life hanging around Preston Park, drinking with my feckless cousins or giving the Punch and Judy bloke grief. Did you know that those creepy Punch and Judy dolls originated in Italy?'

'I did not know that.'

'He was called Punchinello. And the crocodile was originally the devil. Which seems a bit dark.'

'Fine to slap Judy around and drop the baby, though – funny how that made the final cut,' Tess grumbled.

Jerome was full of this kind of interesting bullshit. Tess had never met a man like him. It had been awkward working with him at first, what with him being almost offensively attractive. Dark brown skin, defined muscles visible through expensive tailored shirts, and a smile that didn't just invite you to bed but made you breakfast afterwards. Oh, and he always smelled amazing. When they'd first been introduced, Tess had no idea how she was expected to work with a man who looked like an underwear model, but luckily, he hadn't seemed to fancy her in the slightest, and once her cheeks had stopped turning the colour of postboxes every time he spoke, they had fallen into an easy friendship. As it turned out, DS Morgan was a complex ball of contradictions – a ladies' man who treated women with respect right up until the moment they began to get serious, at which point he would cut and run. He was a joker and a clown, but he could throw out the most random nuggets of nerdy general knowledge, and was always the most popular at a pub quiz. But above all, Jerome was a good copper and a loyal friend.

'Looks like we're here.' Jerome motioned up ahead where flashing blue and red reflected in every window, lighting up the street like a macabre circus show. A marked vehicle blocked the long road crammed with high rises that gave way in the distance to Victorian terraces tracing a lane to the skyline.

Tess took in the scene. Eleven-storey flats, central stairways, balconies at both ends of each floor. Twenty-two premises at the front. Were there more at the back? Armed officers guarded the entrance, but Tess spotted the officer in charge immediately. A short, muscular man with dark, close-cropped hair who was barking orders into his radio. A small crown embroidered on each shoulder marked him as a superintendent.

Teenagers in grubby tracksuits, young women with prams and the odd student clasping their A4 lever arches and rucksacks were gathered in clusters, clamouring for a look at what was going on behind the police tape. The old folks had stayed inside – February in Brighton could chill you to your bones and evenings drew in fast – but that didn't stop them standing in their windows, curtains not so much twitching but drawn aside altogether for a better view. Fortunately, the body was in a forensics tent, hidden from prying eyes.

Jerome rolled up to the police car with his window down and waved his warrant card at the PC in the driver's seat. The PC nodded and straightened up his vehicle. Jerome didn't wait for him to finish pulling over before squeezing his BMW through and pulling up behind the forensics van, not bothering to go in straight. Despite the seniority of the officer in charge, this would be their crime scene now.

Tess approached the superintendent with her warrant card held up. 'Acting DI Fox, DS Morgan.' She spoke in confident, clipped tones, checking her watch as she introduced them to indicate that they were up against the clock. It was going to be a fight against the oncoming darkness at this rate, and that was one they wouldn't win.

He reached out to shake her hand. 'Superintendent Taeko. We can't go in until the building is secure.'

Tess frowned. 'Do you think there's a chance our guy might still be inside?' People didn't often hang around after they'd thrown a man from a balcony. 'He's had plenty of chance to get away.'

'We're searching the surrounding areas. As soon as the poor bloke hit the floor, people were streaming out of the flats to get a look – it's been a right job getting everyone back where they should be.' The comment was pointed; he clearly resented that Jerome and Tess had turned up after all the hard work had been done. 'Our killer could have disappeared during any of that, obviously. The thing is, we've got a tentative ID from the building manager, so we think we know which flat he's from. This particular block had CCTV installed last year after a spate of crimes, and we've reviewed the footage from 3 p.m. to now – we haven't found anyone in that corridor or leaving the building since. We're carrying out a search of every flat. And we've secured the entrance and exit routes to the one we believe belongs to the victim.' He pointed up at a balcony on the fourth floor. 'So unless the perp climbed off the balcony after him, he's still in that building.'

The radio in his hand crackled to life. 'Go ahead,' Taeko barked.

'Sir, the corridor is secure. Flats have been searched and tenants advised to stay inside. We're ready to go in on the count of three.'

Tess pictured the corridor full of armed police, adrenaline pumping through the veins of every one of them. She held her breath, listening to the radio for any hint of what was going on inside, half wishing she was in there with them, closer to the action.

'One? Come in, ready on one?' The super's radio counted down to the forced entry.

'One, ready on one.'

'Going in, sir. Armed police! Open up!'

A pause. Tess looked up at the balcony the super had pointed to, scanning for any signs of life. Seconds later, an ear-splitting crash signalled armed police storming the flat. Someone screamed. Tess looked at the super, unable to tell if the scream came from inside the flat or from one of the women hanging over the balcony above. They watched the radio, jumping as voices blared from it again.

'We're in, repeat, boss, we're in. No gunfire, no casualties.'

The super punched the air. 'Have you got him?'

Silence. White noise, then more silence through the radio. Tess moved instinctively closer to the radio, waiting. Was their suspect under arrest?

The radio sprang to life again.

'Negative, sir. The flat is empty.'

Tess swore. She rounded on the superintendent. 'I thought you said your team had checked the CCTV?'

The superintendent looked as confused as she felt.

'They have. I told you, no one walked down that corridor after 3 p.m.'

Tess looked up at the balcony, where an armed officer was visible in the doorway. The other tenants in the building were now shouting out of their flats to the police, some demanding to be told what was going on, others demanding to be let out. Dusk was closing in now and she knew that every minute that passed she was in danger of losing this investigation.

'That's impossible. You must have the wrong flat. We're going to have to search them all again.'

By 16.59, official sunset on an already overcast and drizzly February evening, DI Tess Fox was pushing through the opening of the crime scene tent, where the victim was still sprawled on the small stretch of grass at the foot of the block of flats. The armed response team had concluded that Flat 40, Mortonhurst, was well and truly empty, and were working to secure the rest of the building. Tess took a deep breath as she saw that Kay Langley was the on-call medical examiner. *Great.*

Kay Langley, a small woman with short, spiky grey hair and piercing blue eyes, pulled her mask down and held up her hand in greeting. Kay and her partner, Beth, had been friends with Tess's ex-fiancé growing up, and the four of them had shared an easy friendship right up until the moment Tess had got cold feet and called off their engagement. Things had been awkward between them ever since, to say the least. Tess remembered the last time they had all hung out together, wrestling with the pull-out sofa with Beth because all four of them had stayed up until three in the morning discussing the merits of criminal profiling – Tess being on the side of the profilers, Kay and Chris staunchly against. Beth, a photographer, hadn't given a toss either way and had proved a brilliant referee. Tess got the feeling she was well versed in Kay's passionate outbursts and knew how to manage her perfectly. Truth be told, she missed Kay and Beth's friendship almost as much as she missed Chris. And she did miss Chris. He might not have been the man she wanted to marry, but he was a good man, a good friend. Tess had wondered more than once since the break-up if she'd made the wrong decision. If being with the wrong man was better than being alone. She wasn't about to let thoughts like that get in her way today though. She was unstoppable. She was a force to be reckoned with. She was made for this job.

'Tess, great to see you again,' Kay said, walking over and waving a gloved hand. 'I won't hug you for obvious reasons.'

To anyone watching, this was a perfectly friendly exchange between colleagues. To Tess, it was the cringiest greeting of her life. She much preferred loud, sweary Kay, the one who would have put her instantly at ease, despite the presence of the dead man between them.

'Good to see you too.' Tess cleared her throat. 'Cause of death?' she asked, knowing what the reply would be.

Spotlights illuminated the corpse making a macabre centre-piece. He was spreadeagled on the ground, his neck contorted at an unnatural angle, blood staining his chest and the pavement below. One knee was turned outwards, the other pointing in. The thick black wound on his throat twisted upwards in a demonic smile.

'This isn't a post-mortem, DI Fox,' Kay admonished, as

14

Tess knew she would. 'There are two obvious places we will start. The throat wound would have killed him, but so would the impact – I'll need to take a closer look at the other injuries. It's going to be near impossible to tell which was the definitive cause. There's a lot of blood here, that much I can tell you. I'm not going to be able to bag his head – the blood is too fresh.'

'Which tells me what?'

'Just that the injuries occurred almost simultaneously.' She mimed a thumb across her throat and then a shove as if from a cliff.

Tess bit her lip. 'Why bother throwing him off a balcony if he's going to die from the throat injury anyway?'

Kay stayed silent, another indication that they were no longer friends. Once upon a time, she'd have speculated with her. Tess suddenly felt more alone than she had since she had called off her engagement. Her friends had been his friends, her colleagues had been his colleagues. She had no family other than her mother, with whom her relationship could only be described as strained.

Breaking the silence, Kay said, 'I've bagged the rope that was around his wrists. It wasn't tied tightly, just wrapped. Seems like he could have got out of it if he'd tried. Might have been done just before he was pushed so he didn't have time.'

'Anything else? Any identifying marks?'

'Just this tattoo,' Kay replied. She lifted the man's stiffened arm and Tess was confronted with a close-up view of the marks on his pale wrist. Later, Acting DI Tess Fox would pinpoint this as the exact moment that her first big case turned into her personal living nightmare.

Chapter Two

Tess leaned against the wall behind the flats and tried not to be sick. She was grateful for the rough brick snagging against her back, the coldness helping to anchor her to her senses. She had to keep it together, although God only knew how she was going to do that – from the moment she'd seen the tattoo on the wrist of the victim, she'd felt as though she was underwater, everything slower and duller. She wasn't even sure now how she'd left things with Kay – a vague memory of stumbling out of the tent and trying not to fall to her knees in front of the dozens of police officers. Somehow, she had managed to direct them to various tasks without screaming, breaking down or running away, instructing them to meet back at her car in an hour. Now that hour was up, and she was having trouble concentrating on anything. Her vision went in and out of focus, heat flooding her face.

It might not even be him, Tess, she tried to tell herself. *You don't know anything for certain yet. Don't fuck this up.* She leaned forwards, hands on her knees for support, and took a few steadying breaths, closed her eyes and counted slowly down from ten. When she got to one, she would open her eyes and that would be it. She would be back at the scene, no feelings allowed. She just needed to get past this part without any questions asked, then she could go somewhere to gather her thoughts properly.

Three . . . two . . . one. Exhale.

She walked over to where her team was gathered around her car, awaiting further instructions. She sat against the bonnet and gestured for everyone to come closer. 'Everyone okay?'

Jerome gave her a look that clearly said, *Are* you *okay?* She gave him the smallest of nods and hoped it looked convincing. Perhaps she could pass her flushed face and her shaking hands off as first-case-in-charge nerves. It wasn't ideal to have a briefing outdoors, in the dark, at a crime scene, but it seemed counter-intuitive to go back to the station when she needed to be here when the flat was opened. They greeted her with murmurs of *yeah* and *bloody brilliant*, leaving her in no doubt that everyone was annoyed at being yanked away from *Coronation Street* and their children's bedtimes, knowing that Brighton Police Station would now be their home from home until this murder was solved, or at least until they could reassure the public that they weren't in any danger. Tess glanced at her watch – 7.30 p.m. – and held up a hand, relieved to see it had stopped shaking.

'Yeah, okay, I know this isn't how we wanted to spend our evening but try to remember that he didn't want to spend his like this either.' She avoided looking at the crime scene tent, trying to forget what, or who, was inside. Most of the collected group had the good grace to look shame-faced.

Armed Response were still doing a thorough job of securing the scene, searching each and every flat in the building before allowing officers or forensics in. Tess was desperate to get a look inside, even more so now that she'd seen the body. Before, she'd just wanted to solve her first homicide as quickly and neatly as possible. Now she needed to know what else she might find inside that flat, and if any of it would connect her to the victim.

She shivered and instinctively pulled her wrists up into the sleeves of her coat.

In front of her were at least twenty officers; most she recognized as DCs from the Surrey and Sussex MCT. These would be her eyes and ears, and she was glad to see that DS Fahra Nasir was at the front of the group, standing with Jerome. She noticed how nicely turned-out Fahra looked, well after her shift had ended. Her long, dark hair was tied back into a sleek ponytail and her make-up was still perfect. She wore designer black-rimmed glasses that made her look quirky, and about sixteen years old. In fact, Fahra's youthful looks often worked in the team's favour. People underestimated her, and that was a mistake you should never make. She was sharp as a tack and had a higher IQ than half the department put together. She had known Chris, as had everyone on the MCT, but much like Jerome, Fahra had never seemed particularly close to him. A couple of the DCs had joined after he'd gone, which only left a handful of people in front of her who probably hated her on sight. It wasn't the best odds but it could have been worse. DI Walker could have been standing here too.

'I appreciate that you're all pulling overtime now, so I'll make it quick.' Her voice didn't even tremble. She could get through this. She nodded to a young-looking Brighton PC at the front of the group. Given his age, and the fact that he'd had to scrape a human off the pavement a few hours prior, he looked impressively calm and collected, far more so than she felt. 'I gather you were first on the scene?'

He pushed back his short ginger hair and nodded, yes. 'I'm PC Campbell Heath. I responded to a call from Control saying there had been a suicide and an ambulance was on its way. When we got here, we moved the crowds back and made a route for the ambulance. People were pushing and shoving to get a look.' He shook his head sadly. 'It never fails to surprise me how low people will go. I had them park the ambulance across to cut off the view and we've moved them back behind the car three times.'

'Who called it in?'

Heath spoke. 'French woman, Emilie Jasper. Speaks really good English, although she was so upset that she tried to give half her statement in French. On her way for an interview as a childminder. She was released about half an hour ago, I have her full statement and contact details. She was a bit of a mess.'

'I'm not surprised. What happened when you got here?'

Heath looked at the car, where his partner was sitting scrolling through his phone. He sighed. 'The paramedic took one look and said that the man was definitely dead, and that he probably hadn't been killed by the fall because his throat was cut. I called Control and asked them to get you guys down here as soon as, and asked for my super to take charge of the scene until you arrived.'

Tess looked at her watch, mentally spinning back through

the chain of calls that led them to now. 'Quick work, well done. Campbell, wasn't it?'

Campbell nodded.

'You handled it well, thank you. You want some work with MCT?'

Campbell nodded, looking pleased.

'I'll see if I can get you put on our team. Jerome, tell us what you found out about victim ID.'

Jerome turned to face the group. 'According to the manager of the building, the victim was Shaun Mitchell, forty-one-year-old white male, living alone. I've got a copy of his rental application, and his place of work is listed as a garage in the city centre. His references were given by one Luca Mancini, who owns the place. I've got the number for it here.'

Tess tried not to let anything show on her face as she heard the victim's name. Shaun Mitchell. *So it was definitely him*. She felt the blood rush to her head, flooding her with momentary dizziness. *Don't pass out, don't pass out*. Someone nudged her, holding out a bottle of water. Tess looked up into the dark brown eyes of Fahra, who smiled encouragingly. She took the bottle, trying to express exactly how grateful she was in that moment.

'Thank you,' she said, unscrewing the top and taking a sip. It wasn't exactly chilled but it was cold enough to help her recover sufficiently to lean over and look at the sticky note Jerome was holding up and jot down the name and number. She had to pull herself together. If Fahra had noticed how rattled she was, then the others might too – although she suspected Fahra was more astute than everyone here put together. Still, the last thing she needed was questions. 'Okay. Find out if our guy still worked there, and if so when he last worked; if he has a girlfriend, or boyfriend. Get me everything you can about his usual movements but especially last night and today. Next?'

'I spoke to the tenants of the four flats on Mitchell's floor,' Fahra offered. 'We've got PCs on the rest of the floors taking statements.'

'What did his neighbours say?'

'They said he wasn't a good sort. All four of them said they thought he was a drug dealer. One had reported him to the police several times but nothing was done. One of them said that they thought he'd moved out because they hadn't seen him for weeks, then yesterday, about 5 p.m., they heard banging in his flat.'

'Like fighting?'

'No.' Fahra shook her head and her ponytail bobbed. 'Like hammering. As if someone was fixing something. The person I spoke to said he thought it meant Mitchell might be moving out, because he'd never done any improvements in the whole time he'd been there.'

'Okay, anything else?'

'Yeah, something big.' Fahra turned over her immaculate-looking notes. 'Next door said they heard banging at about ten to four today, not hammering but like banging on the door, really aggressively, as if someone was trying to get in. They heard men shouting.'

'Men? Plural?' Tess began to feel relief calm her. If some-one had seen a group of men getting into Shaun Mitchell's flat, there was no way this murder would be connected to her. A simple case of drug dealer meets sticky end.

'Yeah, but when they looked out of the door a few minutes

later, there was no one there. They can't be sure it was coming from Shaun's flat – the building is old and draughty and you can hear all sorts, apparently. They said it could as easily have been from downstairs.'

'Okay, well, CCTV should confirm,' Tess said. For the first time in over an hour she felt as though her feet were on stable ground. If anything, this could end up being good for her. Shaun Mitchell being dead was no bad thing. 'Great work, Fahra. If this does turn out to be drugs-related, at least the general public will feel better. And if Mitchell is a small-time dealer, that should keep organized crime off our back too, so fingers crossed.'

'Oh.' Fahra held up a hand again. 'The woman across from him said his sister visited last week so we know he has family – we just need to find a way to trace them. No next of kin on his application form.'

'Okay, thanks.' Tess became aware of a small buzz going around the team, a couple of them glancing between themselves. 'What?' she snapped. 'Come on, spit it out.' What did they know?

'Is it true that we don't know how the killer got out?' The officer looked embarrassed, but everyone was waiting for an answer. 'That he's not on any CCTV?'

Tess sighed, stupidly relieved that it wasn't a question about the victim's identity or past. 'We don't know how he got out *yet*. But look, I don't want this going any further for as long as I can help it. The CCTV has been sent to the tech team for review in case there was some sort of editing – although we know that's a movie trick, not a real-life thing. For now, our job is the *who*, not the *how*. I don't need to remind you how crucial the next couple of hours are. Our main job is to find out as much about the victim as possible, and why someone would cut his throat before throwing him off a balcony.' Tess spoke with confidence. No one watching from the outside would know how close she had been to crumbling. 'Someone get me a list of every CCTV camera in the surrounding area.' A PC held up his hand and Tess pointed at him. 'Brilliant, thanks. Fahra, I want you to find out the route our perpetrator used to get away – ask about every car in the area and talk to everyone on the ground to see if they saw anyone moving at speed straight after the guy landed. Preferably covered in blood, waving a knife in the air. CCTV images if you can. When we get back to the station, I'm putting you on handling the case log, so make a note for someone to look into the rope that was around his wrists, where it was from, what it was cut with. Jerome, can you find out what the response team are up to? I want to get in that flat.'

As if by magic, the superintendent strode over to them and gestured to the flat. 'My team have given the all-clear. You can take your forensics up now.'

Tess took a deep breath that to everyone else looked like steeling herself for the job. She looked at Jerome and raised her eyebrows. 'Fast work. I didn't even see you move. Come on, you can come in with me.'

Chapter Three

The smell hit her before she was even through the door.

'Jesus.' Tess gagged and stepped back. 'I thought the flat was empty? Have you checked for another body?'

'No second body,' one of the forensic officers confirmed. 'It seems like whoever lived here wasn't big on cleaning.'

That was a contender for understatement of the year. The flat was small and dark, but as her eyes adjusted to the lack of light, Tess could see where the smells originated from. Filth-encrusted bowls were stacked in a sink filled with brown water in a kitchenette to her left. The stench of rotten food emanated from an overflowing bin in the corner. Half-empty pizza boxes and Pot Noodle cartons were littered around like pot plants. Cans of lager topped with extinguished cigarettes added to the decades-old-smoke scent, and the walls were stained yellow. The corners of the wallpaper were peeling away and damp patches all but obliterated any pattern there might once have been. Was this how Shaun Mitchell had been living all these years? Tess couldn't help but think that this squalor, and his murder, were a fitting end for the nasty little man. She had to stay impartial and concentrate on justice, whoever the victim was, but it gave her a small sense of satisfaction. Two forensic officers were already inside, one taking samples and the other photographs. With Taeko, Tess and Jerome, it was going to be a squeeze.

Tess stepped over the threshold and the first thing she noticed was splintered wood hammered into the back of the door frame.

'Wait, he boarded up the door?' she asked.

'That must have been the hammering his neighbour heard the day before,' Jerome remarked.

'But then how did the men his other neighbour heard get in?'

'Perhaps they didn't.' Jerome ran a gloved finger across the splintered wood. 'Perhaps it wasn't them who killed him.'

'It has to be,' Tess murmured. Her life depended on this being a drug-related crime.

'There was a CCTV outage the night before,' Superintendent Taeko said, appearing in the ruined doorway. 'Around 4.30 p.m. I'd guess that his killer got in then, just before Mitchell started boarding the place up, from what the witness said. It looks like he boarded them in together, which means it was someone he thought he could trust.'

'You mean two people could stand the smell long enough to stay in here?' Tess wrinkled up her nose.

'Maybe you're looking for a killer without a sense of smell,' the technician commented. 'Other than that, it's pretty clean. For an exposed internal jugular, that is. It's clear the victim was living like a pig, and you've got the wreck caused by ten police officers busting open the door and storming through the place like it's a train station, obviously.' Taeko bristled but didn't comment. 'When I heard your victim had had his throat cut, I was expecting a whole lot more blood.'

'So was I,' Tess conceded. She was about to check the bedroom when something over the technician's shoulder caught her eye. A leaflet was pinned to the wall above the desk, standing out by virtue of the fact that the rest of the wall was bare, and because it was adorned with a lurid pink logo, a logo she would have recognized anywhere. And it was pinned there by a dart.

Just when she had been stupid enough to hope that the direction of the case would take her away from the Three Flamingos and that night fifteen years ago.

'Boss?'

'Sorry, what?' Her attention snapped back to Jerome, who was giving her a concerned look.

'I *said* the killer might have bought their own tarps and taken them away with them,' Jerome repeated.

'Sorry.' Tess shook her head. 'I was distracted.' And now she was wondering how she could get that piece of paper off the wall before the CSM decided to admit it into evidence. The fact that it would be in the crime scene photographs was bad enough, but she was still running this investigation and it was still within her control, for now. 'It's a possibility, I suppose,' she replied to Jerome. 'We took almost an hour to secure the building, that's enough time to clean up.'

'Except, if they were here all that time cleaning up, how did they get out?' Taeko asked.

'Once they'd made it past the CCTV – and no, I don't know how they did that – it would have been easy to slip into another flat, or into the crowd of people watching.'

'And board up the door behind them?' Jerome said quietly.

'Shit,' was the only concession Tess would make that he was right.

'There were four wraps of cocaine in the cupboard under what I think is supposed to be a sink,' the tech interrupted. 'Not that you can be sure in this place. LSD on the coffee table. Some other tablets in the bedroom, unidentified.'

'As expected,' Tess said.

'Nothing really unusual in the bedroom. All the clothes look like they've been pulled from the wardrobe and thrown across the room, but it's unclear if that's of importance or just this guy being untidy. We've fingerprinted everything in case the killer was looking for the drugs, but if they were, they missed the pretty obvious stash in the kitchen.'

'They could have been removing evidence,' Tess said. 'If it were a woman who had been staying with him, maybe she was making sure none of her clothes were in the bedroom.'

'Possibly,' said the tech. 'Maybe he was . . .' – he mimicked holding a throat wound closed – 'looking for something to stem the bleeding. Take a look in the surrounding areas for blood-soaked clothing that might have been dumped in a bin or a skip. Oh, and look at this.'

He handed her a camera. On the screen was a photo of a small black waste-paper bin. Tess glanced around, spotting the bin underneath a desk in the corner of the room. 'Is it that bin there? Where's the writing from the photo gone?'

'It only shows up under the luminal. Here.' The tech pulled his light from the black bag at his feet and handed it to her. 'Run that over the bin.'

Tess crossed the room and crouched down on the disgusting, threadbare carpet, not wanting her knee to actually make contact with the floor. She flicked on the light and shone it over the bin. 'C? And an A? Is it in blood? Whatever it was, it isn't there now.'

The tech shrugged. 'Won't know until the swabs come back. But CA was what we came up with too. Mean anything to you?'

Callum.

She was overthinking it. CA could mean anything. It didn't mean this was connected to Callum Rodgers. And even if it was – it could have been Callum who killed him. Fifteen years ago, they had been thick as thieves, but they were both volatile human beings. 'Vic's name is Shaun Mitchell,' she said, after realizing she'd paused for too long. 'If he was trying to leave a message, he might have written the initials of the killer . . . ?'

'If you were going to do that, would you do it on a bin under a desk? And why not write the full name?'

'I thought you were supposed to give me answers, not more questions.'

Another shrug. 'Answers are your job. Evidence is mine. Good luck. I'll call you when we have the results.'

The first responders had searched the entire flat, but Tess checked again for any space big enough to hide in. The wardrobe, under the bed, the kitchen cupboards; even the electricity box, which would barely fit a baby inside it.

'It's no use,' Jerome complained, watching her trying to yank off the bath panel. 'You know there was a guy on the door the whole time once we arrived. There's no way someone could have got out after they broke down the door.'

'Well, he got out at some point, unless you're suggesting he's still in here?' Tess gave a grunt as the bath panel came away, sending her flying backwards. The space under the bath was empty, nothing but pipes and cobwebs.

'Are you going to take up the floorboards too?'

'If I have to. What about that?' She pointed at an air vent above the front door. 'Could someone get through that?'

Jerome raised his eyebrows and looked her up and down. 'Not even your skinny ass could fit through there. If the victim had been shot, it could have been done through the vent, but the idea of a maniac waving a knife on a pole and managing to cut our victim's throat then poke him off the balcony with it . . .'

'Point made. What's your big idea then?'

'Okay, so what about this . . .' Jerome walked towards the door. 'There's a knock at the door. Our guy opens it and is immediately met by our assailant, CA someone or other, who reaches forwards.' He mimed a swooshing motion with his fist. 'Cuts his throat. Our guy manages to slam the door on him and lock it, but he needs help, right? So he goes to the balcony and opens it up, hoping to maybe climb out onto one of the other balconies, but it's getting dark and he's dying, so he slips, falls over' – Jerome whirled his arms, miming the somersault of a body falling – 'and splat.'

Tess raised her eyebrows. 'But first using the blood to write his killer's initials on the bin, cleaning it up and boarding the door shut?'

'Fuck.' Jerome grinned. 'Don't forget the CCTV. It's not directly on the door but it doesn't show anyone in the corridor. So the only way in and out is the balcony.'

Tess wandered over to where the French doors were obscured by long, grubby curtains. She pushed them aside to reveal the partially open glass door. The balcony outside was as dirty as the inside but there was no blood. Tess pointed this out. 'If his throat was slit, why isn't there more blood?'

'Like we said before, the guy could have cleaned most of it up before he left,' Jerome said.

Tess raised her eyebrows. 'Does this place look like it's been cleaned to you? At all? Ever? Even if someone was only cleaning up blood, they couldn't help but accidentally clean up some of the filth with it.'

'Touché.' Jerome nodded. 'But until we know time of death, we don't have any idea what time our victim had his throat cut. It could have been an hour before he shoved him off the balcony – he could have let him bleed out in the bath, then when he was done wrapped him in a sheet, bleached the bath, carried Mitchell over to the balcony and slid him off. Ta da.'

'And then disappeared into thin air,' Tess murmured, remembering what Kay had said about the amount of blood still on the victim. His heart had still been pumping long enough after hitting the floor to bleed all over himself. And the SOCOs had luminol'd everywhere and not turned up any evidence of a clean-up. Slit throats weren't clean and easy. They were horrible and messy. Still, his throat could have been cut while leaning over the balcony – it was possible to do it without getting blood all over the flat, just tricky. But why throw someone off a balcony if you've already cut their throat? Their victim's death was pretty much guaranteed – there really wasn't any need for a grand finale.

'He wanted him found quickly,' she said to herself. Jerome was looking over the balcony and onto next door's. They were little more than six foot long and three foot wide, hardly enough room for some plant pots, but the next-door flat was technically reachable via a small ledge.

'Why?' he asked.

'I don't know, but it's the only reason for the extra flourish. Otherwise why not just leave him to bleed out in here? If he knew the victim, he knew that he didn't have visitors and likely worked odd shifts somewhere they were used to employees not turning up. By the time someone noticed him missing and reported it to us, it could have been a week.'

'So?'

Tess looked around. 'I don't know. But he wanted this guy found, otherwise he'd leave him to bleed out up here. He wanted us here immediately.'

'Okay, so our killer climbed over the balcony himself and got out through one of the other flats. It's the only way. Which of us is going to try climbing onto next-door's balcony?' Jerome asked.

'You'd have to be an idiot to do that this high up. So that would be you, I guess,' Tess said. 'Seriously – that's not how he got away. If a body drops from the sky, what's the first thing you do?'

'Look up?'

'Exactly. Don't you think that the minute Mitchell landed at their feet, people weren't going to look up to see where he'd jumped from? And the first thing they'd see up there would be our killer, swinging across the balcony like Tarzan. No, he must have moved pretty quickly to get off the balcony, but it's doable if you just take a couple of steps backwards. It's not doable sideways four floors up. He'd have been spotted.'

Jerome sighed. 'So he didn't go over the balcony, he didn't

go out the front door and he didn't hide in here – unless he managed to sneak past the police officer on the front door, who we are assuming is competent enough to notice someone covered in blood strolling past him and tipping his balaclava. Where does that leave us?'

'Fucksake,' Tess muttered, slamming her hand against the wall. 'It leaves us with a boarded-up door and a disappearing killer.'

Chapter Four

Redesigned in 2018 to look like local government had mated a spaceship with a TARDIS, Brighton Police Station was a sleek grey and blue building with huge white, open-plan offices, and it would be Tess's home for the foreseeable future. It was clean, modern, and twice as spacious as it used to be, yet the Major Incident Room still smelled of coffee and despair. The top half of one wall was entirely glass, and every time she saw it, Tess imagined walking in there to find that everyone was naked from the top down. The far wall was dominated by a huge whiteboard. Today, it bore a photograph of a dead man on a steel gurney, a livid gash arcing across his windpipe. The name Shaun Mitchell was written over the top in black marker, and underneath was a list of everything they knew about their victim, what they had confirmed on the left and unconfirmed on the right. The unconfirmed list looked like this:

Victim: Shaun Mitchell
Worked at Mancini's Garage

Early 40s
Lived alone
Drug connections

On the *confirmed* list, someone, likely Jerome, had helpfully scrawled *victim definitely dead*. Pinned to the board was a floor plan of the flat, with arrows indicating all routes in and out.

When Tess walked in, her team were already gathered around the conference table in the middle of the room, cups of coffee and pastries dotted between pieces of paper and pocket-books, and their trousers definitely on. Jerome was sitting on a corner of the table, leaning over Fahra, reading something she'd written. Two DCs were watching something so intently on a mobile phone that Tess was fairly certain it involved breasts or a football. And at the end of the table sat her rival for the current promotion on offer, Acting DI Geoff Walker, the extremely thin case file unopened before him. *Fucksake*.

'What are you doing here?' Tess asked with a weary sigh. The leaflet she had managed to slip from an evidence bag into her briefcase was weighing heavily on her mind. Taking something from a crime scene, even something as insignificant as what looked like junk mail and a dart – her career wouldn't survive that. Why had she done something so stupid, anyway? No one would know what the flyer for the Three Flamingos meant, or how it related to her. She hadn't been thinking. She had panicked, and she had to put a stop to that now, regain control. Having Walker breathing down her neck wasn't going to help.

Geoff Walker leaned back in his chair and put his hands up, his face a picture of innocence. An incredibly punchable face, thought Tess, and a satisfyingly receding hairline. He was also, in her opinion, an utter arsehole. Worse, she was certain the rest of the Major Crime Team considered him a total gas. He had thought very highly of her ex-fiancé, taking Chris's ability to be nice to absolutely anyone for a genuine connection. With middle age now firmly in his rear-view mirror, Walker still saw himself as 'one of the lads', and Chris only served to validate that feeling. A distinct paunch strained against his shirt, mocking his claim that he was in the gym four times a week, and Tess was sure his hair was a Just4Men job.

'What kind of a greeting is that?' he asked in faux innocence. 'Not going to ask how my course went then?'

'Another equality and diversity refresher, was it?' Tess replied.

Geoff clutched his heart in mock shock while she caught Jerome hiding a smirk.

'I was at the COP actually, discussing my DI qualifications.'

Tess nodded absently. Usually she'd be asking herself who he was talking to at the College of Policing, whether she should be doing her share of networking – for networking in Walker's case, read arse-licking – but she had bigger things to worry about at the moment, and they consisted of finding out who killed Shaun Mitchell and, more importantly, if his death had been a total coincidence or some kind of message. A locked room, a disappearing killer, a face from her past – there could only be one person behind this. Tess prayed she was wrong.

'That doesn't explain why you're in my incident room,' Tess said, determined not to give him the reaction he was looking for. 'Get lost on the way to the canteen?'

'Afraid DCI Oswald has sent me to babysit?' Walker smirked. 'I'm just here because I'm interested. The invisible man cuts someone's throat and escapes through the wall – well, beats any case I've had. Thought I'd see what you've got.'

Tess glared her way over the room, wondering how word of the impossible escape had made its way around Sussex already. Unfair though, to blame her team. There were countless others at the scene: paramedics, the first response team, forensics. Any of them could have been flapping their gums with Walker and the rest of the MCT. Of course, DCI Oswald had access to all the details too. He'd probably already had a cosy chat in the pub about it with Walker.

'You don't have a problem with me being here, do you?' Geoff asked. He knew she had no official reason not to want him there. He wasn't her superior – they were on the same team. No reason whatsoever he shouldn't sit in on the briefing. Except that this case was complicated enough without having Walker watching over her shoulder.

'Of course not,' Tess lied. She raised her voice. 'Right, can we get this started please?'

The rest of the faces in the room turned to look at her as if they hadn't been listening to every word that had passed between her and her rival.

'Right, who wants to kick us off? Fahra?'

Fahra picked up a sheet of notes. Tess knew she'd made the right decision to put Fahra in charge of the case file – she was the most organized person Tess had ever met – more so even than Tess herself. 'Door to door was a complete bust. Literally no one saw anything. And that's not to say they weren't around, because they were. Woman opposite was in her front garden fixing a tyre on her bike. She didn't hear any kind of commotion on a balcony or see anyone leaving the flats in a hurry. She heard a crash and a woman scream – that was when the body hit the ground. Nothing else suspicious before or immediately after.'

'I rang Mancini's Garage,' Jerome offered. 'And they have never heard of a Shaun Mitchell, and the owner, Luca Mancini has been dead ten years, his son runs the place now. The references were faked.'

'Right, so Shaun Mitchell was likely unemployed and yet presumably still paying his rent.' Tess let out a breath. 'Anyone got any good news?'

'We got the list of CCTV cameras you asked for.'

'Brilliant.'

Jerome sucked his teeth.

'What?' Tess groaned, keenly aware of Walker, who couldn't hide the gleeful look on his face.

'Well, we marked them all on this map,' he said, sliding the map across the table towards her. 'And this one here' – he pointed to a red dot – 'looks directly at the doors of the flat.'

'And that's a bad thing because?'

'Because I've already seen the footage for the time of the murder. No one—'

'Wait, let me guess. No one goes in or out of that building?'

'Well, yeah. Sorry, boss. I mean, not no one, there are a couple of teenagers and a woman with a toddler, but I'm pretty sure that's not who we're looking for. We don't know how long our guy was in there, so I've asked them to put it all on disc and send us the previous twenty-four hours, but . . .'

'But we know they weren't in there when we turned up,' Tess finished. 'Which means they found another way out of that building. Which is fine, because they could live in the building and just have gone back to their own flat, except Shaun boarded up his door from the inside and CCTV of that corridor doesn't show anyone leaving either.'

'About that,' Fahra said. 'Tech called – that footage hasn't been tampered with. They mentioned the outage from the previous day though, and confirmed it was about thirty minutes. Long enough for someone to get inside without the cameras getting them. But for that to be our suspect, it would mean them engineering the outage and staying in the flat for twenty-four hours before killing the victim.'

'Which is unlikely, unless we're looking at a domestic situation after all. A partner. We don't have any confirmation of that yet?'

One of the DCs held up a hand. 'I pulled his previous records. Drugs, antisocial behaviour, a bit of violence years back but none recently. The complaint about the banging is linked to his address but potentially two others as well – the complainant couldn't be sure which. His next of kin was listed as his mum but she died in 2017. I've got a list of known associates to contact but no girlfriend that we know of.'

Tess wondered if Callum Rodgers would be on that list, and if she'd have to see him face to face after all these years. Not that she'd have to worry about him recognizing her. Callum Rodgers never saw Tess that night. He had been far too busy dealing with Sarah.

Sarah. Somebody else who would want Shaun Mitchell dead, and Callum Rodgers too. Tess knew she was going to have to speak to her before she came across any other surprises. But after last night, Sarah Jacobs was the last person she wanted to see.

'Fox, a word?'

Actually, here was the last person she wanted to see right now. Detective Chief Inspector Oswald.

Jerome froze. His back was to the door of the office that had just opened, so their boss didn't see his mouth twist in an 'oh shit' gesture, but Tess did. It wasn't her paranoia then; Oswald sounded Pissed Off. Oswald was okay most of the time, if not a little old school. Although when he'd had a row with his wife, Janice, the whole office knew about it, and stayed out of his way. Even Walker looked uncomfortable at the tone in his DCI's voice.

Tess crossed the corridor, quickly leaving the rest of the team behind her.

'Shut the door,' Oswald gestured to the door, then stopped suddenly and looked down at Tess. He was a good foot taller than her, with thick dark brown hair and deep brown eyes. He wasn't super-hot like Jerome was, but he was attractive. He was in his late forties and always looked and smelled expensive and spoke with an RP accent. 'Unless you don't feel comfortable shutting the door? Would you care for a representative present?'

'Er, no, sir, I think I'm okay, thanks,' Tess said. 'Is everything okay?'

'I don't like it here, Fox. I like my office, where everything is where I put it and no one leaves these bloody things on my desk.' He ran a hand through his dark hair and shoved a brightly coloured leaflet at her with the words, *Sexual harassment in the workplace: how to recognize it; how to deal with it; how to avoid doing it* emblazoned across the front in bold yellow lettering. 'Apparently in *Brighton* I have to be more sensitive to your needs, and shit. So: is there anything you need?'

'No, sir, I'm all right for now.' Tess didn't bother suppressing her smile this time. So that was what had pissed him off. She didn't think she'd ever seen her boss so stressed. Clearly the thought of having to be sensitive to any woman's needs other than his wife's or Superintendent Tranter's was too much.

'Good, because I've got a meeting with Tranter in twenty minutes and she's going to want to know why we don't have a suspect in custody.'

'It's very early days, sir,' Tess said. 'But we feel like our door-to-doors will probably end up yielding the results we need.'

'Good.' Oswald nodded, happy to accept what she'd said to mean that they practically had a suspect in custody. 'I fought for you to get this chance, Tess. That's why you're acting DI. I don't have to tell you how much is riding on this in terms of permanent promotion.'

'I know, sir. I won't let you down.' Tess cringed. *I won't let you down? Jesus, Tess, it's not* Saving Private Ryan.

Oswald raised his eyebrows. 'Insert your own piss-take, Fox. I'm busy and trying to be more politically correct. Go on, we're done.'

'Thank you, sir.'

I don't have to tell you how much is riding on this in terms of permanent promotion. Tess couldn't believe that just a few short hours ago, her chances of promotion had been the only thing on her mind. What she couldn't tell DCI Oswald was that she had much more riding on this case now. If she didn't catch Shaun Mitchell's killer, her entire life was at stake. There was only one person who would know what Shaun Mitchell's death meant to her, someone she hadn't seen in fourteen years, since that day on the Palace Pier, when her sister had walked away, leaving her clutching a giant green lion. *Sarah.* Like it or not, she was going to have to track down the best conwoman in Brighton.

Chapter Five

Sarah Jacobs's dark eyes were fixed on the corner of North Street as she waited for her mark to appear. She'd been watching him for two weeks now and he was nearly ten minutes later than usual. Today's mark was Lars Friedman, one of three men running a multi-level marketing scam, the kind of thing where the only people who got rich were the ones at the top. And certainly not the elderly women Friedman and his associates were targeting. Well, this 'elderly woman' was about to take the sting out of his tail.

A seagull screamed overhead and Sarah threw another surreptitious glance at the clock opposite. The street was relatively quiet today, grey and slightly drizzly. Brighton was yet to be overrun by tourists in brightly coloured T-shirts taking photos of the graffiti murals that adorned the terraces. Nothing but a steady stream of workers and pushchair-wielding mums trickled past as she lurked in the shop doorway. No one looked her way. She was an old woman resting on her walking stick, and that rendered her invisible to most of the population. She blew a strand of long grey hair from her eyes and almost sighed in relief when she saw him round the corner. It was time.

She didn't need to see his face to know it was him. The sunlight glinting off his hair gel gave him away immediately. Same sharp grey suit and salmon-coloured tie that made him look more like an usher or a used-car salesman than the suave businessman he thought he was. Anyone might wonder how he could be taken seriously enough for people to give him their money. But Sarah knew why. This man was selling a dream. Everybody wants to buy a dream.

Her fingers tightened on the brightly coloured box in her hand and the buzz of anticipation rose and swelled in her chest. She knew she didn't have to do these short cons any more. Her father's organization ticked over so neatly that she need never put herself in the firing line ever again if she didn't want to. But where was the fun in sitting behind a desk, ordering other people to take all the risks? She didn't do this for the money. She did it for the very feeling she had right this second.

A teenage girl dipped into the doorway, music resonating from the inside of a rucksack – some irritating soundtrack from the latest hit family movie. Sarah cursed silently as the girl dropped to her knees and began rifling through her bag.

'Sorry,' she apologized, glancing up at Sarah. 'I can never find it when I need it. You'd think I'd learn and put it in the other side, or inside my jacket or something. If I had a brain, I'd be dangerous.'

Sarah ignored her, hoping she'd leave quickly. The hardest person to fool is the casual observer – if this girl decided to focus her attention on Sarah at the wrong moment, she'd see that the accident that was about to happen wasn't an accident at all.

Friedman's shrewd, rat-like eyes were still fixed to his smartphone as he approached, and he unconsciously stroked his salmon tie with his free hand. Yet he navigated through the pedestrians as easily as if there was a second pair attached to the top of his head.

Now.

Sarah shuffled out into the street, grasping her walking stick as though for support. As the distance between them closed, movement on the other side of the road caught her attention.

A face she hadn't seen in a long, long time.

The woman was leaning on a Ford Mondeo the colour of dried blood, her eyes darting up and down the street like a rabbit anticipating a fox. Her dark blonde hair was tied up in a ponytail that looked anything but casual. Sarah had never seen someone look less relaxed in a leather jacket and jeans. She was still pretty. And she was the last person Sarah needed to see today.

There was no time to panic about this unexpected develop-ment – Friedman was directly in front of her now. Five steps away, four, three . . .

'Oh!' Sarah shrieked, stepping directly into the path of the man in the suit and letting the full force of his body slam into hers. Her arms flailed backwards, her walking stick flew from one hand, the box from the other. It hit the floor with the sickening smash of broken glass, and she landed next to it, a heap of grey hair and voluminous skirt. Her wig hadn't shifted. Friedman looked down aghast at the old woman in a crumpled heap at his feet.

'Oh shit!' He shoved his phone into his pocket and threw himself down at her side. 'I'm so sorry! Are you okay?'

'I'm fi . . . oh.' Her eyes found the destroyed parcel and she let her face crumple into distress. 'My vase . . . oh dear.' Sarah groaned again, casting a sideways look at him. She had to be careful of overdoing it. 'It was a gift, a wedding present for my granddaughter. Cost me all my savings, hundreds of pounds! And now look at it.'

Friedman picked up the box, wincing at the sound of broken glass. 'Oh God,' he muttered. 'Hundreds of pounds? Really?'

'I know it probably sounds like a cheap gift to a young businessman like you,' Sarah said, hands covering her face. 'But it's all I had. Since my husband died . . .' She broke off and began to wail. One of the bystanders let out a loud tut and Friedman cringed once more.

'You should pay for that,' a woman remarked. 'You knocked her flying. You okay, love? I know a good claims advisor.'

Bingo. She couldn't have set a shill up with better timing. He was on the hook – time to reel this fish in. 'Oh no, no no, no. It was an accident, after all. These days everyone is so *distracted*. Claims lawyer, did you say?'

His cheeks coloured. God, she loved this job. When it went well, it was like a concerto played by the finest orchestra. One beat missed and the rest of the score was ruined, but Sarah didn't miss beats. She knew that she would never give this up, despite her father's insistence that she spend more time learning the minutiae of the business, stop messing around on short cons and set pieces. Because you can't conduct an orchestra if you never pick up an instrument.

Friedman grabbed up her walking stick and leaned in to

take her elbow, lifting her to her feet. 'No, no need for that, I'll pay for the vase. Really, I insist. It was my fault. No need for lawyers . . .'

As she let him guide her to standing, Sarah glanced at Tess, who was still leaning against the unmarked across the street. She was looking down the street towards Queen's Street, her back turned away from a tall, shifty-looking man advancing quickly, his eyes fixed on her and his hand groping the inside of his jacket – for a knife? A gun? What had Tess got herself into? Sarah saw the glint of the weapon and reacted without thinking.

'No!' she screamed, shoving Friedman aside. She sprinted out into the middle of the road with the speed and agility of someone forty years younger than she looked, her long skirt flowing behind her and her generous bosom slapping up and down. One of her boobs flew from under her blouse and landed in the path of an oncoming car.

Sarah knew she didn't have time to shout another warning to Tess, so she did the only thing she could think to do. She launched herself at the man, colliding with the side of his body as though hitting a wall, then landed in a heap at his feet. The impact barely knocked him sideways.

'What the hell?' The tall, muscular, shaven-headed man looked down at her, the phone he'd just pulled from his jacket pocket in his hand. 'What are you playing at?'

'I'm sorry, I . . .' Sarah stammered. 'I thought . . .'

'You're a bloody maniac,' the man said, walking away shaking his head.

Sarah looked up to find Tess Fox inches from her face, hands already clasping hers and pulling her to her feet.

'Sarah?'

Oh shit, Sarah thought, *I must look a right sight.* She looked down at her chest. One side was voluminous, the other flat, as though one of her breasts had burst. Sarah could see it lying in the middle of the road where her collision had thrown it. Her grey-streaked wig had dislodged and was hanging over her face. She wondered if her wrinkles had smudged. They had taken ages to paint on.

'Don't let her get away!'

Friedman's booming voice followed Sarah across the street. Oh bollocks! He was carrying her ruined parcel, only now the lid had been removed to reveal the pile of broken glass inside – glass that clearly never even resembled a vase. Fuckity fuck fuck fuck.

Tess kept a tight grip on Sarah's arm as she pulled her to standing. 'What the hell is going on here?' she demanded, looking between Sarah and Friedman.

'That woman tried to con me out of hundreds of pounds!'

Tess's eyebrows creased in a frown. 'Now that can't be right, can it?' she said in a mocking tone.

Sarah groaned. It was obvious to both women that Friedman was telling the truth. 'I don't know what he's talking about,' Sarah said. 'I was on my way to a dress rehearsal for a play when this guy barrelled into me and knocked my box from my hands. He offered to pay for it, and I *declined* his generous offer. That's when I saw that wall of a bloke coming at you with a knife and ran across a busy road to save your life. Which I'm beginning to regret,' she added under her breath.

Sarah knew Friedman couldn't dispute any of what she'd

46

just said. She hadn't accepted his money when she went running across the street, thank goodness.

'So, you saved me from the man taking his mobile phone out of his pocket?'

Sarah cringed. 'It looked like a knife, I swear. Anyway, that isn't the point. The point is that I was doing the right thing.'

'That must feel awfully novel for you, Sarah,' Tess remarked.

Sarah scowled. 'Okay, Tess, lovely to see you again. Let's not leave it fourteen years next time, eh?' Sarah turned to walk away.

Friedman looked between the two women, bewilderment on his face, unable to comprehend what had just happened.

'Sarah, wait,' Tess called. 'You dropped this.' Tess leaned down to the floor and picked up an iPhone from the pavement.

Sarah froze. Shit, she'd forgotten she'd taken that. An old habit: take what you can get.

'That's mine!' Friedman exclaimed, feeling his pockets.

'And this just fell into your costume, did it?' Tess asked Sarah, her eyebrows raised.

'Never seen it.' Sarah shrugged. 'Are you sure he didn't drop it himself?' The battle was lost but there was no way she was going to wave a white flag.

'All right.' Tess sighed. 'You're under arrest. Come on, turn around.'

Sarah couldn't believe what was happening. 'Are you kidding me? I just saved your life!'

This was not good. Not good at all. In the space of twenty minutes, she had probably broken about twenty of her father's rules – she had abandoned a con, tried to save the life of a police officer, broken character and got herself arrested.

Sarah sighed, holding out her arms for Tess to slip on the handcuffs, and allowed herself to be guided towards the Mondeo.

'I'm arresting you on suspicion of theft. You do not have to say anything . . .'

Sarah knew the score. She had grown up reciting her rights in the same way other families recited the Lord's Prayer. This, however, was the first time she'd ever heard them coming from an actual police officer, let alone her half-sister.

Chapter Six

Tess glanced at the rear-view mirror, appraising her prisoner as she drove in the vague direction of the police station. She had no intention of actually taking her half-sister into her place of work – especially not to have this conversation.

Sarah looked no less than terrifying. Her carefully applied wrinkles were peeling off her face, and her dark hair stuck out at odd angles from her hairnet, giving her the appearance of a guerrilla scarecrow. The rest of the wig now lay in her lap like a manky old cat. Tess felt a stab of something when she noticed that Sarah was still wearing the necklace Tess had given her for her birthday all those years ago. Interlocking rings inlaid with her birthstone – citrine for November. Sarah saw her watching and narrowed her dark eyes. 'You know you won't make this theft charge stick, Tess. You might not know, but Frank's lawyer these days is Wayne Castro. Plus, I was trying to save your bloody life.' She scowled.

Tess smiled. 'I'm touched, really I am. After all this time, you still care. And you're right, this theft charge probably won't stick – Castro will destroy it in minutes. But imagine the inconvenience of having your fingerprints in our system. I don't believe we've ever had the pleasure before.'

Sarah opened her mouth and closed it again, her face furious. 'How long have you been back in Sussex?' she asked.

Tess inhaled deeply. She'd known when she transferred to Surrey and Sussex MCT that there was a chance she would run into Sarah and her family again. She knew Sarah must have been wondering why she'd taken that chance. 'Nearly five years. I was mostly working out of Surrey until I got acting DI here a few months ago.'

She indicated left and pulled the car into an empty car park.

'What are you doing?' Sarah demanded.

She stopped the car and switched off the engine. 'I attended a homicide last night, Sarah.'

'Isn't that your job?'

'Correct. But this one was a little out of the ordinary. A locked room, a slit throat and a body falling from the sky. Right up your street, wouldn't you say?'

Sarah shrugged. 'I do illusions, not murders. Although that does sound like a neat trick. You want me to figure it out for you? Do I get a cool badge like yours?'

'Don't flatter yourself,' Tess snapped. Just a few minutes in her estranged half-sister's company and her pulse was racing with irritation already. It had been fourteen years since Tess had last seen Sarah, although her little sister had always been on the edge of her mind. Now, their attempt to go their separate ways for good had dissolved before their eyes. She should have known they could never have put something so huge behind them – the secret they shared was always going to find a way

50

to pull them back together eventually, and here they were, running into trouble again with horrible inevitability.

They say two can keep a secret as long as one of them is dead, Tess thought. Except Shaun Mitchell was the one who was dead now.

Sarah had always been a joker, never one to take anything seriously. To her, life was a bloody cabaret, and Tess both envied and resented her for it. 'It takes more than an obsession with puzzles to be a police officer,' she said.

'If you don't want my help, then why did you bother with that whole charade back there?' Sarah asked. 'And that cost me seven hundred quid by the way. Seems like a lot of trouble to go to, a fake knife attack at exactly the place I was pulling off a melon drop, just to insult my intelligence. Don't you have a boyfriend you can insult, like normal people? And how the hell did you find me after all this time?'

Tess ignored the onslaught of questions. 'How did you know it was a fake knife attack?'

Sarah snorted. 'Um, the fact that I'm sitting in the back of your police car rather than receiving my medal for services to Sussex Police Force? Plus, that bloke you used is a terrible actor. I know I saw a knife, which means he swapped it for a phone to make it look like my mistake. Of course, I'd already thrown myself at him by then. Not that I'm complaining – he was pretty hot. You wanted me in the back of this car and we both know you're not going to charge me with stealing that mobile phone. It was on the ground and could have come from anywhere. So why not ask whatever you got me here to ask?'

'You always were a smartass.' Tess pulled her phone from her jacket pocket, flipped through and held up a photo she'd taken of the crime scene photograph of Shaun Mitchell's tattoo. It wasn't as clear as the original, but it was still obvious what it was. 'Recognize this?'

Sarah leaned forwards, and Tess took no satisfaction in the look of horror that crossed her face. She watched Sarah's right hand go instinctively to her left arm, cradling it protectively, and she remembered all too well the scars underneath her little sister's sleeve. Scars caused by Shaun Mitchell, Darren Lane and Callum Rodgers. *CA . . .*

'What . . . ?'

'On our victim,' Tess said. She didn't ask what she really wanted to know. *Did you kill him?* She'd needed to see Sarah's face when she saw the photo to be sure, but even now, even after seeing the way her sister had reacted, she still couldn't be sure. After all, fourteen years changes a person. She really didn't know Sarah Jacobs at all.

'Is it definitely him?' Sarah whispered. All hint of her self-assured, mocking tone was gone. She looked like a teenager again, like the last time Tess had seen her briefly at eighteen years old, pretending to be a fairground stall assistant. 'He's really dead?'

Tess nodded. 'I'm pretty certain it's him, although there won't be an official ID until we find out next of kin. I found this in his flat. Stuck to the wall with this.'

She handed her the bag containing the leaflet for the Three Flamingos nightclub and the dart that had been used to stick it to the wall.

Sarah's eyes widened slightly. 'Do you think it's the same dart? The one—'

'I don't know,' Tess said quickly, cutting her sister off. She didn't need to hear the words.

Sarah closed her eyes and let out a breath. She looked as though she was steeling herself, putting her defences back in place. 'Well, I'm not sorry he's dead. But I didn't kill him,' she said at last, handing Tess the bag back. Her voice had hardened again. 'And I don't know what this means – honestly I don't. I never wanted to be reminded of that man again in my life, Tess – I swear to you.'

She was a liar and a conwoman, but Tess believed her. She didn't know Sarah any more, which meant that she didn't know if she was capable of murder, she supposed, but she did know that it was unlikely that the other woman would have left a direct link to the Three Flamingos at the crime scene. It made no sense.

'Then do you know anyone who might've . . . ?' Tess raised her eyebrows at Sarah in the rear-view mirror. 'Did you tell anyone about what happened that night?'

Sarah shook her head. 'Of course not. Jesus, Tess, no. And if I knew anyone else who had a grudge against Mitchell, I wouldn't tell you anyway. I'm not a grass and some mobile phone theft charge isn't enough to turn me into one. I'll just burn my fingerprints off. I told you, I don't care that he's dead. He deserved to be dead a long time ago.'

Tess sighed. 'I'm not asking you to snitch, Sarah. Don't you see how dangerous this is for us? If we have to start digging through his past to find people who might want him dead . . . well, let's just say we're pretty close to the top of that list. And if he's linked to the other . . .' She couldn't bring herself to say the word.

'How can he be?' Sarah said. 'It was fifteen years ago. No one knows we were in the nightclub that night and we

53

don't have any links to these assholes. You're being paranoid, Tess. If you're taking me to the police station, can we just get on with it? If I spend too much time with police I come out in a rash.'

Tess could have screamed in frustration. 'Do you not get how serious this is?' she snapped. 'Is everything just a joke to you? We could both go to prison if this comes out. Police officers don't do well in prison, and neither do pretty little smart mouths. And it's not my job to sort this out, not all on my own. I can't do this on my own.'

To her horror she realized she was close to tears. The pressure that had been rising inside her ever since seeing Shaun Mitchell was pushing her close to breaking point. She had tried so hard to forget what she had done the last time she'd seen Mitchell. All these years spent in the police force, getting justice for victims, atoning for murder, and it had all been extinguished at the sight of that tattoo, and then the logo of the Three Flamingos nightclub on an innocent-looking flyer.

Sarah looked away, as though Tess's show of emotion made her uncomfortable. Tess wasn't surprised. After Sarah's mother had died of cancer when she was three, she had been raised by their father, Frank Jacobs, and his makeshift family of crooks and con artists. Tess hadn't met either her father or her sister until Sarah was seventeen, and by then her attitude had been like a suit of armour. Always a witty comment, a flippant tone to mask what she really felt.

When Sarah didn't speak, Tess played her trump card. 'None of this even would have happened if you had just listened to—'

'Oh, that's just perfect!' Sarah threw up her hands. 'I should have known this was coming!' She stabbed a finger at Tess.

'*Fifteen years* and you still had to get "I told you so" into the conversation. You didn't have to follow me there that night, you know. You made that choice yourself.'

Tess opened her mouth to speak. But not knowing what to say, she just stared dumbfounded at the little sister she had tried to save. 'So you aren't even the slightest bit grateful that I turned up that night?' she asked.

'Of course I'm grateful, Tess,' Sarah snapped. 'You killed a man to save my life. I know what that cost you, and I will forever be grateful. But I didn't ask you to follow me there and it doesn't mean I owe you anything.'

'That's all life's about for you, isn't it?' Tess shook her head. 'Who owes who, who you can use as a means to an end, who is the most useful to you. The great Jacobs family, like a bunch of bloody pirates, every man for themselves. I know they say there's no honour among thieves but you lot take the—'

'I do not have to sit here and be insulted by you!' Sarah's face was bright red with fury. Tess had hit a nerve. She knew how much Sarah and her family claimed to value loyalty. And seeing as they were severely lacking morals in any other area of their lives, their family code really was all they had. 'You keep your bloody moral code and I'll keep my family and we'll see who lives happily ever after, hey?'

'Actually, seeing as you are still under arrest, in handcuffs and in a police-issue vehicle, *locked in the back*,' Tess snapped, 'I'm afraid you're stuck here until I'm finished having my say for a change.'

'Oh *please*.' Sarah held up her hands, perfectly free from the cuffs that had held them moments before. Without saying another word, she opened the back door of the police car and slammed it behind her, leaving Tess staring after her, open-mouthed.

Chapter Seven

Sarah's feet crunched on the gravel as she approached the abandoned warehouse on the outskirts of Brighton. She glanced behind her once again – the third time she had checked in as many minutes – but no one had followed her here. She let out a sigh. Her dad had always taught her to be careful – awareness was key in their job, after all – but she had never felt so actively paranoid before. Damn Tess, freaking her out like this. Picturing the photograph of Shaun Mitchell's tattoo, Sarah picked up her step, keen to get inside. She'd spent far too long thinking about that man and what he and his friends had done to her. His death was a godsend. She wished she could meet whoever had finally finished him off and shake him by the hand.

The dilapidated building looming before her was huge: six hundred square feet and three floors, to be exact, though only two of them were visible above ground. Boards appeared to hang loosely from smashed windows, but Sarah knew that in reality the place was more secure than Azkaban. Behind the boarded-up windows, out of the sights of prying eyes, was a layer of two-inch-thick steel, and the rusted old doors were fitted with alarm systems and motion sensors. The doorbell, its weathered yellow plastic shell hanging off leaving the wires exposed, hid a video monitoring system that Ring would kill to get their hands on. Sarah pushed the doorbell, knowing her fingerprints were being scanned and her face run through recognition software that very second. Nothing happened. Nothing was supposed to happen – another level of deterrent for anyone who shouldn't be there. The place looked like it had been deserted for years.

After what felt like longer than usual – *paranoid much?* – came the familiar clunk of the automatic bolt, and Sarah was able to swing the door inwards.

As always, dust hit the back of her throat with a vengeance. Her footsteps echoed as she hurried across the wide empty space, stepping over the rusty pipes strewn on the floor for authenticity. Graffitied shutters adorned the insides of the windows, disguising the steel protection once again. A faded and peeling sign that once warned *Staff Only* hung above a wooden door. Sarah pushed it open, stepped into the service lift beyond, pressed her thumb to the fingerprint scanner inside and waited for the lift to descend.

The space below couldn't have looked more different to the floor above. Sarah was met with the stark white walls and bright lights that always made her blink a few times before her eyes adjusted to the contrast. Down here was anything but silent. The space was set up like an open-plan office floor, people filling every corner, like WeWork on acid. Sarah glanced over to where one of their street grifters was teaching his protégé the three card monte. He held up a hand as she passed, revealing a card pinched underneath his fingers. On the other side of her, one of their forgers peered through a microscope as she turned an imitation ruby held by tweezers. A printer in the corner of the room turned out dry cleaners' receipts – a scam that brought in a few thousand a month if they chose their marks right and rotated dry cleaners often enough. Boxes of broken glass wrapped in bright colours were stacked in another corner – the team had a further three melon drops running in different parts of the city today. Sarah doubted any of them had gone as badly as hers.

As she passed each desk, heads looked up, her employees greeting her in turn. Well, her father's employees really, but everyone knew that Frank and Sarah were practically the same person when it came to the job; they were treated with equal respect from the crew. She stopped on more than one occasion to examine the spoils of a particularly large take, or answer a question about the best way to ring the changes. Frank was in charge – he was the one who knew every con their crew pulled, the right places to fence anything that had been stolen – but he liked Sarah to keep her hand in, to know what was going on so that she was ready to take over if anything happened to him: death or – worse – jail.

'Sarah, hey.' A middle-aged man in a blood-red polo-neck jumper gestured for her to come over. He was sitting in front of a faded document that looked to be hundreds of years old, rubbing his bald head over and over with the palm of his hand. Something he did when he was agitated.

'What is it, Mark?' she asked, squinting at the papers.

'Ancient Mormon documents,' he said. 'But I can't get the ink to soak in enough. It'll fail the inspection in minutes.'

'I'll mention it to Frank,' she promised. 'He'll think of something. We had that ink guy who did Lady Chockley's will – he might be able to help.'

Mark grinned. 'Thanks, Sarah.'

Frank Jacobs, the head of their crew, sat on the dark blue sofa in the corner of what he called his office, although Sarah had always remarked it was more like a bachelor pad. A widescreen TV was mounted on one wall, a fully stocked fridge underneath containing soft drinks (Frank didn't allow alcohol on the premises), snacks, and usually leftovers of whatever Uncle Mac was cooking. Today it smelled like garlic and onions. Frank's dark eyes brightened when he saw his daughter and a smile crossed his handsome face. With his dark hair sprinkled grey and his country-club tan, Sarah knew her father looked every inch the attractive and charismatic businessman.

'Something smells good.' She tossed her bag onto the floor and plonked herself down opposite her dad, resisting the urge to put her feet up on his coffee table. Today had been a close call. Her pulse had been in cardio mode ever since she'd flown across North Street to save Tess's life and she hadn't stopped thinking about it ever since. Who did Tess think she was, anyway, trying to hold her like that? Surely it was entrapment or something. She would ask her dad, but the mere mention of his 'other' daughter would be shut down in seconds. He'd been so happy when Tess showed up on their doorstep fifteen years ago; the result of a fling he'd had before his marriage to Sarah's mum. Family meant the world to him, and the fact that he'd welcomed Tess into theirs so easily meant that he'd been quietly devastated when she decided after only six months to cast them aside and apply for the police. The thing was, Frank knew nothing of what had happened to make Tess leave, and if he did, Sarah would be in big trouble. It was her fault – she'd got them into the mess that resulted in Darren's death after her father had explicitly told her to stay away from the three men.

She'd be in twice the trouble if she got involved with helping Tess now, though. God, she'd better not even think that too loudly in case her dad heard . . . The way he felt about Tess, he'd disinherit her faster than she could say three card monte. 'Uncle Mac been cooking again?'

'Hmmm,' her father said, raising an eyebrow. They both knew what that meant – her father's best friend and mentor had something on his mind. They all had their distractions; Uncle Mac's was feeding the five thousand. She remembered the time he'd been waiting on the results of a betting scam they'd been running for six months. They'd all eaten like kings. Sarah could think of worse ways for him to deal with stress – at least this way they all got fed.

As though speaking of the devil would raise him, Alan 'Mac' Adams appeared from the canteen with a tea towel slung over his shoulder. Uncle Mac had been a grifter his whole life, according to her father, and was one of the best thieves he'd ever known. According to Frank, if you shook Uncle Mac's hand, you'd better count your fingers when he walked away.

'How did it go today?' Her dad took a sip of his coffee and Sarah knew he was eyeing her over the rim of the mug. 'I thought you'd have called.'

Sarah shrugged, trying her absolute best for nonchalance,

but she knew that lying to her father was a mug's game. Not because it made her feel guilty, but because lying was his profession. He made shit up for a living. Sarah had never met a better liar than Frank Jacobs. He knew every trick in the book – literally. He had studied *The Book of Tells* by Peter Collet and used to quiz Sarah on it as if it were a SATS paper. But even while she knew it was stupid to try to deceive him, there was still no way she could tell him that she'd screwed up the con. She couldn't bear to see the disappointment on his face.

'It was a simple job,' she replied. 'He coughed it up no problems.'

Sarah took the seven hundred pounds she'd taken from her bank on the way there out of her bag and tossed it onto the table.

Frank smiled. 'I don't know why you still get involved with these small cons, Sarah, but I've got to admit, you're good at them.'

Sarah preened at his words, so pleased with the smallest compliment that she didn't regret lying to him, even though she didn't know how she was able to get away with it. The reason he didn't understand why she still pulled the melon drops and her psychic cold reads, her street hustles and her sleight of hands was because for Frank, the con was a means to an end. A way to make money and usually get one over on a big business. Sarah had no real interest in the long cons, the ones that mostly involved money transfers and investment bankers, even though those were the ones that made them the real money. She much preferred the performance side, getting dressed up and becoming someone else, playing with illusions and magic tricks until no one was sure what was real and what was fake. All the fun of the fair, she sometimes thought.

'Sarah?'

Wes Carter stuck his head round the door to the office. Wes was their tech guy. He was twenty-seven, five years younger than Sarah and, with his floppy jet-black hair that frequently fell across his clear blue eyes, he was a teenage girl's dream version of a computer geek. In Sarah's humble opinion, he was the single most important member of the family, a fact that she reminded Frank of constantly. She was always trying to get him to increase Wes's cut of the profits. In her opinion Wes should be on equal footing with Frank himself, that was how important she thought he was, and how much money he was worth. If they didn't pay him enough, someone else might. Wes could do wonders on a laptop and if he ever shifted allegiance, they were in trouble. 'What took you so long?'

Sarah cringed. Leave it to Wes to inadvertently drop her in it. She opened her mouth in mock outrage.

'You're complaining about my timekeeping?' she said. 'At least I wasn't hiding in my room playing Zelda – some of us have to work, you know.' The teasing was good-natured and Wes faked grumpy.

'I work,' he grumbled. 'I just do it fast enough to take some extra leisure time. And Zelda? When was the last time you played anything, 1999?'

She grinned. 'My life is a cabaret, my friend – I don't have time for games.' She went over to give him a hug and he dropped a kiss on the top of her head. Wes was the closest thing to a brother she'd ever had. 'Speaking of which, the guys working the Rusco con need the website updating. Something about the parrot being unavailable so they're using an octopus.'

Wes raised his eyebrows. 'A fortune-telling octopus?' he snorted. 'Like anyone will believe that.'

Sarah shrugged. 'We're in it for ten grand so they'd better. Oh, and I need some invitations to an art gallery opening in Liverpool next month – can you hack into the guest list?'

'Drop the details into Slack and I'll get it done,' Wes promised. Just as she knew he would. Indispensable. She stood up and gave him a kiss on the cheek.

'Stay for food, Wes,' Frank instructed. Wes spent so much time at his laptop that if they didn't force him, sometimes he would forget to eat altogether. 'Gabe is coming down too, and Mac. About time we had a family dinner.'

Sarah looked at her father, her eyebrows furrowed. Despite their crew consisting of forgers, illusionists, actors, street magicians and all manner of other grifters, the 'family' only consisted of Frank's top team. There was Sarah, of course, Wes, who Frank had taken out of foster care when Wes hacked into his impenetrable security system when he was thirteen, Uncle Mac, and Gabe, who – according to the overly dramatic and flamboyant man himself – literally owed Frank his life, although he'd never disclosed why. Gabe was their special-effects man, responsible for their costumes and transformations; he put the 'artist' in con artist. The entire top floor of the warehouse was devoted to his costumes and prosthetics collection. Sarah knew she was his favourite dress-up toy. There wasn't much he could do with Frank and Mac – a fancy suit or a workman's uniform – but Sarah had been anything from a teenage boy to a clown performing on Brighton Pier.

Costumes and visuals were Gabe's passion – he had more make-up than the Charlotte Tilbury counter at Selfridges.

'Sarah!' Gabe made his entrance to Frank's office in his usual loud and colourful way. He was wearing a Cadbury-purple blazer with a black lapel, a light pink shirt and tight black jeans.

'Fucksake, Gabe, we're supposed to be inconspicuous here, and you rock up looking like Elton John,' Frank complained. 'Did you arrive in a limo that shits out glitter?'

Gabe pretended to shoot an offended look at him, then turned back to Sarah and made a sweeping gesture towards her chest. 'Where are your breasts?'

Wes snorted, then quickly managed to turn it into a cough.

Sarah scowled and wrapped her arms around her chest. 'Where's the need, Gabe?' Sarah snapped. 'You know what they say: more than a handful's a waste.'

Gabe cackled. 'Oh God, honey, as if I'd risk my life talking about your funbags in front of your father. No sweetie, I'm talking about your saggy old woman breasts – they weren't in the bag you brought back.'

A picture of her fake boob flying into the road and being flattened by an oncoming vehicle flitted into her mind. 'I thought I'd shoved them back in there,' she lied. 'Maybe I dropped them. I was changing behind a skip.'

'You should be more careful in the future,' Gabe grumbled. 'Those titties cost almost as much as Katie Price's. Her first set, anyway.'

'Sorry, Gabe,' Sarah said. 'I'll book a room at the Grand to change in next time.'

Gabe pouted, then smiled. He could never really be mad at

Sarah and she knew it. 'I'll be upstairs if anyone needs me.' He went to leave and Frank frowned.

'You're not staying for food, Gabe?'

Gabe shuddered. 'You know how I hate being this close to all the criminal stuff, Frank. Sets off my phobia.'

Sarah smiled, resisting the urge to ask which one. Gabe liked to claim he had a phobia about something at least twice a day, but his favourite phobia was criminal activity. Just the mention of a credit card cloning machine or a five-finger discount had him reaching for the smelling salts. A shame he refused to get involved in the cons, really – with all those colours and his ability to go from one to a hundred, he would make a perfect distraction.

'Hey, Sarah, you wanna help me dish up?' Mac asked her loudly, nodding towards the kitchen.

'Sure.' When she followed him into the empty canteen, however, he rounded on her.

'What went wrong?' His blue eyes searched her face.

'Nothing went wrong,' she hissed, her eyes flicking to the open doorway. 'Like I said, I got the money, no worries.'

Uncle Mac nodded, his slightly too long grey hair falling forwards into his face. He wasn't her real uncle, just like Wes wasn't her real brother and Gabe was no relation either. It didn't stop them being a family. Mac had been her dad's best friend and confidant since before she was born. They were so close that Mac was almost like the mother she'd never really had. If a mother could be a sixty-year-old, six-foot-two hustler who cooked like an angel and had the confidence skills of the devil himself.

'Yeah, I heard you, sweetheart,' Mac said, his voice soft. 'I just wondered why you were lying.'

Sarah groaned. Dammit. 'Don't tell Dad,' she said quickly. 'It doesn't matter what happened, but it went a bit south.'

'You get caught?'

'No, not exactly. We don't have anything to worry about.' That might be true for Mac but it wasn't the case for her. She couldn't stop thinking about Tess, and what trouble her reappearance was going to cause.

Mac nodded. 'Fine. Your secret's safe. But if your father finds out, you're on your own.'

'I don't get it though,' Sarah said as she helped Mac ladle spaghetti bolognese onto plates. 'If you could tell I was lying, why couldn't Dad? He's the master at spotting deception, remember?'

Mac smiled. 'You really don't know? It's his Achilles heel – the one thing I've always warned him will get him into trouble one day.'

'What is?' Sarah asked, confused. As far as she was aware, her father didn't have any weaknesses.

'You, Sarah. The only blind spot Frank has is you.'

Chapter Eight

Chocolate powder swirled around in the tiny vortex of her mug as Tess stood in her galley kitchen stirring hot milk, almost in a trance. The stress was making her head hurt and even now at home in her empty flat, she was having trouble putting her thoughts in order. There was no one she could talk to about what had happened today. Only Sarah knew the truth and, as her little sister had so sweetly stated, she had no time for police officers. Tess had chosen her path, morals over family. If she'd known how lonely it would have made her, would she have chosen differently?

Why now, for God's sake? Why after all these years did that asshole Shaun Mitchell have to show up in her life? Of course, like Sarah, she wasn't sorry he was dead. She just wished he'd go and be dead in someone else's investigation.

It's not a coincidence, the little voice in the back of her mind told her. The leaflet, the dart . . . *someone knows*. She honestly couldn't bring herself to believe that Sarah was a killer, and maybe part of her didn't think that her little sister would be able to lie to her face so easily, even after all this time. But if not Sarah, then who? Someone who knew that she had recently become acting DI, and that Walker wasn't around to take the case that day. Could it have been planned that meticulously? And why let her know in such a dramatic fashion? A door boarded shut from the inside, clothes ripped from a wardrobe, an invisible man who could walk through walls. The banging and shouting – had that really been outside Mitchell's flat? Or another coincidence?

She poured the chocolate into a mug, squirted cream over the top and tossed in a handful of marshmallows. This was her bottle of whisky, her prescription pills. Unlike some of her colleagues, she'd never dealt with the horrors of the job by taking mind-altering substances, drinking to forget. No, her punishment for the things she had done – for killing a man – was to *remember*. To stay clean and sober and remember every mistake. Maybe that's why Shaun Mitchell had shown up now: because she'd finally begun to forget what she'd done, to feel like she'd atoned. She wouldn't take anything to make her sleep better tonight; she was certain the nightmares would come and she would be back in that dark, empty nightclub. Tess grabbed a cloth, wiped the spilled powder from the countertop, and tossed the cloth into the empty washing basket.

What would Sarah be doing now? Had she told Frank about seeing Tess this afternoon? She doubted it. Tess wondered if Sarah had been telling the truth when she swore she hadn't told anyone at all what happened fifteen years ago. Perhaps she had a boyfriend, a husband even. She imagined them sitting around a huge table, Sarah and her family. *She could have been there.* No one had kicked her out; if anything she had been as much part of that family as any of them for half a year. She had realized, just before it was too late, that her relationship with

69

Chris had been so appealing because he was the direct opposite of everything the Jacobs family was. Chris had been her way of proving to herself that she was not the same as them, that she was normal. But when the chips had been down, she hadn't been able to go through with committing to marry someone so pure, someone without her past. And now she had none of them by her side. She was completely alone.

It was unlikely Sarah was partnered up, though not impossible. Frank had always been so cautious about who he allowed to get close to his family. It was hard to start a relationship when your dad was running surveillance on the guy before you finished your first date (Sarah said she had actually caught him doing that once; she had got a glimpse of one of their crew watching her and a boy called Martin on Brighton Pier). But if Sarah had confided in a boyfriend, then that could account for what had happened to Shaun Mitchell, if it were some twisted declaration of love.

Her microwave beeped and she pulled out the pasta bake for one, wafted away the steam and tipped it into a bowl – it looked slightly less depressing than eating it out of the plastic. She carried it the few steps into the sitting room to complete the stereotype spinster-eating-her-TV-dinner look. Her one-bedroom flat had been advertised as an 'open-plan apartment in Chichester' to make it sound chic, when all it really meant was small. From her front door she could see the whole of her kitchen and front room, the door to her bedroom and bathroom. Nowhere to hide if a serial killer came looking for her here.

Tess positioned herself into the ass-shaped divot on the sofa that she had begun to worry she would die on one day, and flicked on the TV. She could no longer bear to watch crime dramas – she spent too long yelling at the TV that it wouldn't happen like that in a real investigation – and soaps didn't interest her, so most of the time she ended up watching reruns of *Friends* and wondered if anyone really had grown-up friendships where they let themselves into each other's houses and ate out of their fridges. How anyone growing up with that show as a benchmark for relationships ever made it through life without severe issues was beyond her.

She picked up a three-day-old pile of post and began to flick through. Bill, bill, junk mail . . .

Her chest tightened as she saw the last piece of junk mail. Black with a lurid pink logo. Almost as lurid as the nightclub really was. It was at the bottom of the pile – had this come separately to the rest of the mail? Had it been delivered by hand? The Three Flamingos had closed down years ago, so whoever had sent this flyer had to have put some serious effort into finding or making one that looked so realistic.

Unable to comprehend what it might mean, Tess instinctively got to her feet and looked out of the window. Was someone watching her? There was no one out there – no one she could see, anyway.

The Three Flamingos. How Tess wished to God she'd never heard of that place. Frank had warned Sarah to stay away from the three men they met there that night, Callum Rodgers, Shaun Mitchell and Darren Lane, but at seventeen her little sister had thought herself invincible. She was a good ringer, that much was clear, and she'd inherited Frank's quick thinking, but that hadn't been enough. The nightclub was run by the oldest of the three, Darren Lane, and Tess had begged her not to go, but Sarah thought she knew best. At seventeen, didn't everyone? Although not everyone ended up in life-or-death situations, and Tess had ruined her own life to save Sarah's. She had never been able to let go of what she'd done that night; the impact of taking a life and then having to live with the secret had spread like a disease through every area of her life. She had known the moment Lane had ended up dead that she would never be the same person; it was part of the reason that Tess had made it clear that she never wanted to see or speak to Sarah again. Until now.

Tess ripped the leaflet down the middle, over and over again, until there were only tiny pieces left. Not wanting to even have it in her bin, Tess made the trip down the three flights of stairs and threw open the door to the apartment block.

Outside, night had fallen, picking out pools of light into people's lives. Residents on the street had begun to close their curtains to the outside world. The houses that hadn't were lit up, their lives on display like some kind of street play. Across the way she watched the woman whose name she could never remember breastfeeding her newborn (whose name she could never remember) on the sofa, one hand supporting the baby's head while the other flicked idly at the TV remote. Her husband – nope, his name eluded her too – entered the room and she put down the remote to take the glass of water he handed her. He crossed the room to close the curtains and Tess looked away before he noticed her voyeurism.

She took a few steps out into the street, barely registering the rain soaking through her socks and bent down, shoving the leaflet confetti into the drain outside her front wall. They floated on the top of the drain water, still taunting her as she turned her back on them and went inside to throw away the remains of her wasted dinner. She wouldn't be eating or sleeping tonight.

Chapter Nine

The sound of her mobile phone ringing pulled Sarah from a deep sleep in her king-size bed. She'd been having a pretty thrilling dream about a long-lost family member who wanted to take over the crew and her first thought on waking was annoyance that she wasn't going to find out how it ended. Her indignation was short-lived when she found her mobile phone on the shelf next to her bed and, holding it up above her face, saw the caller was Uncle Mac. Her heart began to thud. Mac never called her just to say hi. Something must be wrong. She grappled with her duvet and sat up, listening for any sounds beyond her bedroom. Everything was quiet. It was 10.30 a.m. She must have slept through the first part of the day. Had her dad said he was going somewhere today? Or had she forgotten where?

'Mac, you okay?' she asked by way of a greeting. Her voice came out sharper than she intended, that familiar worry resurfacing, the one that said that one day something would happen to her dad and she would be all alone. Well, she'd never be alone – she had Mac of course, and Wes and Gabe. But none of them was Frank.

'Fine, yeah. Um, is your dad at home?'

His casual tone wasn't fooling Sarah. She dropped the phone from her ear and listened again. There was no sound from the house beyond, but that didn't mean much. Sarah and Frank lived in one of the most spacious homes in Brighton. 'I can't hear him but let me check. Isn't he at the unit?'

Mac hesitated. 'No, he had a meeting this morning, but he didn't tell me where. I thought he'd be back by now, that's all.'

Sarah slid out of bed and pulled on her dressing gown. She looked over the balcony to the kitchen, then padded down the hall to her father's study. The door to his bedroom was closed and when she knocked, there was no reply.

'He's not here,' Sarah said, her mind working quickly. Yesterday, Tess came to see her about a murder, Mac was acting cagey and cooking up a storm. Now her dad was having clandestine meetings and going dark . . . 'Should I be worried, Mac? Is Dad in trouble?'

What she really wanted to ask was, *Does Dad know what happened fifteen years ago? Did he kill Shaun Mitchell because of it?* But she knew that if she was wildly off track, then she'd be rewarded with more questions than answers. And if she was right, then her father wasn't the man she thought he was.

'No,' Mac answered, a little too quickly for Sarah's liking. Both men knew how she hated to be shielded from things. She'd proved over and over that she wasn't a child any more, orchestrating some of the biggest cons they'd pulled off in recent years. But still she often felt like there were things going on below the surface that she wasn't privy to. And it pissed her

74

off. 'He's probably just got a property meeting. You know he doesn't always bother me with the boring stuff.'

'If Dad's in trouble you need to tell me,' she said. 'I need to know where he's gone and who he's meeting. I . . .' She took a deep breath. 'I saw Tess yesterday.'

'You saw Tess?' Mac sounded predictably shocked. They never spoke about Tess any more. 'How? Where?'

'She's in Brighton for a case. That guy who was murdered on Grove Hill. I ran into her on my melon drop.'

'And she recognized you? Gabe is losing his touch.'

'She was looking for me. She wanted to know if I had any information about it.'

'Why would you have information on a murder? Does she think you're involved?'

'No, nothing like that,' Sarah assured him quickly. 'She's just out of her depth. Wanted some help. Don't worry, I told her we don't help the police. I just wondered, what with her popping up after all these years, and Dad sneaking off to meetings without us . . .'

'You wondered if your dad is a rat?' It was Mac's turn to be sharp.

'Of course not!' The suggestion was worse than if she'd called him a murderer. If he had killed that man, he would have had a good reason. There was no good reason to turn rat, not ever. 'I just thought it was a weird coincidence.'

'Yeah, it is,' Mac mused. 'And you're sure she didn't have any other intentions when she came looking for you?'

Sarah wondered if he could sense her cheeks burning from down the phone. Should she tell him? He was family. He would help her, he would understand. She thought about what had happened all those years ago, the shame . . . no, if there was a chance this could blow over without her family finding out, then she had to take it.

A sound downstairs made her jump. 'Oh,' she said. 'I think he's back.' She covered the phone with her hand. 'Dad? Dad, is that you?' She took the stairs a couple at a time but there was just a pile of post behind the door.

'Is it him?' Mac questioned from the other end. 'Sarah? Who's there?'

'It's no one,' Sarah said disappointed, 'just the post.'

She picked up the pile while holding the phone between her ear and shoulder and was about to toss it straight on the table when she saw the bright pink logo of the Three Flamingos that Tess had shown her yesterday. Twice in two days. A flyer for a nightclub that had been closed down for years. The club was the reason she'd avoided Kemp Town – once one of her favourite places in Brighton – for years, until they had ripped the sign for the club down and split it into a trendy coffee shop downstairs and office units upstairs, with no hint of its unsavoury past. It was only recently that she had been able to actually go inside to find that the entire topography of the building had changed, like a caterpillar into a butterfly. Sarah actually did believe in coincidences, but this leaflet wasn't one.

Had Tess sent her this? Was it a reminder? A warning?

If it wasn't Tess – and this really didn't seem her style – then someone else knew about Darren Lane's murder. She didn't believe that Tess would have told anyone, and she certainly hadn't. No one had even known she was connected to the Three Flamingos; that night was the only time she had ever set foot in there, planning on teaching those men a lesson by conning them out of thousands of pounds. Her first solo con, trying to run before she could walk. And Lane had been the perfect mark – he was the worst kind of criminal. The three of them had been using their drugs to control their workers, getting them hooked on their substance of choice then putting them to work to pay off debts they wouldn't clear in years, if ever. Sarah had been so determined to stop them, and she had. But the price she had paid had been the loss of her sister. Tess hadn't been able to cope with the guilt and Sarah had always known that joining the police was some kind of redemption quest for her. That was one way they were definitely different – Sarah had never lost a moment's sleep over the death of that scumbag. If she could turn back time and take her sister's place, could have killed Lane with her own hand and saved Tess the guilt, she would.

If Tess hadn't followed her to the club that night, then Sarah knew she would either have ended up dead, or worse. Darren Lane had told her as much when he'd whispered in her ear exactly how he was going to make her pay for trying to screw them over. She could almost feel the heat of his breath on her cheek, smell the beer he'd been drinking. The memory made her nauseous, but she had to pull herself together – this was about her dad. If Frank was involved in Shaun Mitchell's death, she was going to need Tess's help again to keep him out of prison.

'Sarah? You still there?' Mac's voice cut through the silence. She put the post down on the coffee table and went over to the window to look out between the blinds, unable to shake the feeling of paranoia that had been hanging over her since seeing Tess. There was nothing beyond but their perfect view of Brighton Marina and the beautiful turquoise sea.

'Yeah, all good, Mac. Listen, let me know if you hear from Dad, okay? And I'll do the same. I've got some errands to run this morning but my phone will be on. And tell him he'd better have a good excuse for worrying us all to death. Speak later.' And without waiting for him to reply, she hung up. For only the second time in her life, she had no idea what to do. Well, actually she knew what she had to do – she just really, really didn't want to do it. Getting involved in a murder investigation was about as close to the police as you could get without actually signing up, and for a Jacobs, close to the police was not a place you wanted to be. But if her dad had found out what happened all those years ago, and if he had got himself into trouble trying to make it right, Sarah had no choice. She needed help, but she was damned if she was going to tell Tess that.

Chapter Ten

Tess knocked on the wall of Shaun Mitchell's flat, listening for any signs of hollowness. She knew the forensic team had already searched the flat for false walls, secret hiding spots and hidden passageways, but there had to be another way out of here. Perhaps Mitchell's killer had been in league with the old lady downstairs and had made some sort of hatch in the floor. Hell, for all she knew, maybe Mitchell's killer *was* the old lady downstairs. That was how much of a clue she had right now.

'Makes you wish you hadn't bothered, eh?'

Tess jumped at the thick Geordie accent and spun around to see a crime scene technician standing behind her. She had been so engrossed in looking for escape routes that she hadn't even noticed there was anyone else in the room. Besides, she thought the forensics team had finished yesterday – hadn't someone told her the scene had been released? *Please don't say I've screwed up the scene,* she prayed silently. That would be just her luck. Five years in MCT and she'd compromised the only scene she was in charge of.

'Hadn't bothered what?' she asked, wondering if the tech had seen her touch anything. She was *certain* it had been signed off, dammit.

The tech shrugged and pushed a strand of bleach-blonde hair behind her mask. 'Coming all this way for something so mundane.'

'Mundane?' Tess repeated, not certain she'd heard correctly. 'Am I missing something? What exactly about this is mundane? The killer has literally disappeared into thin air.'

'Uh huh. Booor-ring. Well, it will be once you figure out how it was done. The best cons always are. You take your time though.'

'Take my . . . excuse me?' Tess snapped. *The best cons always are*. Wait a second . . . 'What the . . . ?'

The tech pulled her mask from her mouth, grinned and gave a wink. 'Miss me?'

Tess froze. 'What the fuck are you doing here?' Jesus Christ. If anyone found out that her criminal half-sister was at a crime scene . . . She scowled, furious. 'Is your hair blonde now? Don't you know it's a crime to impersonate a police officer?'

'And yet not to impersonate a scene of crime officer. You should get that looked into.' Sarah looked around at the scene. 'So, you haven't figured this out yet?'

'No, and neither have you, so don't pretend you have. What are you doing here, Sarah?' Tess rubbed at her eyes. This was her fault. She never should have sought Sarah out and then expected her to stay out of the whole situation. 'Do you have information that can help me find out who did this?' Tess almost asked her about the leaflet that had been shoved through her door yesterday, but stopped herself. She hadn't been able to trust her in the past and she doubted anything had changed. She had to remember that. Sarah Jacobs and her family couldn't be trusted.

Sarah looked uncertain. 'I thought you wanted my help. That's why you came to find me, right?'

Tess sighed. 'Usually when I ask people what they know, they just give me the information – they don't break into my crime scenes. Where did you get that suit, anyway?'

'You can get these things to fumigate your office. Maybe you should consider having something embroidered on them – at least give us a challenge. So, do you want to know how this asshole died or not?'

Tess shook her head, seriously regretting ever getting her sister involved. But she was here now, and forensics had released the scene. What harm could Sarah do?

'Look,' Tess said, in her firmest down-to-business voice. 'You shouldn't be here. I came to find you to see if you knew anything about Mitchell's death, not for you to impersonate a SOCO and come here making out like this is a game. It's not a game. This is real life. The real world. You should come join the rest of us in it.'

'Is that a "yes, Sarah, please help me"?'

Tess sighed. 'Fine. You can take a look around. The landlord wants to get this place cleaned up today so it's the last chance you'll have.'

'Good call!' Sarah held up a hand for a high-five. Tess ignored it and Sarah mock-pouted. 'Okay, I get it. We're not quite there yet.'

'I'd keep quiet if I were you, before I change my mind,' Tess muttered.

'Consider it zipped, partner.'

'You are not my—'

'Sorry, boss. I'll keep quiet and listen. If we could get this solved by seven, I have an Uber Eats booked.'

'Stop with the "partner" and "boss" bullshit. You are not involved in this; you are taking a quick look around. Speaking of which . . .' She held out her hand for the camera Sarah had been using to take photos before she'd caught Tess's attention.

Sarah sighed and handed it over. It hardly mattered; she'd switched the SD card out five minutes ago. 'What can you tell me?'

Tess hesitated, but if there was anything she knew about Sarah and her crew it was that they could do discretion. She briefly ran through the details they had so far. When she got to the part about the initials on the bin, Sarah's eyes lit up.

'Oooh, a secret message from the killer to the police?'

Tess rolled her eyes. 'There you go with the detective fiction again. In real life, killers don't leave the police messages on the walls. And definitely not on the bins.'

'Well, somebody put it there.' Sarah crawled out from under the desk. 'And this desk has been moved recently. Look at the indentations on the carpet – when it was put back, it wasn't put back in the right place. Why would someone move the desk?'

Tess sighed. 'There are a million reasons someone outside of a detective novel might have moved the desk. He might have moved it when he hoovered . . .'

Sarah raised her eyebrows and gave a theatrical look around.

'Okay, maybe not hoovered,' Tess conceded. 'But you see what I'm saying. In your stories, the detective can see something like that and wonder what it means for the case, but in

my world, we need things like DNA evidence, witness statements, murder weapons. An indent in the carpet where the
desk has moved an inch . . .'

'Okay, okay, I get it. Fine. You need more, but I'm keeping
one eye on that desk.'

'You do that. You wanna see the balcony?'

'Okay, yeah. Take me to the murder weapon.'

At some point the tiles on the balcony must have been white,
but there was very little evidence of that now, they were so slick
with filth. The dirt was dried and had retained little in the way
of footprints, although it had been disturbed in a clear path
to the edge. An old ceramic plant pot lay on its side at the end
farthest from the door, but apart from that it was empty. Sarah
leaned over the edge.

'There's a bit of this drainpipe hanging loose up here,' she
said, heaving herself onto the thin balustrade. 'Looks like it
might have been cut.'

'Jesus Christ, Sarah, get down.' Tess moved quickly over to
her sister's side and looked up at where she was pointing. She
took hold of a fistful of Sarah's forensic suit. 'We've swabbed
all that for DNA, fingerprints, all the usual. There's nothing
useful there.'

'Except a broken pipe,' Sarah countered. Her leg wobbled
slightly and Tess's heart jumped.

'That could have been broken for ages. Look at the state of
the rest of the place. Get down.'

Sarah pointed to the floor. 'But there's no sign of a constant
leak onto the balcony, and this is twisted to point right at it.
The balcony would be wetter, that dirt wouldn't be so old.
When was the last time we had heavy rain?'

Tess thought. 'Last Thursday, I think. What difference does it . . . oh God, please don't stand up on that ledge.'

'Fine, pass me that plant pot,' Sarah said, jumping down and turning over the empty ceramic plant pot Tess had pulled over. It was tall enough to almost reach the pipe she'd been looking at. 'Pass me up your phone,' Sarah instructed, leaning backwards slightly, keeping her balance neatly. 'I need the torch on. And the camera.'

Tess turned on her phone's torch and passed it to Sarah. 'Don't drop it,' she warned. She watched Sarah reach as far as she could towards the drainpipe, click a few times, then pass the phone back down. She jumped down off the plant pot then took the phone back out of Tess's hand and peered at the photographs, zooming in and holding the phone close to her face. Suddenly she stood up straight and asked, 'Did you check the fire stairs?'

'We checked them but they weren't much use. They're accessed by the corridor that we know no one left by, because of the CCTV. What's with the drainpipe?'

'It's been damaged. And it looks intentional, although I don't know why. Like you say, not everything has to be a clue. And from the looks of all this, there is only one obvious route in and one obvious route out of this flat. The front door.'

Tess tried to keep the impatience out of her voice. 'Do you think I tracked you all the way around Brighton before ascertaining that he didn't walk out of the bloody front door? That would be impossible.'

Sarah smiled. 'Not impossible. In fact, I'll bet half the proceeds of my next con that he walked out of the front door.'

Tess raised her eyebrows. 'Oooh, half of an old iPhone. Brilliant. Are you planning on showing me how?'

'I'll need access to that CCTV.'

'No chance. I already told you we looked at—'

'Yes, but you didn't know what you were looking for.'

Tess had to force down a growl. How had she forgotten how infuriating Sarah Jacobs was? Or was it only apparent now they were on different sides of the law? She shouldn't be letting her sister anywhere near the police station, she knew that. Sarah and her family couldn't be trusted, she reminded herself like a broken record.

But what if she can figure this out? Sarah was smart. When it came to illusions and sleight of hand, Sarah had been an expert, even fifteen years ago. If she could solve the mystery of how the killer got away, Tess would be one step closer to getting this whole case off her back and perhaps salvaging her career.

Sarah had already taken her silence as assent and was pulling her fake forensic suit off.

'Can we stop at the library on the way to the station?' she asked.

Tess raised her eyebrows. 'Books overdue?'

'It's the life of a hardened criminal. I like to live on the edge.'

On the street outside the block of flats, footsteps away from where Shaun Mitchell's body had landed, Sarah took advantage of Tess making a phone call to make one of her own. This was a beautiful mystery. The flat was completely sealed – one way in and one way out covered by a camera – no large mirror propped strategically to reflect the other end of the corridor and no chimney breast to poke a long blade down and retract it when the deed was done. Too high up to jump from the balcony – too low down for a hatch to the roof. No snake lowered through a vent here. Just a man who had been sliced from one side of his neck to the other and thrown from a third-floor balcony by the invisible man himself. If anyone could pull this off, it was Frank, and Sarah had seen nothing so far to prove or disprove her theory that her dad was involved, although she couldn't for the life of her think why he would go to these lengths.

'Wes? I need a favour. I'm leaving an SD card inside a book at the library, *Hag's Nook* by Dickson Carr. I need you to retrieve and store it at one of our dead drops.'

Wes was as unruffled as ever. Literally nothing fazed him. Sarah had never really seen him display any emotion stronger than mild irritation when a firewall was proving stubborn.

'Everything okay?'

'Sure it is.' She knew he would have other questions later, but he would do as she'd asked. They were always sneaking around and keeping things from the grown-ups, coming up with the idea of the 'dead drops' – locations around Brighton where they hid things for each other if they needed to pass them around without Frank or Mac knowing. But there was a price – no secrets. And now she was skirting dangerously close to breaking that rule.

'Okay, cool. I'll leave it with the twins.'

'Thanks.' Sarah put up a hand to Tess who had hung up on her call and was waiting on the other side of the street, tapping her watch. Sarah had walked to Shaun Mitchell's flat, so they were going to make the journey back to the police station – via the library at Sarah's request – in Tess's car. 'I've got to go.'

'Er.' Wes sounded unsure. 'Should I tell you to be careful or something?'

Sarah smiled. 'You could do. That's what Mac would do.'

'Well then, be careful. And if your dad ever finds out, I had no idea what was going on.'

'You don't have any idea what's going on,' Sarah said.

'And yet somehow, I know he would disapprove.'

Chapter Eleven

'Are you going to tell me what you're getting from the library?' Tess gripped the steering wheel and glanced at Sarah, who was rummaging in her bag. 'Oh no, oh no you don't. Not in here.'

Sarah froze with the cigarette halfway to her lips. 'What?'

'You can't smoke in a police car.'

'Oh, stop clutching your pearls, do. You can't inject heroin in a police car. Smoking isn't illegal, yet.'

'This isn't 1999. You can't smoke in public places. That includes work vehicles.'

Sarah groaned, pulling her feet underneath her legs so she was sitting cross-legged in the front of the car. Tess resisted the urge to tell her to get her feet off the seat. 'Isn't it exhausting being so *good* all the time? Don't you ever want to tell someone to fuck off, or get wasted and throw up in your neighbour's wheelie bin? Have you ever done anything wrong in the last fifteen years?'

Tess gritted her teeth. 'What, you think my life would be

infinitely better if I smoked inside my work vehicle? If I went about my duties smelling like an ashtray, I'd be jolly all the time?'

Sarah snorted. She grappled in her pocket for her lighter and lit her cigarette, rolled down the window. 'I think it's going to take more than that.'

'Put that out or I'll pull this car over,' Tess warned.

'Jesus, calm down, *Mum*.'

'Don't be childish.' Tess scowled and wound down her own window.

'Tell me about your life these days.' Sarah changed the subject but didn't put out the cigarette. 'Boyfriend?'

'No.'

'Girlfriend?'

'Also no. Stop talking. We're not friends.'

'Don't I know it.' Sarah inhaled deeply, then blew the smoke out of the window. 'I don't need any more friends anyway. I didn't ask you to come and look for me.'

'And I didn't ask for my breakout case to be the murder of a man whose best friend I killed. *For you*,' Tess snapped back. 'But here we are. And I don't think you're taking this anywhere near seriously enough. I'm not sure what goes on in that head of yours, but if Shaun Mitchell gets linked to what we did—'

'What you did,' Sarah corrected. Tess gave her a mutinous glare and Sarah pulled an imaginary zipper across her lips.

Tess sighed. 'Fine, what *I* did . . . well, that's the end of my career. The end of my life. All these years getting justice for victims, trying to make amends, all for nothing.'

They drove in silence until Sarah spoke, her voice serious now. 'You honestly still feel guilty for what happened, don't you? That stuff you said about making amends when you walked away from our family – that's real to you?'

Tess nodded, biting her lower lip. 'I told you then, I was joining the force so I could do some good. I don't understand how you don't feel guilty. I took a man's life.'

'If you'd chosen to let him live then he would have killed me,' Sarah reminded her. 'Probably you too. As far as I'm concerned that makes you balanced in the justice scales. Take a life, save a life. You're even.'

Tess gave a weak smile. 'I wish I had your outlook on life. Everything's pretty easy for you, huh? No rules.'

'Are you kidding?' Sarah said. 'My life is all about rules. Don't own anything you can't walk away from. Don't get attached to anyone outside the family. Don't keep anything you steal, always tell someone where you are . . . and the most important?' She looked at Tess, who nodded, and they both intoned in unison, 'You have the right to remain silent.'

'At least we agree on that,' Sarah said.

'No getting attached? Still no boyfriend then?'

Sarah hesitated. Then she shrugged.

'There was a guy, once, after you left us. His name was Jefferson. But it was never going to work, was it? Not unless I told him the truth about who I was. And then either he'd dump me because I'm in an unusual line of work—'

'A diplomatic way of putting it,' Tess snorted.

Sarah glared at her but didn't comment. 'Or he joins the family. I just wasn't sure I was ready to do that to him, you know?'

Tess raised her eyebrows. 'I thought being a grifter was the best job on earth?'

'It is. For me. But Jefferson was just too . . . too *nice*.'

'Your dad married your mum though,' Tess pointed out.

'*Our* dad. My mum was a carny, remember? Her family travelled with the fair all her life. She wasn't some naive townie.'

Tess did remember, now that Sarah had said it. She hadn't spent long with the Jacobs family, about six months from the time she first met Frank Jacobs to the time she left, but she had been fascinated by them. It made sense to Tess that Sarah was the daughter of a carny; her outlook on life had been so different, so free-spirited. Tess was certain the only reason she'd settled in Brighton was because she was terrified of leaving Frank.

'Mum was used to living by a different set of rules to the rest of society,' Sarah was saying. 'The grift was more a part of her blood than Dad's, I think. He doesn't really talk about his childhood, but I get the sense it was pretty normal until he met Mum.'

'All in all, sounds like a pretty lonely life for you,' Tess remarked.

Sarah shrugged. 'I have the family, I'm never alone.'

Tess shook her head. 'That's not the same as not being lonely.'

'And you?' Sarah asked, looking at her and raising her eyebrows. 'Is your cup overflowing with happiness and companionship?'

Tess snorted. 'Touché.'

'Do you ever miss us at all?'

The sarcastic comment was almost out of her mouth when Tess realized that Sarah was serious. She almost sounded hurt. But it wasn't exactly a straightforward question, and one that had become infinitely more complicated since seeing her sister again. Because of course she missed them. She hadn't spent a lot of time with the family, but she had felt an immediate sense of acceptance when she was with them. She'd been able to cut ties from them easily at first, because of the immediate horror she'd felt at having to take another man's life, but now, with the horror of the incident so far behind her . . . it wasn't quite as easy to pretend she didn't crave a family again. Thankfully, the appearance of the library let her avoid the question.

'Look, we're here.'

Sarah let out an exaggerated sigh and Tess looked pointedly at the cigarette still between Sarah's fingers. 'Are you going to smoke that thing in there?'

'Hell, no.' Sarah opened the door and threw the cigarette into the drain. 'You think I've got no respect?'

Tess had dropped Sarah at Jubilee Library with the promise that they would meet back at the police station on John Street in forty minutes. Sarah figured that gave Tess long enough to park the car and find somewhere in the station to put her where she couldn't cause too much trouble. She thought about how anxious Tess must be every day, working for the police and carrying such a huge secret. Not just the murder, but the secret of who she really was and where she came from.

'Don't speak to anyone in here,' Tess warned Sarah when she arrived, springing out like a jack in a box. Clearly she'd been waiting just inside the door for her. 'Don't be a smart-ass. Don't steal anything. Do not defraud anyone. This is not a reconnaissance opportunity. We can use this room.' Tess opened a door marked *Private* and gestured her in. It was barely bigger than a stationery cupboard and contained only a desk, a computer and an antique printer.

'What, I don't get invited into the murder room?' Sarah clocked the layout of the corridor as she entered after Tess. 'I was hoping for a grand tour – I've never been here before. For which I'm very grateful.' She tipped a nod at Tess, who rewarded her with a scowl. 'It looks more like an office block than somewhere drunken idiots are thrown in cells to sleep it off.'

'I'm sure there's plenty of time for you to see the rest of it if you keep trying to con bankers out of their cash. It's hardly a long-term career path.'

Tell that to Frank. Sarah had to bite inside her lip to stop from replying to the snide comment. Her career so far had been pretty lucrative. As a crew they brought in over quarter of a million on a bad month, with none of that pesky law-abiding tax the likes of Tess had to pay.

'Look, it's what I'm good at. A girl's got to eat,' she said.

Tess raised her eyebrows. 'And you have to steal to do that? Who are you, Aladdin? Somehow I doubt that.'

'You have no idea how much it warms my heart to hear that you know Disney.'

'I had a childhood too, you know. Just because I wasn't raised by Fagin doesn't mean I wasn't young once.'

'You'd be welcome back, you know,' Sarah said quietly.

'Here's the CCTV,' Tess said, ignoring her. 'I'll make us a coffee.'

She placed the coffee down next to Sarah and glanced over her shoulder.

'Any divine inspiration yet?'

The screen was frozen on the moment the police officers entered the flat. Sarah was scrawling descriptions and time stamps onto a notepad.

'What are you doing?' Tess asked. 'Have you found something?'

'Not sure yet. I need your help.' Sarah looked up at her. 'I'm pretty sure this is the bit where I explain how he walked out of the door without being noticed.'

'Go on.'

Sarah spun in the chair to face her. She pointed at the screen. 'The art of illusion is about one thing, primarily. Misdirection. When was there the biggest smokescreen at the crime?'

'When the victim landed on the pavement,' Tess replied, feeling clever. 'That's when all the attention was on the street.'

'Wrong,' Sarah replied. Tess's face fell. 'Our guy – or girl, sorry – is clever. He or she knows that it doesn't matter how many people are out front looking at the victim, there is still the matter of getting out without the camera seeing. We know he knows about the camera because he tampered with it to get in. So he arranged for a power outage twenty-four hours before the murder, but he can't do that again from inside the flat. So he had to have a bigger diversion that will render the camera useless. The guy falling from the balcony doesn't affect the camera. What else does?'

'There's nothing until our guys go in.'

'Exactly.' Sarah pulled the book she'd borrowed from the library after hiding the SD card for Wes to find and handed it to Tess.

'*The Hollow Man*,' Tess read, turning the book over in her hands. 'I think I've seen the film. About a man who can turn invisible, right?'

'Wrong. The film was about a man who turned invisible. This story is about a killer who *seems* invisible. John Dickson Carr is considered one of the best locked-room mystery writers who ever lived. And in this book he – or his main character, Dr Gideon Fell – dedicates an entire chapter to giving a lecture on the locked-room mystery and all the ways in which it can be achieved. He does this for no other reason than to show how clever he is – and cement Carr's place as a true master of the impossible crime.' Sarah took the book from Tess and flicked through. 'See here. Fell's talking about a magician who's disappeared from a horse in the middle of the field. He explains that the guy they are looking for never even left the field. He just pulled off his paper clothes, jumps off the horse and joins the rest of the people in the field searching. As long as no one counts the stagehands before the trick they can go off without him being noticed.' Sarah pointed at the screen. 'It's all about creating a big smokescreen so the sleight of hand can go undetected.' She jabbed her finger at the screen. 'It's a classic disappearing act, all the magicians use them. They have ten or so stagehands surrounding him. When the time comes for them to disappear, poof! The smoke hides the magician from sight long enough for him to join the stagehands. Does anybody notice there are now eleven? No, they do not. Misdirection 101.'

'But he didn't have ten or twelve stagehands. The only people in there were us.'

'That's the beauty of it. The stagehands don't have to know that's what they are. Just so long as they all look the same – or are wearing a uniform – and no one clocks each one in and out. He could have slipped past the guy on the front door in a police uniform in the middle of a lockdown. Seen by all, noticed by no one.'

'Bastard,' Tess hissed.

'Clever bastard,' Sarah corrected. 'Now we just have to identify which of these guys went out who never went in, and you have your man. And with this little speech I cement myself as a student of Dr Fell, a rival perhaps to Merivale and Dr Hawthorne. Impressed?'

Except there was no extra officer.

Every one of the police officers who left the flat after the murder had been caught on camera at some point going in. Added to that, Tess took warrant IDs and managed to cross-reference every single one against the confirmed list of officers who were called to the scene. Sarah and Tess watched the footage six times, Sarah each time becoming more and more irritable, obsession taking over, to the point that she knew what every officer on the team looked like, along with their name, nickname and warrant number. When Tess glanced at her watch again, they had been there two hours. If she didn't get back to her team soon, DCI Oswald would be wondering what the hell she was doing.

'I'm really sorry, Tess. I was wrong.' The words seemed to stick in Sarah's throat. Clearly she was not used to being wrong and didn't like it. 'There's no way your killer slipped out after the door was opened. I don't know how they did it yet, but they got out sometime before your lot even showed up. Maybe across the balcony?'

Tess shook her head. 'The balcony is the most visible place. All eyes would have been on it as soon as the victim hit the ground.'

'Someone falls from the sky and you look up,' Sarah agreed. She took a sip of her drink and picked up her mobile phone when it beeped. Her face paled and she screwed up her nose.

'What?' Tess asked.

Sarah held up the phone for her to see. The words *WHY ARE YOU AT THE POLICE STATION* were written across the screen in capital letters.

'Frank?'

Sarah nodded. She glanced down again. 'Oh shit.'

She held up the phone for Tess to see the words on the screen. *BLACK DOVE NOW. BOTH OF YOU.*

Chapter Twelve

Tess ducked her head as she descended the stairs into the darkness below the Black Dove. Sarah, in front, took a left turn in a cramped basement corridor, rapped three times, then twice, once, paused, then another three times on the heavy mahogany door tucked away in the corner. There was the sound of a key turning in the lock and the door opened slightly. Tess raised her eyebrows.

'Sam lends us the key when we need privacy,' Sarah explained, gesturing back upstairs to the pub. The hidden room was a well-known secret in Brighton, a long narrow room underneath the pub, designed to mimic the shape of a ship, artwork adorning every wall and exposed pipes still visible from when it was a toilet block.

'Does Sam know what your business is down here?' Tess asked, following her through the door.

'Not that you could ever prove,' Frank's voice answered from the gloom beyond.

Even though Tess had been steeling herself for this the entire journey to the meeting, seeing him standing in front of her still made her heart pound. The famous Frank Jacobs, conman extraordinaire. He was an attractive man, and an imposing presence. Dark eyes bored into her as she stepped forwards. Tess forced herself to nod. 'Frank.'

Everyone in the room was watching the pair as though they were expecting them to take ten paces back and draw guns. Tess glanced around, absorbing the scene. A twenty-something guy who looked like a boyband member's nerdy older brother was sitting at one of the tables behind a laptop, sheets of paper fanned out and a can of Red Bull next to it. He was now looking at Sarah, concern on his face. Gabe sat opposite him, dressed like Willy Wonka in a purple crush velvet suit, legs and arms spread wide. He gave a subtle wink when she looked over at him. And in the corner was Mac Adams. He'd aged since Tess last saw him, of course, but not necessarily badly. Mac had been kind to Tess when she had first found her father, seeming to understand more easily than Frank did what a new world it was that had opened up in front of her; she'd always thought of him fondly. She'd always thought of them all fondly, when she'd allowed herself to think of them at all. It wasn't the people she'd run away from; it was their life choices.

Frank looked her up and down and nodded back slowly. 'Tess. You look well.' No mention of their lost years, or her betrayal. He just turned his focus straight to Sarah and narrowed his eyes. 'What's going on?'

'Sarah is helping me with an enquiry,' Tess answered for her. 'She's not in any trouble. Related to this, anyway,' she added as an afterthought. She figured Sarah was always in some kind of trouble. It went with the territory.

'I was going to tell you,' Sarah said, her voice sounding slightly petulant. Frank scowled.

'When?'

'Tonight? How did you know, anyway? Do you have people following me?'

'Not specifically,' Frank said, and Tess couldn't tell if he was lying. Infuriatingly, she never had been able to.

'Liar,' Sarah snapped. Clearly she could. It made sense – she had spent her whole life with him – but still Tess felt her chest tighten. Yet another reminder that she wasn't part of the family.

'Have you patted her down?' Frank demanded.

Tess rolled her eyes.

'She's not wired, Dad.'

'Sarah.'

She sighed, mouthed 'sorry' at Tess, who lifted her arms up for Sarah to pat her back, under her arms and down her sides, like she'd been taught to do.

'If you're so concerned that I'm going to arrest you, Frank, why bring me here in the first place?' Tess asked.

'I want you to tell me what's going on,' he said, pointing at her. 'From your mouth. She's a natural liar' – he swung a finger at Sarah – 'gets it from her old man. But I'll know if you're telling the truth. And whatever the truth is, DI Fox, it's not this shower of shite you're feeding me. You've been MIA from this family for over ten years. Now you show up, and Sarah is following you to crime scenes and hanging round at the police station.' He said the words 'police station' like they tasted bad. 'So how about you stop insulting my intelligence and tell me what's going on. All of it. From the start.'

Tess hesitated. Behind Frank, Sarah was glaring at her as though she was trying to beam a plausible story directly into Tess's brain. The other three men watched her in silence.

Frank was right; she was a terrible liar. Sarah was much better, and yet she didn't seem to be volunteering any help. What was it that Frank used to say? A good lie is ninety per cent truth. Best to start there then.

'As you apparently well know,' Tess said, 'it's about the murder at the Grove Hill flats.' She saw Sarah's jaw tighten. 'A man was pushed off a balcony after having his throat slit.'

'Sarah has an alibi,' Frank said, his words quick and well-oiled. She expected certain phrases like 'no comment' and 'lacking in evidence' would trip just as easily off his tongue.

'I haven't told you what time it was,' Tess replied dryly.

Frank shrugged. 'It's been all over the news this morning.'

'Fine.' Tess crossed her arms and glared daggers at Frank. 'What's her alibi?' she demanded.

'Will you two stop it?' Sarah interrupted before Frank had a chance to speak. 'This bickering isn't helping. I'm not a suspect, Dad, so you don't need to alibi me. Tess asked for my help because they can't find out how the killer got out of the flat. The door was boarded up from the inside and the CCTV in the corridor doesn't show anyone going in or out. She was looking for some professional advice.'

Ninety per cent truth, Tess thought. *Nice.*

Frank looked at her. 'Is this true?'

'All of it.'

Tess caught the small glance that passed between Frank and Mac, and she shot her own questioning look at Sarah.

'What?' Tess asked. 'What is it?' But Sarah looked as confused as Tess felt. 'What was that look?'

'Did you check *everywhere* in the flat?' Frank asked. 'Any hiding places . . . however small?'

Tess banged her palm against her forehead. 'You mean I was supposed to *search the flat*? Shit! You take one measly month off detective school and look what happens.'

Ignoring her sarcasm, Sarah turned to face her father. 'Why did you say *however small*?'

Frank looked as though he was about to speak, then caught himself and glared at Tess in defiance.

She sighed. 'I get it, Frank. You don't want to tell me anything. I'm the filth, you're not a snitch, yada yada. But if you know who might be involved in this, then I would really appreciate a heads-up. Not as a police officer, but as . . .' She breathed in and forced the next word out as quietly as possible and through gritted teeth: 'Family.'

Frank looked at her for another beat and in that second Tess wondered what she would do if he tried to hug her.

Instead he sighed. 'I need to make some enquiries, ask around. I'll see if I can help you on this occasion, because I don't want Sarah mixed up in this any more. But next time you have a disappearing killer, find yourself a different magician to play with. You made your choice and it wasn't this family.'

Tess looked to Sarah for help but none was forthcoming. He was right; she had chosen the police over her dad and sister, so why did his words hurt so much? Could she honestly say that she'd never questioned her choice over the years? Of course not – especially after her break-up with Chris and when her friends at work had deserted her. But it was clear that her reasons for what she'd done didn't hold water with Frank.

'Thank you,' she said, with all the grace she could muster. 'And don't worry. When this is done, I won't darken your doorway again.'

Chapter Thirteen

'Shaun Mitchell.' Tess stood at the whiteboard and pinned up a picture of the victim. She wished she could cover up that disgusting face, still somehow sneering in death, but that would, of course, arouse suspicion. She would just have to avoid glancing in its direction. 'Forty-one years old. Small-time drug dealer, a record of drug and violence going back to childhood. He served a few years inside for battery. The only thing that surprises me about his murder is that it didn't happen sooner, to be honest. In all likelihood this is a dispute between rival dealers.'

Her hands hadn't stopped shaking since she'd left the Black Dove and she still felt slightly sick. It had been so long since she'd talked to her father. Now, just seeing them all there had made her veins pump with adrenaline. The man she'd been so desperate to impress when she was twenty-two and found out her real father was a celebrated businessman, a *someone*. And then to find out the real nature of the Jacobs business . . .

She'd been young, yes, but old enough to know that she wasn't a natural thief, or a con artist. Sarah had been excited to meet her. Tess got the distinct impression that her half-sister had a lonely life with only a handful of people she could trust, no one to talk to about any doubts or concerns she might have. Tess had vowed that she would convince Sarah to go straight with her, to leave Frank's way of life and get a real job. It hadn't worked out that way.

Tess noticed that Walker had his feet up on the desk at the back of the room. *On the fucking desk.* God, she hated him. She tried her best to ignore him, like she would an attention-seeking child.

'This case will most likely be solved by good old-fashioned legwork, I'm afraid. I'm going to extend the interview radius. Our main aim is to get someone to talk. In disputes like this they always do, eventually. Hopefully forensics will pull up something to link to when we get a name.' She let out a sigh. 'Yes, DI Walker?'

Walker smiled, held up a hand as if he were some kind of minor celebrity. 'I was just wondering, DI Fox, whether there was any news on how the perpetrator left the scene yet? I heard your latest theory was that he was hooked up to a helicopter and hoisted out. Or perhaps he scaled the building, like Spiderman?'

There were a few wry smiles but it seemed her team knew better than to snigger.

'All excellent theories, DI Walker, thank you as always for your input.' Tess gritted her teeth and counted to three. She wasn't about to let Walker be the reason she lost her cool. 'But we've interviewed both Spiderman and James Bond and they have alibis. Which leaves us with the local drug dealing scum as our only suspects at this present time. And no,' she said as his hand shot up again, 'we don't yet have an exact picture of the killer's movements following the crime, but we are working on that. If that's all, I'll get back to the real world and do my job, shall I?'

She looked around quickly, not wanting to give Walker a chance to disrupt her briefing further. 'I have forensics at eleven, then the PM this afternoon. Any luck and we'll have a suspect in custody in time for *EastEnders*. Don't let the door hit you on the way out, DI Walker.'

She was relieved when Walker left without further comment. Tess had managed to hold things together but she didn't want to end up saying something she'd regret and having her colleagues ask difficult questions. Obviously nobody on the force knew that Frank Jacobs was her father, and the strain of carrying that as well as her connection to the victim – it was more than it had been in years. The Sussex Police Force had tried a few times to prove that Frank had been involved in criminal activity, but since his early twenties, when he'd been on first-name terms with the police, he'd managed to leave no trace of his involvement in anything illegal and they hadn't ever been able to get hard evidence that he was involved in anything. Yet still, there was no way Tess wanted anyone to know she had any association with Frank whatsoever. And if anyone found out she'd been withholding evidence, she'd be fired. Yet the idea that Frank had something to do with the murder had been playing on her mind since the Black Dove, and her stress levels weren't helped by the persistent voice asking her what she was going to do if she found out that her father had killed this man.

'DS Morgan.' Davit Shah, head of the Forensic Identification Services Unit for Surrey and Sussex greeted Jerome with a firm handshake, bordering on manic pumping. Everyone was always so pleased to see Jerome; it was beyond irritating. 'DI Fox, good to see you again.' Davit nodded at her, and shook the hand she stretched out considerably less manically. 'I'm afraid we don't have a great deal. Despite being an absolute horror movie, forensically speaking, your crime scene was cleaner than I imagine Jerome's kitchen to be.'

'The Manson crime scene was cleaner than Jerome's kitchen,' Tess retorted, gaining herself a small smile. Something was clearly bothering Shah. Usually a true-crime-related joke would have earned her a much bigger laugh. 'What is it?' she asked. 'What do you think it means?'

'Here, look at this. Doesn't even fill a side of A4.' Davit passed her the exhibits log which was, as he suggested, unusually sparse. At a normal crime scene – any crime scene, let alone a murder – there would have been blood results, fingerprint analysis, countless other DNA profiles. Tess had never come across a murder like the ones that happened in books, where the killer hid their identity so completely and successfully. Until now, it seemed.

'But his flat was filthy!'

'It was,' Davit agreed. 'But the only prints we found were your victim's. The only blood and hair – your victim's. The only semen . . . ' He wrinkled up his nose. 'Your victim's. He was a disgusting specimen, it seems. But your killer was the cleanest one I've encountered. If I didn't know better, I'd doubt it was a crime scene at all.'

'Okay, so what do we actually have?'

'Forensics found the same substance on the light switch and

the door as on the bin,' Davit said, pointing to a line of codes and indecipherable words, 'but there was no blood on any of them. It was something other than blood that made the luminol react – likely, judging from its composition, horseradish.'

'Horseradish? So what, Shaun Mitchell didn't wash his hands after eating his sandwich? Great. We have one less clue than before.'

'Except for the bin,' Jerome pointed out. 'It wasn't just the smears of a messy eater. It was initials, CA, remember?'

'How could I forget?' Tess muttered. 'Okay, we'll find out if our vic had horseradish on his hands at the PM, or if the stuff on the bin, the door and the light was older. What else is there?'

'Handprint on the balcony, consistent with someone gripping the rail. Partial print matches the victim – obviously, as it was his flat, we don't know when that print was left there. The only thing was, the rest of the balcony was fairly clean print-wise. I'd have expected a lot more.'

'And a bucket-load of blood,' Jerome commented. 'The guy had his throat slashed on there.'

'Except,' Tess said slowly, 'what if we've got this all wrong?' Tess looked at Jerome, a horrific idea forming in her mind. The crime scene not looking like a crime scene, the lack of blood on the balcony . . . 'We're presuming he was thrown off *this* balcony because this was his flat. But what if we've got the wrong flat? It could have been the one above, or below even.' The horror of what she was saying hit her.

'Fucksake, Jerome, what if we've got the wrong crime scene?'

'So what, we get warrants for every flat that faces that side of the street?' Jerome kicked relentlessly at a piece of moss stuck to the wall he'd perched himself on.

Tess wanted desperately to tell him to knock it off but chose to ignore it. She couldn't think properly; the idea that she'd been searching the wrong flat had taken root in her brain and she was trying to come to terms with what a monumental fuck-up that would be. Any evidence from a crime scene could have been completely destroyed by now – it didn't bear thinking about. And yet thinking about it was all she'd done since leaving the forensics lab. She could hear Davit's voice. *If I didn't know better, I'd doubt it was a crime scene at all.* Well, what if it wasn't? What if the reason no one was seen leaving the flat on the CCTV was because they were walking out of the flat above?

'The PM is in less than an hour, and then I suppose I'll have to go and speak to Oswald. It wouldn't be every flat we need to reconsider. Our witness says he landed with some force, which rules out the first floor and likely the second. Hopefully Kay can help, give us some indication of how far he's fallen from the injuries. Only the end flats have balconies. That's eleven.'

'Eleven potential crime scenes. Oswald is going to love that.'

'Cheers, *mate*. I'm not exactly dancing a jig about it myself,' Tess grunted. She eyed him hopefully. 'Are you stepping in on the PM?'

'Why, are you scared of Kay?'

'Why would I be scared of Kay?' Tess snapped. Jerome's eyes flew towards what had once been his hairline. He'd shaved his head for charity eighteen months ago and discovered that – if possible – he was even more attractive without hair, and so he'd kept it that way ever since.

'Because everyone's afraid of her. She spends all day with dead people and likes them more than the rest of us. Except . . .' He stopped short, but Tess knew what he wasn't saying. *Except Chris.*

'Yes, okay, I get it.' Tess rubbed her hands over her face. '*Everybody* loved bloody Saint Christopher. I didn't force him to transfer, you know; it was his choice to leave. The Chris Hart Fan Club could always get off their arses and actually go and see him if they are all so in love with him.'

Jerome unscrewed a bottle of Coke and let the fizz die down before taking a swig. 'Well, they do, don't they? I thought he was at Iron Man's retirement party?'

Iron Man – so called because he'd had so many metal plates and spare parts stuck into him that he took an hour to get through airport security – had retired two months earlier. Tess had been invited – in the least enthusiastic way possible – and had, predictably, declined to attend. She hadn't known Chris would be there.

'What do you mean, you thought? Weren't you there?'

Jerome grinned. 'Nah, I gave it a miss, out of solidarity.'

'You had a date.'

'She was ten times hotter than Iron Man, that's for sure.'

'You're a real pal, you know that?' Tess sighed, took a deep breath.

'I actually am the best friend you have.'

Tess groaned. The worst part of that sentence was that it was very possibly true. She had some friends from training college but most of her adult friends had been mutuals with

Chris. Jerome was the only one she'd got full custody of when they had split. She picked the skin at the edge of her thumbnail. If she'd stayed with Chris, would she have told him about Shaun Mitchell? And about what his friends had done to Sarah, and what she'd done to protect her sister? Had to do. Would she have had to tell him about Frank? Lying to Chris about who she was, who her family were and what they did for a living had been the hardest part of her relationship with him. Possibly even the reason it hadn't worked out. How can you give yourself to someone fully when you can't admit who you really are? For the first time in months, she desperately wanted to speak to the man she had almost been ready to marry.

'But they can orgasm for thirty minutes!' Jerome said.

'What?' Tess said, confused. She wasn't entirely sure she wanted to know what she'd missed at the start of that interesting fact.

'Pigs,' he said, as if it were fully obvious. 'Don't sweat. Like I was saying about whoever killed Shaun Mitchell not leaving any DNA. No sweat or anything. Like a pig.'

'Right.' Tess nodded. She'd guessed correctly: she hadn't wanted to know. 'So are you coming in on the PM or not? You might even be able to interest Kay in some of your bullshit facts.'

Jerome shook his head. 'Thought I'd prep the list of other occupants of the Grove Hill flats and pull their interviews ready for when you talk to Oswald. Unless you want me there to hold your hand?'

'Fuck off, Jerome,' Tess muttered, when what she really wanted to say was 'yes please.'

When Tess walked into the mortuary, the body of Shaun Mitchell was laid out on the table. Kay's assistant had done all the usual prep work. He looked up when Tess walked in and gave what she assumed to be a smile, although she couldn't really tell behind his mask – it could have been a grimace.

'I'm hoping you can tell me a bit more than forensics,' Tess said. 'There's nothing like the words "cleanest killer I've encountered" to strike fear in the heart of a detective.'

Kay cringed. 'Yes, not what you want to hear. What I can tell you straight off is that there are some serious injuries from the fall.'

'Can you tell which floor he fell from?'

'I thought you might ask that, so I took the liberty of looking up your flats.' This is what made Kay so good: she could always anticipate your next question and usually had an answer. 'In my opinion it wouldn't be any lower than the third, by which I mean I couldn't rule out a third-floor fall, but it's much more likely to be the fourth or higher. If it helps, he was most likely upright and facing forwards when he left the balcony. If he'd been lifted over the balcony we would see injury patterns here.' She pointed at the side of the head and shoulders. 'Much more consistent with gravity taking effect.' She mimicked picking up someone and rolling them over the side of a balcony. 'Whereas the significant injuries to the front of the body and face indicate he landed face down.'

'He's face up in all the pictures, but presumably the paramedics turned him over to check for signs of life. So you're saying this guy walked himself to the balcony and climbed over himself?' Tess nodded. 'That explains the lack of blood in the flat – someone with a knife forces him to the edge, makes him climb over, then slits his throat and shoves him.'

'The evidence from the body points that way,' Kay agreed. 'I'm not sure your evidence from the scene does.'

'I know, I know. Fuck, Kay, this case . . .' Tess stopped short. Once upon a time she'd have talked to Kay about anything. They would have finished up the post-mortem and gone for a glass of wine so that Tess could bitch and moan about a killer who managed to move through a door boarded up on the inside and stroll past a CCTV camera without being seen.

Kay sighed. Tess knew this was as weird for the pathologist as it was for her.

'Any other injuries?' Tess asked, before the tension in the room could thicken further.

Kay shook her head. 'Drug abuse, a lifetime of bad habits, some old scars but nothing that might help you. I've listed and photographed each one for the report. Looks like the throat slash was from left to right, which is consistent with a right-handed person standing behind him, or a left-handed person in front – although that's a much harder position to be in to get a cut as deep as this, and obviously he would be better positioned to defend himself if that were the case – there are no defensive marks whatsoever.'

'Was it the throat-slit that killed him?'

'It's impossible to tell which injury actually caused his death. If he hadn't fallen from the balcony, the throat wound would have killed him in less than three minutes. There was a lot of blood . . . I had to take all of the head evidence at the scene – if I'd bagged his head it would just have been covered in blood – that's how fresh the wound was. His heart carried on beating while he was on the ground for a short period of time but, because the injuries were practically simultaneous, I can't tell you if he bled to death first or if his organs gave up before he bled out.'

'They are a lot more precise on *Silent Witness*.'

Kay gave a wry smile. 'The killers are a damn sight more considerate. They only kill their victim once, for a start.'

'A regular run-of-the-mill murder case? I'd forgotten those existed. What did you get from the fingernails?'

'Nothing. Clean as a whistle. But there was one thing I've been dying to show you.'

Tess raised her eyebrows.

Kay held up her hands in defence. 'Sorry. Here.' She moved over to where a pile of sealed exhibits bags lay on the counter. 'Most of these are swabs, checking for things I might not be able to see. But this – this was very visible.' She slid out a bag and passed it to Tess, who held it up, frowning.

'Where did you get this? Is it a moth? Or a butterfly?'

'A butterfly,' Kay confirmed. 'Found in your victim's mouth.'

Chapter Fourteen

'I'm really sorry, I only have a twenty-pound note.' Sarah tried to look apologetic as she handed it over to the Bagel Man cashier. The young girl behind the counter smiled back at her. Her blonde hair was pinned back into a ponytail, dyed bright blue at the ends where it swished about her shoulders. She looked maybe seventeen, like she probably had a boyfriend and friends she went to clubs with, spending her money as fast as she made it on clothes and shoes. Worlds apart from where Sarah had been at her age.

'It's fine, I can change that.' The cashier handed her a ten-pound note, a five-pound note and two pounds eighty in change. Sarah pocketed the ten-pound note.

'Wait there, oh, God sorry, I have two twenty in the bottom of my bag – can you swap that for a ten for me?' The cashier pulled out a ten and handed it over, Sarah's change still in her other hand. 'Great, thanks.' Sarah didn't wait for the girl to put the money away. It was crucial the cashier kept the ten pounds in change in her hand.

'Actually, I may as well give you this back and take the twenty, sorry, here. Sorry to be such a pain.' Sarah giggled self-consciously and handed over the ten pounds the cashier had just given her from the till. The other girl smiled, swishing her blue ponytail as she gave Sarah back her original twenty-pound note.

'No worries, here you go. Have a great day.'

'Oh I will. Sorry again to be a pain.' Sarah gave her a winning smile, thirty pounds now in her pocket. All right, it was the shortest of short cons and she'd never make a living lifting ten quid here and there, but the thought of a free lunch was too tempting to resist. *Doesn't hurt to flex the grifting muscles every now and then.*

As Sarah walked towards the door, she noticed a familiar face coming towards her. Jesus, that was close. Tess Fox might be her half-sister, but she wasn't going to keep getting free passes for ever.

'Paid for this.' Sarah held up her bag. 'So you've got nothing on me today. Good to see you again, detective.'

'So you're done now, are you? Daddy's told you to stay away from me and that's that?' Tess looked genuinely hurt.

Sarah scowled. The woman had a cheek.

'I thought you were the one avoiding us? Or did I miss the fifteen years' worth of emails and phone calls?'

'You know why I left, Sarah.' Tess glanced around. 'Look, do you think we could do this somewhere else? Just get some lunch maybe?'

Sarah glanced at the pre-packaged sandwich and packet of crisps in her plastic bag. A grifter never turned down a free lunch.

'Fine,' she acquiesced. 'Go out of here and left at the end of the street. Then take the next right and straight on for two streets. The Poco Loco. I'll go separately in case anyone sees us. My reputation would be ruined.'

Tess had already found a seat and ordered a drink when Sarah arrived at the Poco Loco.

She reached into her bag and slipped on a pair of red-rimmed glasses and fixed a huge bow in her hair.

'I thought we were supposed to be keeping a low profile,' Tess muttered.

'Misdirection is my job – not yours. I don't tell you how to solve murders. Oh . . . wait . . . I take it that's what I'm here for?' She grinned.

'Very funny,' Tess said. 'Has your dad found out anything that might help me?'

'I don't know why you keep doing that. He's your dad too. You can't keep denying it for ever.'

Tess scowled. 'Except I have to, don't I? If anyone on the force found out what my father did for a living, I would be fired.'

'Well that's unfair. You can't choose your family.'

'Can you imagine the embarrassment it would cause to the force if it came out that one of their DIs was linked to Brighton and Hove's biggest confidence men? Every case I've ever worked on would be called into question.'

They sat in silence, Tess looking like she wanted to lock herself in a dark room and never come out. Sarah wanted to feel for her, but she also wanted to hate her for not caring about their family enough to stick around. She was beginning to realize just how effectively she'd boxed away everything that had happened to her all those years ago – including losing her sister.

Sarah picked up the menu and glanced at it – anything to break the tense silence. 'I'll have the steak baguette with chips and a side of onion rings. It's more likely to be pigeon in here but it'll have to do. I wouldn't usually be caught dead in a dump like this.'

Tess looked around. Low flickering lights, shadowy corners and a bar so sopping wet you could get a day's takings if you wiped it down and wrung the cloth out. 'I'd have thought this was exactly the kind of place you people would love.'

'*You people*?' Sarah raised her eyebrows. 'If we're going to be partners, you're going to have to start sounding a lot less elitist. I'll have you know that *our* people are more "wine bar" than "backstreet dive". And I speak four different languages fluently. How many of *your people* can do that?' Sarah didn't wait for a reply. 'I'll have a glass of red with mine.'

When Tess returned from the bar, she handed Sarah her drink and put her own Diet Coke on the table. Sarah nodded towards the glass. 'Let me guess, you don't drink. Recovering alcoholic?'

'You read too many crime novels.'

'Maybe. But even tired old clichés come from somewhere.'

'You have an exceptional mind, Sarah. Don't you ever want to use it for something good?'

'Like what you do, you mean?'

'Yes, actually. You're exactly the kind of person we could use in Major Crimes.'

'Is that a job offer?' Sarah shook her head. 'That was your problem from the start, Tess. From the moment you met me, you thought you knew what was best for me. You thought you could change me. When, in actual fact, you weren't sure of who you really were, were you? Why else would you leave your mum to come and find a father who didn't even know you existed?'

Tess breathed in sharply. 'Harsh, but perhaps fair. You're right, I wasn't like my mum, and I didn't ever want to be. I wanted to know if I was like my dad.'

Sarah snorted. 'Must have been a disappointment.'

'I didn't know how to feel, if I'm honest with you. My mum was a bit of a bitch but she raised me to know right from wrong. Then I find you and the rules don't apply.'

'I know,' Sarah said, beaming. 'You should try it. The feeling that you could get caught at any moment – it's like the best sex you've ever had. Assuming you've had sex.'

'Funny,' Tess replied. 'I'm fine with sticking to the rules, thanks. I don't think I'll be throwing away my career to become a two-bit grifter.'

'Am I supposed to be insulted by that? There's one thing you can count on: a grifter is always the smartest person in the room.'

'Don't get carried away with yourself. I've never fallen for a con and I never intend to.'

Sarah laughed. 'Ah, that's because the grift is in your blood. Although if you'd fallen foul of *us lot*, you'd never even know about it.'

'Okay.' Tess smiled and leaned back. 'If you say so.'

'You think you're so clever?' Sarah raised an eyebrow and pulled a deck of cards from her handbag. She slammed three cards onto the table. 'Here. First trick *our* dad ever taught me. He'd have taught you too if you'd stuck around. I'll bet you one English pound that you can't follow the ace.' She handed Tess the cards, inviting her to study them. Two jokers and an ace. 'I'll give you the first hand for free – as a practice.'

Sarah rolled up her sleeves and demonstrated she wasn't hiding anything. She laid all three cards face up, picked them up and showed Tess. 'Here, follow the ace, got it?'

She placed the cards face down and began to shuffle them back and forth, fast enough not to patronize, slow enough so Tess kept track. 'Well?'

Tess pointed at the middle card. 'It's there.'

Sarah flipped over the card and looked triumphant. When she saw the ace facing up, Sarah's face fell. 'Okay, it's been a while since I did this. Give me another chance.'

She flipped the cards and shuffled again. Tess pointed to the far-right card. Sarah flipped them all over, crestfallen to see the ace on the far right. 'Wait—'

'You owe me a pound.' Tess grinned.

'Look, one more chance, double or quits. I can do this, honest!'

'Fine.' Tess watched as Sarah moved the cards around again, the ace clearly resting in the middle. She sighed impatiently. 'Middle. Look, I . . .'

Tess stopped as Sarah flipped over the cards, the ace on the far right again. She sat back, genuinely triumphant this time.

Tess groaned. 'You knew where it was the whole time – you were just trying to get me to up the stakes.'

'Of course I did,' Sarah replied. 'Magic isn't just about sleight of hand or misdirection, it's about the stories we tell ourselves. Life is just one big story, Tess. You've spun yourself a story about me – I'm a two-bit criminal, a chancer, arrogant and cocky – and one about yourself – you're the heroic detective, moral and intelligent. In stories, the good guys win, and so that's what you're expecting to happen. Me losing twice confirms your story must be true: you're cleverer than me and I'm a chancer. We use people's stories about themselves, about us, about the world – we study and read people. I know what your next move will be before you know you're going to make one. That's what it means to be two steps ahead. Keep your two quid – it was worth it to be part of your first ever con.'

Tess sat back and let out a breath. 'Wow. How about I buy us another drink, in recognition of all the money you've just saved poor, naive, future me?'

Sarah nodded in satisfaction. 'Sounds good to me.'

As Tess went to stand up, Sarah's eyes flicked to the door, where a man in a faded denim jacket and black jeans had just walked in.

'Shit,' she hissed. 'Sit down!'

Tess dropped back into her seat. 'What?' she asked, looking at the man Sarah had hastily turned her back on. 'What's Mac doing in here?'

'That's what I'd like to know,' Sarah muttered from between clenched teeth. 'What's he doing?'

Tess glanced over. 'He's just standing by the bar, staring at his phone. Doesn't look very happy. He's just turned the barman away – I don't think he's staying. I thought you said your people wouldn't be caught dead in a place like this?'

'Yeah, well, usually we wouldn't. Which means he was probably doing exactly the same as I was – hoping not to be seen.' Sarah turned and took a quick glance over her shoulder in time to see Mac shove his phone back into his pocket angrily. 'He's leaving,' she muttered. Her relief quickly turned to curiosity. 'I wonder why?'

'Maybe he got stood up,' Tess offered. 'He didn't see you, anyway. Shall I get us those drinks?'

But Sarah was already grabbing her bag.

'Come on,' she said. 'Something's going on.'

Chapter Fifteen

When they left the pub, Sarah ditched her hair bow and sunglasses for a baseball cap pulled from an inside pocket. She scanned the street to see which way Mac had gone.

'There.' Tess grabbed her arm and pointed at where the black jeans were disappearing around a corner. Sarah broke into a sprint and heard Tess running behind her. When they reached the corner, Sarah flung out an arm to stop Tess from rounding it. She stuck her head around in time to see him push open the door to a small, trendy-looking coffee shop – outside painted in Farrow & Ball, windows stencilled with a hand-drawn logo, chalkboard out front inclusive of witty caption – and take a seat far enough away from the window that he was hidden in shadow.

'Over here,' Tess said, dragging Sarah across the road to a partially crumbling wall. They both crouched behind it, earning themselves a glance from a passer-by. Mac was nursing a cup of something, a newspaper spread out in front of him. He looked up and Sarah started: he seemed to be looking straight at her. Then she noticed the woman who had just walked into the café. Her back was to the door, she had long brown hair and was wearing a black leather jacket and jeans, but she was facing away from Sarah and she couldn't get any handle on how old she was. Not as old as Mac, judging by the posture, hair and outfit. More Sarah's age, possibly. She made her way over to the table Mac was sitting at, but he didn't move to hug her or even smile. Who was she?

'Who's that?' Tess muttered. 'You know her?'

'I can't get a good look at her.' Sarah grimaced. 'But I don't think I've seen her before.'

It wasn't the family's business to know everything about each other. They weren't some sort of controlling cult; they all had their own separate lives, the same as any other family would – the difference being that only Sarah and Frank shared the same blood. But even though they didn't have to know every detail of each other's lives, their close proximity meant they kind of did. For example, Sarah knew that Mac, just like her father, had no contact with his real family. He'd never married; she had heard him and her dad talk about a couple of short-term relationships, but she had never been introduced to a girlfriend. Especially not one who looked to be Sarah's own age. The idea that Mac might have a girlfriend, or even a daughter, that Sarah didn't know about was like finding out your grandad had another family. Weird. It occurred to her to call Wes to find out if Mac was on a job, but that same instinct that stopped her calling out when she saw him on the street stopped her picking up the phone.

She had always just assumed that Mac's life began and ended

with the family, and the idea that he might have a whole other side of his life made her feel . . . deeply strange.

The waitress brought the woman a drink and Sarah saw Mac's lips were moving. Part of her skillset as a grifter was being able to read lips, and expressions. Mac wasn't happy with this woman. He wasn't frowning or yelling, but there was a hardness in his face, and certain words such as 'not a chance' and 'can't' were easy to make out, each time accompanied with a slight head shake. He was refusing her something, and she was insistent. Although Sarah couldn't see her face, her shoulders were hunched; she hadn't relaxed for a second. God, what she'd give to be able to hear both sides of this conversation.

After less than ten minutes since her arrival, the woman pushed aside a half-drunk cup of coffee, threw a note on the table and shoved back her seat. She was getting up. Sarah held her breath as the woman turned around, and she had half a second to catch a glimpse of pretty, feline features, perfect eyebrows, a small straight nose, before the woman started to leave the café and Sarah had to duck behind the wall.

Sarah longed to follow her, but if she moved now Mac would spot her as he left the café. Shit. The woman stalked down the street, away from where Sarah was hiding, and disappeared down a right turn. Mac sat in the café, head in his hands, looking completely lost, and she knew one thing for certain – if she ever asked him about this meeting, he would lie.

'Are you going to tell me what that was all about?' Tess asked when Sarah aimed a kick at the wall. 'Or do I not want to know?'

'I don't even know if I want to know,' Sarah groaned. 'Want to go get crepes?'

'I've got to get back to the station.' Tess glanced at her watch. 'Despite what a good team we make, both of our futures might depend on me making sure I keep on top of what my team is uncovering.'

'Good team, eh?' Sarah grinned, ignoring Tess's implication. 'Maybe I'll make a confidence woman of you yet.'

'Or maybe I'll make a police officer of you.'

Sarah grimaced. 'Now that *is* funny.'

Chapter Sixteen

The statue stood on Brighton seafront, a constant breeze whipping around its face. It had one arm in the air, as though it had been frozen in time while hailing a taxi. A young girl of about four approached, gingerly taking one step towards it then stopping, edging ever so slightly forwards, encouraged by her mother. When she was almost close enough to touch it, she threw her coins into the hat by its feet and the statue bowed, dropping its arm into a thank you.

The girl shrieked; the small watching crowd laughed. Her home town at its purest - entertainment and fun.

Brighton in February wasn't the Brighton most people saw. Most people – tourists, in other words – saw a crowded seafront, smelled doughnuts and candy floss and the scent of bacon wafting from the cafés, and heard the music from the pier, the excited shrieks of children. Outside the school holidays it slowed down, quietened down, like its senses had been dulled. There were still children, but they were not quite of school age, like the girl watching the statue, and the odd group of teenagers bunking off – or on 'study leave'. The seagulls still hovered overhead in February, though, their beady eyes watching and waiting for any sign of an unguarded churro or some discarded chips.

As Sarah walked, she stared out across the sea, the salty breeze chilling her arms and face. She needed to talk things over with somebody she could confide in who wasn't her father. Pulling out her phone, she typed out a message.

You free?

Wes replied almost instantly. *Where?*

Meet me at the twins.

Preston Park was once home to the Preston Twins which, at four hundred years old, were the oldest English Elm trees in Europe. Now though, only one of the twins remained. High winds in 2017 had felled a bough from the second twin, revealing an entirely hollow trunk, and Brighton Council had made the difficult decision to channel between the trees, disconnect the roots and cut the rest of the tree back. The remaining tree, although still a majestic sight, looked down on the mutilated remains of its twin in sorrow. Sarah always thought it one of the saddest places she'd ever seen, yet still one of her favourites. Gabe had brought her here once when she was about six and they had played hide and seek for what felt like hours. She knew now that there was probably a reason Gabe had been told to keep her out of the way, but she tried not to view her every memory through the glasses of a criminal life.

She leaned against the small fence surrounding the second twin, waiting for Wes to arrive. After dark it was much easier to hop the fence and climb inside the hollow, but she didn't need any extra attention drawn to herself today. When Wes arrived, he looked concerned.

'Everything okay?' he asked.

'Not really. I need to go over something with you, but' – Sarah wetted her lips – 'but I need you not to ask me any questions about context, or, anything really. Just pretend it's a puzzle in a book. And don't tell Dad,' she added.

Wes shrugged. 'Okay,' he agreed easily. 'But I'm not lying to Frank. If he asks me specifically whether you came to me to help with an out-of-context puzzle, I'll say yes, she did. *Boss*.'

Sarah smiled at his acceptance, despite his reluctance to be caught lying to her dad. There was no way Frank would ask Wes specifically about what she was about to discuss with him; therefore he didn't have to lie for her. Just omit the odd detail.

'Thank you.' She pulled out a notebook. 'So let's say, hypothetically, that someone has been killed. And at the scene, the police find traces of blood in only three places: a door between the lounge and the bedroom, a light switch close to the door and on a wastepaper bin. Only on the bin it's not a smear, it's initials. CA. No usable prints.' She looked at him expectantly. 'What are your first thoughts?'

'Why isn't there more blood?'

Sarah nodded and underlined the place in her notes where she'd scrawled *WHERE IS ALL THE BLOOD?* 'That was one of my thoughts. The only trace the luminol picked up was those three places. Nothing else.'

'How do you know it was blood, though? Has it been tested?'

Sarah frowned. 'I assume it was swabbed, but if it was picked up by luminol then it was blood, right?'

'Not necessarily. Got anything to eat?'

'I'll go get us something in a bit,' Sarah replied impatiently. 'What do you mean, not necessarily?'

Wes looked like he was about to argue on the food front but thought better of it. 'Luminol picks up a couple of other things too. Blood is one, faeces . . .'

Sarah screwed up her nose.

'And horseradish.'

'Excuse me?'

He nodded enthusiastically. 'Yeah, weird, right? Horseradish peroxidase catalyses the oxidation in luminol.'

Sarah made him repeat the exact wording while she wrote it down in her notebook, marvelling about what a fountain of weird knowledge her family was. She wondered if Tess knew there might be even less blood in the flat than she'd first thought.

'Okay, so let's say for a second that the reason there was only the three traces of blood was because there was actually no blood at all, and these marks were made by something else – possibly horseradish.' She raised her eyebrows but Wes nodded. 'So the light switch and the door could actually have been an accident – say our victim being gross and not washing his hands after he's eaten. But the bin . . . that was done deliberately.'

'Had to have bin,' Wes quipped, a goofy grin on his face. 'Get it? Bin?' His face fell. 'God, my talents are wasted around here.'

Sarah ignored him and carried on talking, mostly to herself. 'So what does CA mean? And who put it there, killer or victim?'

129

Sarah remembered what Tess had said earlier. *In real life, killers don't leave the police messages on the walls.*

Unless maybe the clue wasn't for the police. Sarah pictured the leaflet for the Three Flamingos – stuck to the wall with a dart, Tess had said. Something threatened to click into place in her subconscious, something just out of reach . . . The door, the light . . .

'What if it wasn't one word . . .' she muttered, scribbling some more in her notebook. 'How about three . . . but why?'

'What are you talking about?' Wes craned his neck to get a better look at the paper. 'What three words?'

Sarah snapped her fingers. 'That's it! Wes, you are a genius!' She picked up her phone and began typing furiously.

The young hacker looked as if he'd never felt more stupid in his life. 'Usually I am, but right now I haven't got the foggiest id—'

'I'll tell you when I've figured it all out,' Sarah promised, scribbling furiously in her notebook. To determine if Shaun Mitchell's murder had anything to do with her, she was going to have to get back into that flat.

'Detective Inspector Tess Fox.' Sarah held out her hand to the manager of Shaun Mitchell's building, a man called Phil Gonsall, hoping he wouldn't take it. He was really, ridiculously tall and thin, dark hair past his ears and slick with grease. Sarah didn't like touching people at the best of times, let alone someone quite so shiny looking, and she retracted her hand quickly before he could accept the offer. 'I think we met the night of Mr Mitchell's murder?' She had pulled her hair back into a sharp ponytail, mimicking her sister's, and was dressed in a sharp but stylish trouser suit. She hoped that would be enough to convince him.

Phil shrugged, leaning on the door frame of his flat. He kept shifting position to block her view inside, then shuffling on his feet like he was preparing to do a runner. Sarah thought that detectives probably got that all the time, people acting guilty as all hell. 'Name rings a bell. It was a bit mad that night though, hey? What can I help you with, detective?' Shift, shuffle, shift.

'I need to get back into Mr Mitchell's flat. Is there any way you could help me with that?'

'The officer I talked to said you were done,' Phil said defensively. 'Said I could start cleaning it up. I got the cleaners in yesterday afternoon; it was disgusting in there and the council want to rent it out again soon as possible . . .'

'That's fine,' Sarah assured him. 'We absolutely did say it was okay for you to start cleaning. Are Mr Mitchell's things still in there?' She held her breath, waiting for his reply. If the desk was gone then this was all for nothing. Or if she was wrong about the markings on the bin and the light and the door in the first place. That was a lot of ifs.

'Yeah. No one's picked them up yet. Would you be able to check up on that for me? Because I need it cleared out, you know.'

'If you can just lend me the key for a few minutes, I'll speak to the deceased's next of kin and get that all sorted just for you.' She gave him what she knew was a winning smile. He hadn't even asked for ID; this guy wasn't going to give her any trouble. It was the nosy neighbours she was going to have to worry about.

As soon as he closed the door, Sarah opened the bag she'd brought with her, slipped on a baggy sweater over her cream blouse and pinned her long dark hair under a blonde wig, shoving a baseball hat on top. There was nothing she could do about her height, but the wig and the baggy clothes might fool anyone watching the CCTV back. Hopefully it would be enough to fool her sister, should she ever have cause to check. Tess wasn't exactly a fan of her impersonating police officers and breaking into crime scenes, and Sarah could just imagine her glee at getting to arrest her twice in two weeks. Whatever was hidden in this flat had better be worth all this trouble.

'The police are looking for you,' a voice called from the doorway across the hall.

Sarah almost dropped the bunch of keys in shock.

'Me?' she said, only half turning so the elderly woman couldn't get a good look at her face. 'I don't think so.'

'Oh, I'm sorry, love.' The woman came out of her doorway to stand in front of Sarah. There was no way of getting away from her now; she'd just have to brazen it out. 'I thought you were that sister of his. You look like her a bit, except she had dark hair, longer than yours. Different nose too, now I look at you. My eyes aren't as good as they used to be.'

'Oh, not to worry. I've just been asked to pick up a few things. So the police are looking for his sister?'

'Yes, do you know her? Perhaps you could get her to call that nice girl detective – Freya, was it?'

'Yes, I'll tell her. Although I haven't seen her for ages, I think she's been travelling. I don't know how the police even knew about her. They're so clever, aren't they?'

The old lady beamed. 'Well, it was me who told them about her. I saw her, you see, not long ago. She was visiting, had a bunch of keys like yours and I came out to let her know it was the one with the blue top. I thought it might have been his girlfriend, but she laughed when I said that and said she was his sister. Anyway, I told the police and they said if she came back I was to get her to call them. Poor thing might not even know what happened to him. And then I saw you and thought you were her. Sorry to bother you.'

'Wait.' Sarah stopped the woman as she turned to go. 'If you do see her again, could you give her my number? It's been so long since I saw her. My name's Sarah, here's my number.'

'Sarah?' the old woman repeated. She looked confused. 'Your name's Sarah?'

'Yes,' Sarah said slowly. 'Why, what's strange about that?'

'Well, nothing, I suppose. It's a very common name, no offence, dear. It's just funny that you've got the same name, that's all, but you know that, of course.'

'Yes, funny.' Sarah smiled. 'The same name as . . . ?'

'As his sister – Sarah.'

Of course . . . Of course the woman who had visited would have given her name. Who was she? Was she the one who had hidden something for Sarah to find? Bin . . . door . . . light. CA . . .

The door to the flat swung open; the smell of bleach hit her instantly. She walked quickly over the still filth-encrusted carpet – she bet the landlord was going to have to replace those completely – to where the desk sat and knelt down to run her fingers along the edges and underneath, feeling for anything out of place. It didn't take long for her to find the false panel in the middle drawer. Slipping her fingernail into the crack, she worked the wood loose until it came free with a scraping noise and something small and round tumbled out. Sarah pulled it out and – looking at it in horror – realized she was most definitely dealing with someone who wanted her framed for murder. Because the ring now sitting in her hand, encrusted with dried blood, belonged to her.

Chapter Seventeen

Sarah paced back and forth across her living room, her phone in one hand and the bloodied ring in another. She'd panicked back at Shaun Mitchell's flat – she realized that now – but it was too late to return the ring. And anyway, she didn't want to risk it being found by anyone else, so what else could she have done but pocket it?

She flicked between the two numbers in her phone once more, eventually landing on one. Sarah took a deep breath and dialled her father's number. She didn't have any choice. There was direct evidence linking her to a murder and she'd just stolen it from a crime scene. She was going to have to confide in Frank, tell him everything and let him help her, just like he always did. Perhaps if she'd grown up with her mother, if Lily Jacobs hadn't been ripped away from her by that horrific illness before she had a chance to remember her properly, she would be calling her mum now, or if Tess hadn't taken off after what had happened, she would have chosen her number over her dad's. Hell, perhaps none of them would be in this situation if her mum had been alive, or if Tess hadn't left them. But it was what it was. Now she had to find out how a ring that had always been in her jewellery box at home had managed to find its way to a murder scene. Because there were very few people who could come by that particular piece of jewellery, and they were all people she called family. So right now the only person she could fully trust was her dad – she knew he would never betray her.

'Sarah?' Frank sounded concerned when he answered the phone. 'Everything okay?'

'Dad, where are you?' Sarah sat down on the light grey suede corner sofa. 'I need to talk to you at home. It's about that murder Tess was telling you about the other day . . .'

'Sweetheart, have you forgotten I'm on a job?'

No wonder he'd sounded so concerned – Sarah only contacted him when he was working if there was a risk of exposure. She *was* confused about what he was doing though; she was sure they didn't have anything on this week. They'd had the Jupiter restaurant job, but they hadn't agreed that one yet, and she'd raised serious objections. Surely her father wouldn't go ahead and start it without her? When Mac had first mentioned the place she'd thought it was a chain, some big corporate deal with a fat-cat manager who probably wouldn't notice he'd even been conned. Then she'd been for lunch there. The owner, Remi, had been warm and funny. He'd stopped to talk to her about how long he'd owned the branch, how his family worked with him every evening and weekend to make a go of it. And when Sarah had gone home and checked Companies House, she'd realized that all the hard work Remi and his family had put in was not paying off. The restaurant was in real trouble.

'Wait . . . are you out at the Jupiter?'

Silence.

'We didn't agree that job yet, Dad,' Sarah snapped. 'Jupiter is on the brink; this guy can't afford to lose money. The guy who owns the place isn't some big corporate chain – it's family run.'

Sarah heard her father sigh. 'I know that already, Sarah. Mac has done the grunt work on this. It's okay, he assures me they're good for the cash. He's heard of this guy – he's hungry for money and he'll stump up what we need.'

'He's in a bad place, financially. Losing this money – it could tip his business over the edge.'

Silence on the other end. Then, 'What are you saying?'

'I'm saying' – Sarah paused – 'I don't think we should hit this one. We can get the same money – more maybe – if we just scope out a different mark. If this guy is in trouble, what's to say he'll even foot the cash?'

'He'll foot the cash because he's greedy, Sarah, the same as every other mark we come across. What's got into you all of a sudden?'

She didn't know, truth be told. She couldn't place why all of a sudden she cared that this man could go bankrupt, that he might lose everything. She had come to terms with the fact that they weren't good people years ago. That their fortune was another person's misfortune. Why was this starting to feel so wrong all of a sudden? Because she'd met Remi? Because he'd been kind to her? Or because of Tess?

'Nothing's got into me, Dad,' Sarah said firmly. She got up from the sofa and paced the floor again, returning to the floor-to-ceiling glass window she loved so much to gaze out at the sea. It just felt wrong, surrounded by all this wealth, talking about taking money from a man who was in such a bad place that he'd risk everything his family had for the chance to get out of it. 'And he's not greedy – he's desperate. There's a difference. I just think we could put a little more effort into our work. You know, find someone who is good for more than a grand. This con only works so many times before the police start putting out alerts – why are we wasting our limited opportunities on small fish? Because *Mac* said so?'

It was a low blow to question his leadership and she knew it. Mac had been her father's best friend and mentor ever since Frank broke ties with his own father, when he was just a boy, for reasons he'd never divulged to her. Mac had taught him everything he knew. And when he had overtaken his mentor as one of the most notorious conmen in the South, Mac hadn't even tried to put him back in his place. He'd never overstep the boundaries of their friendship, and yet the suggestion that he might be pulling the strings still struck a nerve with Frank.

'What's that supposed to mean?' he snapped. 'You think Mac is running this show? I make the decisions, you know that.'

'It doesn't look that way from where I'm standing. And that's not how it's going to look from the outside. Mac's old; he's content to pull short con after short con, hitting low-key family-owned businesses, making a grand a day. I remember when you wouldn't get out of bed for a con worth less than ten grand. I thought Frank Jacobs was the cleverest fraudster since Abagnale?'

There was silence on the other end, then her father's voice, hurt but defiant. 'I don't know what you're playing at Sarah, but we're not calling this off now. You know the score – maybe you're the one who needs to think about where you're standing, and what the view would look like from elsewhere.'

The line went dead, leaving Sarah staring out of the window through the tears in her eyes.

Chapter Eighteen

Sarah stood staring at the door of Tess's flat for ten whole minutes. She had turned and walked away three times, at minute four, minute seven and minute nine, before finally pressing her finger to the doorbell and almost walking away again. The smell of the Chinese takeaway radiated through the white plastic bag biting into her fingers.

The door opened almost straight away, owing to the fact, Sarah assumed, that the entire flat beyond was the same size as her bedroom. Not only that but it was practically empty. It looked as though Tess was preparing to move out. Either that or she'd Marie Kondo'd and nothing she'd owned had brought her much joy.

Tess gave her a look so loaded with disbelief that Sarah felt as though she had woken from a sleepwalk.

'What are you doing here?' Tess demanded, her eyes dropping to the bag at Sarah's side.

'I don't know.' Sarah shook her head. 'I genuinely don't know. Pretend I'm not.' She turned around, ready to make a quick getaway. Fortunately, that was something she had experience in.

'Wait.' Tess's voice stopped her short. 'Is that takeaway?'

'Chinese,' Sarah replied, turning back slowly. 'Beef chow mein, special fried rice, crispy duck.'

'Prawn crackers?'

'I mean, would it be a Chinese without prawn crackers?'

Tess glanced around the hallway as if someone might be watching the outside of her flat. 'Quick,' she said. 'Get in.'

'Cutlery is in there,' Tess said, directing Sarah to the kitchen area and pulling out plates. 'So what are you doing here?'

Sarah went to say she didn't know again, but that wouldn't be true. Turning her head away so Tess couldn't see her face and dishing chow mein onto a plate, she muttered, 'I had a row with Dad.'

'Okaaay,' Tess said slowly. 'But that's not really an answer.'

'I know.'

Tess gestured to the sofa and they carried their plates over, piling up the coffee table with the Chinese buffet Sarah had provided. 'This place is really small,' Sarah observed. 'I thought being a detective paid well?'

'I'm saving for a deposit. It's not easy getting a mortgage on your own, you know. Wait.' Tess leaned forwards and grabbed a prawn cracker. 'You own your own place, amiright?'

Sarah shook her head. 'Nah,' she said. 'I live with Dad. Where's your mum these days?'

'Still living in Sheffield. What did you fight with Da . . . Frank over?'

Sarah bit her lip, unsure of what to say. She didn't want to tell Tess that she'd driven to her flat with the intention of convincing Tess to stop the con her dad was on. It had been a desperate idea, because she hadn't known what else to do, but as soon as she'd seen Tess arrive home she'd known she couldn't do it. Not that she didn't want to stop Frank, but she couldn't put her sister in the position to be the one to do it. She'd have to find a way to make good with Remi herself, and deal with the fallout like a grown woman, instead of expecting her big sister to come to her rescue again.

Still, when she'd seen Tess arrive home, she hadn't turned around and left. She'd gone to fetch food and considered telling Tess that she'd solved the mystery of the letters CA. She had been about to tell her dad about the ring before their argument, and she still felt the need to tell someone. But would Tess believe her? Or would she be forced to arrest her?

'We had a disagreement over work,' she settled on. 'I can't really go into it, for obvious reasons.'

The implication hung in the air between them – they were on two very different sides of the coin when it came to work. They sat in silence for a few minutes, each contemplating what a terrible idea it was for them to even be sitting there together.

'My mum is sick,' Tess said eventually. Sarah sniffed. She didn't even need to ask if it was bad – she could see it was from the pain on Tess's face.

'God, I'm sorry. Are you going to go to Sheffield?'

'Maybe,' Tess said. 'Probably not.' She paused. 'No.'

'Wh—'

'She doesn't want me to,' Tess said quickly; if she didn't get it out fast, she wouldn't say it at all. 'We're not on the best of terms.'

'Right.' Sarah wanted to ask more but she also didn't want to push. In her experience, people spoke a lot more honestly if they wanted to speak in the first place. Perhaps this was the real reason Tess had sought her out for help, but she knew that wasn't possible. Tess could hardly go from the police station to a cosy Sunday lunch with Sarah and her criminal family. Could she?

'Do you remember your mum?' Tess asked, breaking into her thoughts.

Sarah closed her eyes for a second, saw the flashing lights, almost heard the carnival music, as she often did when she thought of her childhood. 'I'm not sure. I think so. Sometimes I get snatches of memories that I hope are real, being pushed on a swing at the park, running through woods playing hide and seek. In them, though, my mother is always barefoot, and always wearing the same outfit she's wearing in my favourite photograph of her, so I can never be sure if they're real or imagined.'

'I think they're real,' Tess said kindly. Sarah shook her head.

'I'm not so sure.' She leaned forwards, pointed her fork at Tess. 'You see, the fairground is in my blood – I know it's true because I wake up with the smell of fried dough in my nostrils, flashing coloured lights still behind my mind. I hear the pounding music of the Waltzers and the delighted screams of teenagers being spun around and around and around. The pink of the candyfloss machines, bright yellow rubber ducks and gaping mouthed clown faces, it's all here' – she tapped the side of her head with the fork – 'and yet, I've *never stepped foot in a fairground*. My dad forbade it my entire life. I think it's too hard for him, to bring back all those memories. Memories I *shouldn't even have*. What's that if it isn't wishful thinking?'

'What's Brighton, if not a fairground?' Tess asked, her voice gentle. Sarah sighed.

'You're right. And yet it doesn't feel the same. The feel of mud on your knees and the smell of churned-up grass in the air. It's the fair, Jim, but not as we know it.'

Tess gave a sad smile. 'You were three, weren't you? When she died?'

Sarah nodded. 'Yeah.'

'I'm so sorry.'

Sarah picked up her can of Diet Coke and shrugged. 'Thanks. Are you going to tell me why you're not talking to your mum?'

Tess looked at her with something like admiration. Of course, she could hardly refuse, now that Sarah had opened up about the death of her own mother. She was snookered.

'Why *she* doesn't talk to *me*, remember?'

'Right. What'd you do?'

Tess sighed. 'I didn't do anything. We were never particularly close. She hated that I wanted to know about my real father, so we fought about that, remember? She's never really forgiven me for moving here. She thinks I want to be closer to Frank than I was to her.'

'And do you?'

'No,' Tess scoffed, but she didn't look at Sarah when she said it. Sarah raised her eyebrows until Tess said, 'I guess I've never really let myself believe that I stayed so close to Brighton because you guys were here, but it's hard to find a plausible excuse for why I didn't get the hell out of Dodge when I left the crew.'

'And your mum never forgave you?'

'Every time we spoke after that, she made out like I'd chosen him over her. When in reality I didn't have either of them any more. Like I said, I've never been close to Mum anyway. It always just felt like I belonged somewhere else.'

'Do you still feel like that?'

'I belong in the police,' Tess said, her voice so firm that Sarah wasn't sure who she was trying to convince – Sarah, or herself. 'I don't need anything else.'

'So he says—'

'I just slept with your wife, whisky please!'

Sarah looked devastated and Tess burst out laughing. 'What, because I'm a detective I'm supposed to never have heard a joke before?'

'Well, you could have pretended,' Sarah grumbled, but she grinned too.

The conversation had flowed more easily after she had opened up about her mother. It had turned to magic and illusions, Sarah getting more and more animated as she spoke of the greats – James Randi, Rocco Silano, Val Valentino – who broke the code and showed the audience exactly how the tricks were done. Her passion was infectious, and soon Tess was laughing at the old stories of Sarah's early forays into magic shows, charging her peers 50p to be beguiled by cups and balls, convincing her dad to be her assistant and watching him try to fit inside boxes and avoid death by broomstick as she invented her own versions of the sword tricks. Some of the stories she'd heard back when they'd first met, but they were still just as interesting. Tess could probably listen to Sarah's escapades all night. She even learned a few card tricks herself. She hadn't had a girly night like this since she had joined the police force, and as the evening had progressed it had become less and less important to her what Sarah did for a living. It had felt like having a friend. Or a sister.

'Am I allowed to ask how the investigation is going?' Sarah asked after a while, her voice tentative.

Tess hesitated.

'You don't have to tell me,' Sarah said quickly. 'I get it. I just thought maybe I could help.'

Tess gave her a quick run-down of the latest evidence. After all, the most information she had was an absence of it. But Sarah perked up when she explained what Kay had found at the post-mortem.

'A butterfly?' Sarah had her feet tucked underneath her on the sofa and was taking another swig of wine. 'That's not normal, right? I mean, it's normal on TV – I once saw a programme where a guy's penis had been cut off and shoved down his throat, but in real life?'

'No,' Tess agreed. 'Definitely not normal in real life. But nothing about this is normal in real life. There was nothing in that crime scene, Sarah. My boss gave us the go-ahead to send forensics onto five other balconies in that block of flats. Not a single drop of blood was found on any of them. No murder weapon, no blood-stained clothes. Nothing.'

'Okay, so let's say he was forced to the edge of the balcony and made to climb over. His throat was cut from behind and he was shoved. Would that explain the lack of blood?'

Tess nodded. 'It would be a huge stroke of luck not to get even a couple of spots, but it's possible. Unlikely, but physically possible.'

'Right. But you still have the question of how that person got out of a flat locked from the inside, covered by CCTV.'

'Yeah, the part you were supposed to be figuring out?'

'Can you draw me a picture of the butterfly?'

Tess sat forwards in surprise. Her head swam slightly from the bottle of wine they had just shared, and she steadied herself on the arm of the chair. 'Why? Do you know what it means?'

Sarah shook her head. 'Not yet. But I've been thinking . . . about that drainpipe. If you can draw me a picture, I'll do a bit of research.'

'Okay.' Tess tried not to sound too disappointed. She'd thought Sarah had been about to tell her something a few times that night, but perhaps she was reading too much into everything.

'It's the timeline I'm interested in,' Sarah said instead. 'When did he write the letters on the bin? Obviously not when he was held at knife point. He's not going to go, "oh, hold on, let me write your initials somewhere for the police to find." And even if he did, why the bin? Why not somewhere more obvious?'

'Okaaay.'

'And so then he's walked at knife-point to the balcony, he climbs over the railing. His killer then reaches forwards, slashes his throat, then what? Shoves a butterfly in his mouth before shoving him off the balcony? Every second that guy is on the balcony is a second closer to being seen. Why take the risk for the butterfly?'

'You're forgetting one thing,' Tess noted, rubbing the heel of her hand into her tired eyes. 'He wasn't worried about being seen. He's invisible, remember?'

Chapter Nineteen

'Guv,' Jerome's voice cut through the tangle of thoughts bouncing around Tess's head as she tried for the fourth time to read the statement on the desk in front of her. Her cosy chat with Sarah had kept her up way past her bedtime and this morning she was knackered. 'I grabbed us these.' Jerome tossed her a wrapped bacon bap from the canteen and a can of Diet Coke. 'You look like shit. You sleeping?'

'You treat all your women like this?' Tess looked at the food and back at her partner, who was pulling his 'I'm waiting' face, coat in his hand. She sighed and looked pointedly at the coat. 'We haven't got time to go out to eat. Unless it's escaped your attention, we don't have a single strong lead. Usually by this point we know who we're after and the rest is bureaucratic bollocks. I'm going to fuck up my first ever murder case and be thrown off the force, and you are offering bacon?'

Jerome shoved her own jacket at her. 'You've got a whole team behind you. Everyone is working their ass off to make sure we nail this guy. The investigation is not going to collapse if you eat a sandwich. Come on, we'll call it a meeting. You should see the place I've found us.'

This was something about Jerome that only Tess knew. She trusted him in a way she hadn't trusted anyone in a long while, and he obviously trusted her too, because even the secret group he was part of didn't know who he really was. In fact Tess thought she might be the only person in the world who knew about both sides of her DS.

Jerome was an urban explorer, a pastime which wasn't entirely legal, involving trespassing and sometimes breaking and entering into disused buildings. He was part of an Urbex group who operated around Sussex, exploring closed-down psychiatric facilities, disused railway tracks, sewers . . . you close it, they would open it. Their escapades were documented on Jerome's website, Sussex From Where You Are Not. It meant that whichever station in the county the team happened to be working from, Jerome could always find them somewhere quiet to eat. It was a gift for investigations in the city too.

Today's cafeteria was an abandoned garage on Circus Street, just a street away from Brighton Police Station; so close, in fact, that Tess wondered if she could just make out Fahra at her desk. They entered around the back, Tess following Jerome to where a sheet of MDF had been prised away from a broken glass door panel.

'Are you bloody kidding me? It was bad enough having to climb over that turnstile at the last gourmet diner you took me to. Now I've got to risk being gouged to death by broken glass?'

'Imagine Walker's face though.' Jerome grinned, holding the panel back. Tess stuck up her middle finger and ducked into the dusty darkness beyond.

Jerome turned on his phone torch and led them both to what used to be an office. As he swung the beam around, Tess saw the usual crisp packets and empty beer bottles littering the floor. They were rarely the first people to find these places. At least today there were no used condoms. 'God, the dust makes me want to gag. This place is filthy. We should have borrowed crime scene gear.'

'You'll be telling me you're not coming to eat with me again next,' Jerome teased. 'That there's nothing wrong with a *café*.'

'I wasn't going to say that,' Tess grumbled, even though that had been exactly what she was going to say. 'Although I do live in fear that one day we're going to find a body in one of these places. What do we do then?'

'Anonymous tip-off,' Jerome said, so quickly that she had a feeling he'd been in that exact situation before, or at least had the same thought. 'At least you're not a flamingo,' he said, changing the subject before she could ask.

She fought the urge to shudder at the mention of flamingos. *Jerome knows nothing about the club*, she reminded herself. *It's just one of his ridiculous facts*. 'Why's that then?' she asked.

'They can only eat with their heads upside down,' he said. 'That's why they have those long necks.'

'That's not even true,' Tess said.

'Is too.'

'This place is still a shithole.'

'Okay.' Jerome turned to scrutinize her. 'What's really wrong? Because you are being weird, and I don't think it has anything to do with the case. Is it that woman you brought into the station? One minute you're asking me to help you arrest someone, next thing you're making her cups of coffee in our storeroom. Who is she?'

'Okay.' Tess took a bite of her bap, her eyes adjusting slowly to the gloom around them. The desk to her left was still covered in old paperwork and discarded stationery, a name written in Tippex on a stapler by someone who was protective enough to label it but didn't care enough to take it with them. She scanned the rest of the room, empty water cooler, the obligatory naked girls calendar hanging forgotten on the wall – the owner had decided against taking that home to his wife then; things that had once been important enough to install and display now all seemed so sad and discarded. Tess chewed on her bap. 'Her name is Sarah Jacobs. I wanted to arrest her because I thought that was the only way to get her to help us. She's a conwoman, yes, but she's also wickedly clever. She's got an amazing mind; she sees things the way other people don't. She's obsessed with magic tricks and detective stories.'

'I can see why you like her.'

'I never said I liked her,' Tess replied, a little too quickly. Jerome raised his eyebrows.

'Come on, Tess, did you just hear yourself? That was respect in your voice. Besides, I've never seen you say more than five non-work-related words to anyone in that station in the whole time I've been here. Then suddenly you're making coffee for this woman and letting her paw through evidence? I heard you laughing at something she said on the phone once. *Out loud*.'

Tess felt her cheeks redden. 'Yeah, well maybe I've just not had much to laugh about lately. And for your information, it's the team that doesn't like me, not vice versa.'

'Has anyone actually told you that? That they don't like you? Besides Walker, who is a prick and as far as I can see doesn't like anyone.'

'Well . . . no,' Tess admitted. 'But they don't have to, do they? They're always laughing at Walker's stupid jokes and no one even speaks to me unless they have to, except you.'

'They laugh at Walker's jokes because they don't want to be the butt of the next one. And did it ever occur to you that you're not the most approachable of people? Since whatever happened with your ex, they say you shut down, wouldn't sit with them any more, stopped going to social stuff.'

'I just thought—'

'Yeah, well, I'm just saying that maybe you thought wrong,' Jerome said. He looked like he was going to put a hand on her shoulder but thought better of it. 'I get that everyone liked Chris. But they liked you too. And I happen to think that it was really brave of you not to go through with marrying someone if you didn't feel ready. No one hates you for it.'

'Walker does,' Tess huffed, but she felt a weird pounding in her chest. Had she been wrong all this time? Was it really her fault that she had no friends left?

'I refer you to my previous statement, officer. Walker is a prick. Anyway, this isn't Oprah. You were telling me about how this fraudster is a better detective than you?'

'Fuck off,' Tess muttered. 'So anyway, when Mitchell's murder came through and it turned out whoever killed him escaped through a locked door . . .'

'You went in search of your magician,' Jerome finished.

'Yes.' Tess took the last bite of her bap, chewed and swallowed. 'I asked her to take a look at our crime scene. And before you say anything,' she said quickly, 'forensics were finished with it. She didn't touch anything, I just wanted her to see the layout, to see if there was a way out I'd not thought of.'

'And did she?'

'She came up with a pretty good theory about the CCTV,' Tess replied. 'But it didn't pan out. Like I said, she's clever. Thinks differently to most people. It's like her brain connects things in ways normal people's brains wouldn't.'

'You mentioned that already. I knew you liked her,' Jerome teased, his wide grin visible through the gloom. Tess hoped he couldn't see her face go red in the dark.

'I do not.'

'You do, you like her. Worse – you respect her.'

Tess scowled. There was no point in lying to him: he wasn't her boss or her lover. 'All right – I'll admit it's nice to be dealing with someone who has their wits about them.'

'No offence taken,' Jerome quipped.

'Oh, you know what I mean. Most of the criminals we deal with are gang members barely out of nappies, carrying knives like they are comfort blankets, or drunken husbands beating their wives one too many times. It makes a change, that's all.'

'You know she can't be involved in this case. She's a criminal, not a consultant. She can't be your Sherlock any more, Watson. If that woman stays involved in this case, you are going to end up in big trouble.'

'Thanks, Jerome,' Tess said, her face colouring as she thought of the previous evening, how easy it had been to break her own code of silence when she was with her half-sister. How easy everything felt when she was around Sarah. 'Like I say, her theory about how our killer escaped didn't pan out. I'm absolutely certain that Sarah doesn't know anything we don't already know.'

Chapter Twenty

The ginger wig itched like a bitch. Sarah yearned to shove her fingers underneath the netting and rake her fingernails across her scalp, but the last thing she wanted was to let the middle-aged woman sitting across the small round table think she had nits. She had come to work to take her mind off what she had found in Shaun Mitchell's flat – off the screaming realization that she was more ingrained in Tess's murder case than she'd first thought possible, but it wasn't doing her any good. Today, even becoming someone else wasn't helping.

'I hope the baby is well.' She smiled at the woman across the table, who looked up from picking her fingernails in surprise.

'Oh, thank you. Actually—'

'The colds don't last for ever,' Sarah said, injecting just the smallest amount of mysticism into her voice. Sometimes, with the older ones usually, she had to go full-on zany psychic, crystal ball and everything, but this woman was sceptical enough already without the place looking like a carnival. She probably didn't think 'real' psychics would work out of an abandoned retail unit on Brighton seafront, and she'd be right. Sarah had dumped the ball in the stationery cupboard and swapped out her flowing technicolour dreamboat robe for an all-black number, mysterious enough but not over-egging the pudding. She was regretting keeping the long auburn wig on though. 'Although this one seems to have gone on for an age, right?'

'God yes.' The woman rubbed her face, another sign of exhaustion that came with lack of sleep. That, added to the small purple Calpol stain on her cuff, had been enough to tell Sarah that the woman's young child was suffering from an illness that didn't yet warrant the use of antibiotics – usually a bright yellow. 'Thank you.'

'But you're not here about the baby's cold,' Sarah said as kindly as she could without patronizing her. 'You want to know about your relationship with your husband.'

That threw her. Her eyes widened. 'How did you know?'

Sarah could have told her that she had been fiddling with her wedding band ever since she'd turned up for her appointment fifteen minutes ago, that she had watched her on the baby monitor she'd set up in the makeshift reception area as her eyes narrowed while tapping out angry text messages to her husband on her phone, and that her Facebook page wasn't as private as she suspected – friends of friends' posts were particularly valuable. When the woman had made the appointment a week ago, before Sarah had heard the name Shaun Mitchell for the first time in a decade, the first thing Sarah had done was to use her fake profile to friend one of Hilary's closest friends.

But that would be giving the game away, so she merely smiled and replied, 'That's why you came to me. I'm getting a lot from you, Hilary, a lot of anxiety. You worry about everyone except yourself, and you are wondering when it will be your turn to be worried about. You are searching for answers even though you aren't completely certain of the questions.'

'That's amazing,' Hilary replied.

No, that's motherhood, Sarah thought, *coupled with some Barnum statements,* but she merely smiled. Even with everything that was going on, she was still excellent at her job. It felt good to know that she had a place in the world, a calling. This was who she was.

Hilary leaned forwards. 'What should I do?'

'You have friends who have been in this position before. Why aren't you going to them for advice? Is it because you don't want to look like a failure?'

Hilary's eyes welled up. 'I'm always so in control, so together,' she admitted – although Sarah already knew this from the perfect highlights in her hair, the roots showing through now telling her that they had been neglected of late. Not to mention the smart clothes and the nails that needed infilling desperately. 'I just don't want them to think I can't cope. They were all so much younger when they had children, and they coped fine.'

'They didn't,' Sarah said confidently. Being childless herself, it had taken a lot of time on Mumsnet to understand this side of motherhood, the constant questioning of yourself, the feeling that whatever you did wasn't good enough – but the research had served her well in her side-hustle as a medium. In order to be good enough at this game to get people to open up, you had to understand them, to empathize with every type of person, to get the common problems and worries faced by mums and pensioners, businessmen and the recently bereaved. It was what made her stand out from the other cold readers who graced Brighton occasionally, the ones who knew the signs but not how their marks felt. 'I promise you that your friends had these exact issues. Especially your oldest friend.'

The woman looked confused. 'But my oldest friend doesn't have kids,' she said with a frown.

Oops, she'd got carried away. 'Sorry, I mean oldest in age. The oldest in your group of friends.'

The woman did some mental calculation and nodded. 'Sharon. Yes, she has three kids, you're probably right. God, you're good at this.'

'Thank you. Now I'm getting something else. The letter J. Is there anyone in your life who begins with J?'

'My husband's name is Geoffrey,' she replied. 'But he spells it with a G.'

'Yes, that's it,' Sarah replied without hesitation. She usually would have remembered it was Geoffrey with a G, but with everything that had happened since she'd researched Hilary, it was incredible she could even remember that she had a husband. She needed to try and wrap this up before she screwed up and damaged her reputation. 'I was hearing it rather than seeing it written. This person, I'm getting that they love you very much, but they've had a lot of stress at work recently, and that's stopping them from fully understanding what you are going through.'

'You're right!' Hilary nodded enthusiastically. 'His job is very stressful. He's in stocks and shares and the current climate—'

'It's no excuse for not being there for you, but perhaps you can understand that Geoffrey has had a lot of adjusting to do himself. The baby, was it a surprise?'

'No, we had been trying for years,' Hilary replied.

Sarah smiled, unfazed. 'I feel that it *was* a surprise. I'm afraid your husband had come to believe that it wasn't going to happen. This has been a learning curve for him as well. Do you think you can try to understand how he has been affected by all this? I get the sense that he is feeling pushed out by the new baby and feels like perhaps you don't have as much time for him any more. Does that sound feasible?'

'Yes, absolutely.' Hilary's face flushed, and Sarah felt that rush, that same one she got when she saw a mark's face relax into utter acceptance of whatever she was selling them.

'God, Emma was right about you,' Hilary said. 'You're the real deal.'

Fifty minutes later Sarah was leading the woman to the door. She held out a hand for her to shake but, instead, Hilary leaned forwards and grabbed her in a hug, nearly knocking her off her feet. It had been an exhausting hour – once she'd got to the root of Hilary's reason for being there it had been more like a therapy session than a psychic reading, but that's what her job was like sometimes. In the past she'd had to listen as women sobbed on her shoulder that their husbands were having an affair – *'I see you leaving his ass and having a wonderful life as an independent woman before finding a man who respects and loves you'*; been a grief counsellor – *'I see your wife/sister/cat is in a better place – they loved you very much and wouldn't want you to feel this way;* and a financial advisor – *'I see that taking a second mortgage to finance your dream of opening a topless bookstore is not the path you are destined to take at this point in your life.*' She could feel bad for lying to these people, but she used the fact that she was helping them to sleep soundly at night. And if they wanted to give her £100 an hour – well, it was probably cheaper than seeing a therapist. Those people were all charlatans anyway.

She was in the back of the old shop in a makeshift area separated from the front by an old black curtain. It was one she remembered from her childhood, and when she'd seen that it had gone out of business, a casualty of falling tourism in the summer not quite covering the losses of winter, she'd allowed herself a moment of sadness before seizing it as an opportunity to make some cash and have some fun on the days they had no long cons on the go.

The bell above the door rang.

'Sorry, I don't do walk-in readings,' Sarah called, without looking up. She liked to be prepared for her appointments. Psychic Brenda had a reputation to protect.

'Not even for your sister?'

Her head jerked up at the sound of the woman's voice and her heart picked up speed. Tess Fox was standing in her reception, looking at her sceptically. 'You're a psychic now?'

'How do you think I knew you'd open the door for beef chow mein?' Sarah said. There was a hint of a smile on Tess's face and Sarah thought about the previous evening, when they'd laughed and chatted as if they weren't from two entirely different worlds.

You're glad to see her. The realization was a strange one.

'How did you find me here, goddammit? I'm starting to think being a detective was your true calling, after all.'

Tess smiled but she didn't answer.

'What can I do for you?' Sarah asked. 'I'm guessing you aren't here for me to tell you there's a tall dark handsome man on the horizon.'

'Chance would be a fine thing,' Tess said.

'Was that a joke?' Sarah feigned shock, her dark eyes widening. 'I did not see that coming.'

Tess rolled her eyes, that almost-smile on her lips again.

'You left this at mine last night.' Tess held up a canvas bag and Sarah froze. Her notebook was in there, her theory about the initials on the bin, her drawings of the flat.

'Cheers,' Sarah said, reaching out to take the bag, waiting for Tess to ask her what all her notes meant. Surely she'd have looked through the contents? Sarah herself would have.

'And I wanted to say thanks for the food last night,' Tess said. 'It was nice. To chat, I mean.'

'Weird though, right?' Sarah grinned. Clearly Tess hadn't looked in the bag. And she was trying to say – in her buttoned-up way – that she'd enjoyed Sarah's company.

'Totally weird.' Tess grinned back. 'But nice.'

'But nice,' Sarah agreed. 'It felt like, before. You know, when I was just a crazy teenager in need of guidance.'

'As opposed to a crazy thirty-something in need of guidance?' Tess remarked, looking around at the unit where Sarah spent her time pretending to be psychic.

'Hey,' Sarah said, catching her eye and smiling. 'Everyone needs a personality flaw.'

Chapter Twenty-One

'Right, tell me what you have, and please tell me it's good.'

Tess was back in the murder room, where the whiteboard was looking much fuller than it had that morning. Fahra stood up, looking both proud and embarrassed to be at the forefront of the investigation. Tess had been right in thinking that she had the organizational skills required to collate the details on Shaun Mitchell. Give it a couple of years at the most and she'd be running an investigation of her own.

'I've been going back through the interview notes,' Fahra said, struggling to keep the excitement from her voice. 'I did the interviews with the neighbours, remember? When I interviewed one of Shaun Mitchell's neighbours – an elderly woman, Kath Phillips from across the corridor – she said Mitchell had been visited by his sister a couple of weeks before the murder, but I've checked . . . Shaun Mitchell doesn't have any siblings.'

'Bloody hell, well spotted, Fahra,' Tess praised. Fahra beamed. 'So who was this woman who visited Shaun? And why did she tell the neighbour she was his sister when she wasn't?'

'Apparently the woman called herself Sarah.'

Tess worked to stop her mouth falling open. Sarah definitely hadn't mentioned visiting Shaun Mitchell shortly before the murder. In fact, she'd claimed not to know he even had a flat on Grove Hill. Could it be a different Sarah? It was a common name; it could be a coincidence. Tess wasn't the type of person who claimed that she didn't believe in coincidences – she knew they happened all the time. But she had a bad feeling this wasn't one of those times.

'Do you have a description?' Tess tried to sound casual. Fahra read from her notes.

'Dark hair, just below the shoulder. Bit wavy, she said. Pretty eyes.' Fahra shrugged to acknowledge that this wasn't helpful. 'Oh, she mentioned that she was wearing a necklace, interlocking rings and a gemstone.'

'Right, thanks.' Tess held back a groan as she pictured her sister's necklace. Still a coincidence? Or had Sarah been lying to her when she said she'd never been to Shaun Mitchell's flat? And if so, why?

'I know, not very helpful, sorry, ma'am,' Fahra said, mistaking her boss's shortness for disappointment. 'Shall I speak to her again? See if she remembers anything else?'

'Yes, sure, thanks, Fahra. Jerome—'

Before she could finish her sentence, her phone began to ring. 'Shit, it's Oswald.' She swiped to answer the call. 'Sir?' Her face creased into a frown at his words. 'Right, yes, okay. I'm on my way.'

She shoved her phone into her pocket and reached for her coat. 'Forget that for now. There's been another murder.'

Chapter Twenty-Two

'The Hilton Metropole,' Jerome was saying, 'has arguably one of the most colourful histories of all the hotels in Brighton.'

'You're going to have to give me the potted version – we're less than five minutes away,' Tess said, knowing that to try to stop him imparting his knowledge would be futile.

'It was requisitioned in the Forties to house various units of the Army, Navy and Air Force,' he continued, barely breaking his stride. 'With some very demanding customers. Winston Churchill would insist on cream on his porridge and Marlene Dietrich would demand steak at any hour she pleased.'

'Woman's got to have her steak.'

'Seen its fair share of crimes too,' he said. 'John George Haigh, otherwise known as the Acid Bath Murderer, kidnapped two of his victims from the Metropole in 1948, turning up to pay their bill and collect their luggage. Mr and Mrs Deacon were never seen alive again, having been shot dead and dissolved in a bath of acid.'

'Charming. You should do tours.'

As Jerome promised, the Hilton Metropole was a far cry from the Premier hubs that Tess was used to staying in. She walked into the marbled entrance hall and across to the mahogany reception desk, and a face she knew came forwards to meet her. It felt like the cast from a Broadway show coming together again. Campbell Heath nodded at her.

'Don't tell me you were lucky enough to be first responder here as well?' Tess raised her eyebrows.

Heath shrugged in a 'what can you do?' kind of way. 'I was out and about interviewing Shaun Mitchell's known associates when I heard the call come in. I thought it might be linked so got over here as fast as I could,' Heath confirmed. His Welsh accent had a strange calming effect on her. She'd only known Heath a short time but he was good at his job, dependable and a levelling influence. Despite his chaotic desk driving Fahra to distraction, she was glad to have him on her team. 'Our case just got weirder,' he said. 'You ready to see the body?'

Tess nodded. 'Who called it in?' she asked, as Heath led her towards a block of three lifts hidden away in the corner of the lobby.

'Reception called 999. The victim was found by a guest on the fifth floor. The guest was waiting for the lift and, when the doors opened, our victim was on the floor with a fresh stab wound.'

The victim. It was like she'd been expecting it, and yet the sight of him slumped against the wall of the lift, eyes glassy, made her heart thump faster and heat rise in her face. Callum Rodgers. The other man present the night that she killed Darren Lane a decade and a half ago.

Tess stepped back and focused on a watermark in the

otherwise perfect hotel wallpaper. She tried counting backwards from ten and circular-breathing without catching the attention of the rest of the crew, hoping it looked as though she was thinking. When she'd got control of her heart rate, she turned back to Heath who was watching her closely.

'CCTV?' she asked, as though she hadn't just warded off a breakdown.

'Covers the lobby and both lift entrances,' he replied. 'The receptionist saw the victim walk over to the lifts alone less than ten minutes before the guest found him. SOCO are there now.'

A review of the CCTV showed it was in fact six minutes and forty seconds between Callum Rodgers entering the lift and the moment a woman flew into the lobby in hysterics and practically collapsed at the reception desk. Mrs Bevan, 41, staying in the Metropole for an IT training course, had been waiting for a lift, and would probably spend the rest of her life now taking the stairs. Tess was grateful that Jerome had stepped in to interview her immediately – she had never been good at comforting emotional women and he was something of an expert. From what she could gather, there was no connection between Callum Rodgers and Mrs Bevan, and from the CCTV she could ascertain that Rodgers was already dead on the floor of the lift when the doors opened. And he was completely alone.

Tess rubbed her face. Why was this happening to her? She attempted to smile at the receptionist – was that even what they called them these days? Concierge? Front of house? *Hardly important at this stage, Tess.* She felt as though she was drowning in useless details and missing the key that would tell them who'd killed Callum Rodgers. For a start, where was the murder weapon? The lift was hardly six foot by six foot, with nowhere to hide a knife that hadn't already been searched. Unless the weapon was as invisible as the murderer himself. Jesus Christ, perhaps she should have let Walker have this case – perhaps she wasn't cut out for this, after all.

'So Mr Rodgers was definitely on his own when he entered the lift?' she repeated.

'Well, erm, I didn't say that.' The receptionist cracked his knuckles and Tess cringed. 'He was on his own when he walked across the lobby. The lift is behind that marble wall, so from the front desk I can't see the doors exactly.'

'So, someone else could have entered the lift with Mr Rodgers without anyone seeing anything?'

'Well, yes. He came in alone, walked over alone, but there's nothing to say someone couldn't have been waiting there for him without me noticing. I don't escort guests to their rooms.'

Tess thought back to Shaun Mitchell's killer, who had potentially been waiting in his flat for twenty-four hours before claiming their victim. If they were looking at the same person, she had no doubt they had the patience to wait for their moment to strike.

'We have two of the team reviewing the CCTV for the entire day, noting anyone who goes behind the wall to the lifts and matching them with the guest lists,' Jerome murmured to her. 'In an hour or so we'll have a complete picture of everything that went on in those lifts around the time of the murder.'

'Okay, thank you. So in theory, someone could have come down in the lifts, stabbed Callum Rodgers, shoved him into the other lift and sent him up to the fifth floor without anyone seeing anything?'

Jerome frowned. 'In theory, I suppose they could have. Then gone back to their floor in the second lift.'

'Right.' Tess nodded. It would have relied on excellent timing, and she was fairly certain that wasn't what had happened, but it was the closest thing they had to a theory at this moment in time. As far as they could tell, Rodgers walked into that lift alone and didn't walk out.

'We need to find that weapon,' Tess said. 'Get someone down that shaft.'

Tess and Jerome watched as Heath donned a crime scene gown and gloves and was clipped into the contraption that would lower him into the bottom of the lift shaft. They had found a maintenance hatch on the staff level in the basement and the hotel maintenance crew had offered them the use of their winch and rope, used if there were ever any problems with the lift. Tess peered over the side into the darkness below and looked back at Heath.

'You okay with this?' she asked. 'We can wait for the flood-lights to arrive.'

'It's fine,' he assured her, clicking his torch on and off to demonstrate. 'Lower me in.'

As Heath was dropped into the shaft, Tess watched the beam of his flashlight slide down the wall and disappear, swallowed in darkness. She looked at Jerome. 'How many horror films have you seen that start like this?' she asked.

'I think it needs to have thunder and lightning to qualify,' he replied. 'Plus, he's not a big-breasted blonde teenager. Should be fine.'

'Glad you feel that way,' Tess said. 'Because if he doesn't come out, you're going in after him.'

Jerome made a noise that conveyed a loud '*Hell, no.*' He looked at her, eyebrows raised. 'Good-looking Black dude like me? You must be crazy.'

'Guv?' Heath's voice came up from inside the shaft and Tess's heart began to thump. 'I've got it. I've got the knife.'

Chapter Twenty-Three

The room fell silent the minute Tess walked in. Judging from the smirk on Walker's face, this was probably so she didn't hear the jokes they'd all been telling at her expense. He thought Tess didn't know what he had been muttering ever since the second murder had cropped up. Okay, so they were just childish jokes, jabs about invisible men and magicians, but every one of them meant to undermine her, make her look stupid. Tess didn't even know any more if it really was about Chris leaving the force after their break-up, their competition for the permanent DI job, or if Walker just hated her in general. It wouldn't be beyond him to throw his weight about and be a colossal prick just because she was a woman going for the same job as him. She could imagine how much his pride would take a tumble if she made DI first.

Tess clamped her teeth together and tried not to direct an acerbic comment to her colleagues around the table. It wasn't their fault that Walker was a prick. Besides, her mother used to say you'd catch more flies with honey than vinegar – which was ironic because she was a cranky old bitch with very few friends of her own.

'Okay.' She made her way to the front of the crowd of officers – her team had doubled in size with the second murder victim – and addressed the room. Jerome was sitting at the front next to Fahra, Campbell Heath and six DCs, sent by Oswald as soon as news of the second murder hit. And DI Walker, of course, who – despite having his own team to run – seemed to be as difficult to get rid of as a rancid fart in a lift. 'Who's first?'

She perched herself on the edge of a desk as PC Heath cleared his throat. Tess was glad he had been allowed to stay on with them; he'd proved himself a valuable asset at both crime scenes and she liked having him around. 'We found a handprint. Blood.'

Tess hadn't been expecting that. 'Where? In the lift?' she asked, looking at Jerome. 'Did you know about this?'

'Just found out now, guv.'

She looked back at Heath, who had reddened. 'Go on.'

'It wasn't in the lift, guv. It was on the revolving door at the entrance of the hotel.'

Tess raised her eyebrows and stood up straight. 'Excuse me?'

'That's why we only just found it. SOCO were concentrated around the lift area – they didn't think there was any way the killer walked out of the front doors covered in blood without being seen.'

Tess could see the poor officer cringing. She knew now why there had been a buzz of conversation that had stopped when she had walked into the room. Not only was their killer able to get to the lift unseen – now they'd bloody walked out of the front door. Were they taking the piss?

'Presumably the blood is being tested for a match to the victim?' Tess asked, as if there were nothing untoward about this new information. Heath nodded. 'And any fingerprints being run through the system?'

'It was pretty smeared, according to the tech,' Heath offered. 'They don't think they have workable prints, but they'll let you know the minute they have confirmation.'

'Thank you.' Tess made a mental note to find out more about the positioning of the handprint later. She looked at the rest of the team. 'Next?'

All eyes in the room were fixed on Tess until Walker cleared his throat. 'Erm, guv?'

He didn't have to call her that; they were the same fucking rank. He was taking the piss and loving it. Tess resisted a sigh.

'Do you have new information, Walker?'

'No guv, I was just wondering, does the CCTV show anyone leaving the hotel by the front doors by any chance?'

Tess gritted her teeth. 'No, it does not.'

'So how do you reckon the handprint got there? Do you think the invisible man left it?'

'Or woman, Walker – remember your Equality and Diversity training. How many times have you had to take that this year again?'

Walker scowled as a few sniggers rippled through the people watching the exchange with glee.

Tess clicked her fingers. 'Right, I asked who's next? And if anyone else fancies making quips about bloody magicians, you'll see how quickly I can make you disappear.'

'List of suspects, guv.' Jerome stood up quickly and handed her a sticky note. She resisted the urge to roll her eyes at him. 'Not many, I'm afraid. On-off girlfriend of about twelve months, no history of domestic. No police reports involving the deceased, no pissed-off employees or ex-wives standing to inherit. He was squeaky clean.'

Squeaky clean? That didn't sound like the Callum Rodgers she'd come into contact with in the past. Of course she couldn't say that. But she was going to have to steer the investigation towards his shady past at some point – it was starting to look like her only chance of finding out who else might have wanted him dead.

'Movements that day?'

'He was at home until lunchtime when he said he had to go and meet someone. We've spoken to the girlfriend; it wasn't her and she had no idea why he'd have been at the Hilton. Apparently he didn't have a room there.'

'Do we have a guest list? Was he on it?'

Jerome shuffled through some papers that were laid out on the table next to him and passed over a list of names. At least this one was on actual paper, not the back of a napkin. 'Guests who had a room the night of the murder. No Callum Rodgers on there,' he said.

Tess scanned the names. He was right. Rodgers's name was nowhere to be seen. But there was another name, one that was disturbingly familiar. Sarah Jacobs had booked a room at the Hilton Metropole hotel the night before their second victim was stabbed to death.

Fuck fuck fuck fuck fuck.

This wasn't a coincidence. It couldn't be. She discreetly

passed it back to Jerome, her finger hovering over Sarah's name. He raised his eyebrows in a question, and she nodded slightly to confirm. Fuck.

'Right,' she said to the rest of her team. 'Once again, I would ask you to keep the details – however, um, unique they may be – to yourselves for the time being. This is a murder investigation team, not the magic circle. We will figure this out, even if we have to arrest David Blaine, Dynamo and both Penn and Teller to do so, although I've heard Teller is a no-comment interview.'

That got a few smiles at least. 'Fahra has control of the jobs list – mark down what you're doing so we don't cross over, and report to her at every avenue. Clear?'

Nine heads nodded; Walker's remained still.

'Excellent. Walker, if you're not doing anything constructive, feel free to put the kettle on.'

Tess pulled Jerome to one side as soon as the meeting was done and everyone began to filter out of the room.

'I need to go and find Jacobs; is there any chance you can hold the fort here for me?'

Jerome shook his head. 'You're going to meet her alone? No, Tess. If you think she has anything to do with this, you need to bring her in for questioning. By the book, remember? It's your mantra, not mine. She might be dangerous.'

Tess sighed. He was right but she couldn't bring herself to believe that Sarah was involved in this, and if she could keep the Jacobs name out of this she would, for her own sake. But she couldn't deny that it looked like whoever killed Shaun

Mitchell and Callum Rodgers was linked to Sarah in some way. Otherwise, why give her name at Mitchell's flat, and book a room in Sarah's name at the Hilton?

'Who is she, guv? Who is this woman and how is she involved in what's going on?'

'Look, I can't explain right now. I just don't think she killed anyone. And I don't want to bring her in until we have something concrete to charge her with.'

'This is a bad idea, Tess. If Oswald finds out, then your job is on the line, never mind your promotion.'

Tess almost laughed at the fact that he still thought her promotion was the biggest thing on the line here. If Oswald found out she was related to Frank Jacobs, and that she'd killed a man to protect her half-sister, it would not only be her job she would lose, but her freedom, her whole life.

'I appreciate your concern, Jerome, honestly. But I can't let someone get away with murder, and if we arrest Sarah Jacobs on circumstantial evidence then the real perpetrator walks free.'

Jerome looked like he wanted to say something else but instead he gave a small nod. ' hope you're right, boss, really I do.'

Tess went outside to make the call, keen to get away from prying ears, although as she leaned up against the unmarked police car she could still see Walker watching her from the window of the office upstairs. He was furious that she was leading the case – that much she could tell – and desperate to find a stick to beat her with. She wasn't about to hand him the ammunition by calling her sister from somewhere she could be overheard.

Sarah answered her phone on the first ring. Perhaps she was psychic after all.

'Tess?' she said urgently. 'I wanted to call you. What's going on? I just heard there's been another murder?'

She sounded fraught – something Tess hadn't been expecting. She'd never heard Sarah sound anything but cool and cocky.

'Yeah, there has,' Tess replied, her eyes going from the window where Walker was trying to casually watch her, to the door of the station. No one was in sight but still she kept her voice low. 'I need you to answer some questions. Your name keeps cropping up at every bloody turn and I'm starting to feel more than a bit paranoid that I'm being watched. Can you meet me somewhere?'

'I don't know.' Sarah suddenly sounded cautious. 'You sound stressed. Are you going to clap me in irons?'

'I'm trying not to. Believe me, neither of us wants you attached to this case but still, here we are. So what do you say? You can meet me in private or I'll have to arrest you very publicly. Please don't make me do that.'

'Fine. I'll have to give Dad the slip, though. He doesn't want me anywhere near you.'

Sarah didn't mean any offence, yet still Tess was furious at herself for the stab of pain the words caused her. Hearing that her father didn't want anything to do with her still hurt, even after all these years convincing herself it had been her decision. 'The feeling is mutual, believe me,' she snapped back, knowing it was a lie. 'Text me when you get away and where you want to meet. The sooner we clear this up and go our separate ways, the better.'

'Guv?' Jerome motioned for Tess to follow him as she hung up the phone, feeling exhausted. Her temple pounded and she could feel her body was rigid with tension. She held up her hand.

'Don't try and stop me again, Jerome. I have to go.'

'I'm not – look, it's Rodgers's girlfriend. Fahra tracked her down and she came straight to the station. I wondered if you'd want to speak to her yourself?'

Tess cursed. She *did* want to speak to her, but there was no way she could send someone else to meet with Sarah. God only knew what she might let slip.

'Can you tell her I'm not in the station at the moment? Make sure you keep her here and I'll be back in an hour?'

'Sure. We really need to question her as soon as we can though, you know? Spouse, family members – they are our most likely options at this stage.' His next sentence – *not some wannabe Sherlock grifter* – went unspoken but hung between them. For the first time since they had begun working together, Tess sensed a crack beginning to form between them. She hated it, but she just couldn't tell him what was really going on. It was the one secret she was never going to be able to share with anyone. She was still the DI and Jerome was still her DS, and he was going to have to do as he was told, even if it was do as I say, not as I do.

'Thanks Jerome, I know who our most likely suspects are,'

she said, trying not to snap. From the look on his face, she'd failed. 'Look, I have to follow this lead. I know Jacobs didn't kill anyone, but she has something to do with this and I need to figure out what it is. I'll be back in less than an hour and we'll talk to the girlfriend. Can you get the case file ready?'

Jerome nodded, despite still not looking happy about her choice. 'I'll get everything we've got, *guv*.'

She ignored the emphasis on the word 'guv', but knew she was going to have a bit of making up to do for her premature rank-pulling, five minutes into her temporary promotion. She tried to soften her voice, despite her urgency. 'Jerome, you're a star. Thank you. I promise not to be long.'

Chapter Twenty-Four

Sarah slid the box containing the ring back under her bed and sat on the floor of her bedroom facing the wall, knees pulled up to her chest. She couldn't remember the last time she'd worn the ring she'd found in Mitchell's flat, but she knew it was hers. It had been a gift from Jefferson – her one and only Prince Charming. It was a thick silver band that crossed without meeting, the co-ordinates of their first date engraved on the band. It would have to be a damn fine coincidence for someone else to have the exact same ring, with the exact same engraving, left at a crime scene where someone had pretended to be her two weeks previously.

So who took it? It would help if Sarah could remember the last time she'd seen the ring, but she couldn't. She'd stopped wearing it when she'd ended things with Jefferson – it had all been too raw. But she was sure she'd have put it in her jewellery box, which had been on the shelf in her bedroom for as long as she could remember. Which narrowed down the people who could have planted it in Shaun Mitchell's flat to Gabe, Wes, Mac or her father. Unless someone was ballsy enough to break into Frank Jacobs's house, and clever enough to leave no trace. Probably the only person who fitted that description was Frank himself. But none of her family were supposed to know about what had happened to her all those years ago, and none of them should have any reason to hurt Shaun Mitchell but her.

'Sarah, you okay?'

Speak of the devil, Sarah thought as her father's voice came from outside her door. Their disagreement two days earlier seemed to have been completely forgotten, on Frank's part at least. Sarah still didn't know how to feel. She was a grifter – her heart lay with the thrill of the con – but it had never left such a bitter taste in her mouth before. Was this really the life she wanted? Wrestling with a newfound conscience after every job? If anyone had asked her last year if she'd swap places with her half-sister, she'd have laughed herself hoarse. Tess's life compared to hers looked sterile, lonely, pointless – so she had thought. Now she wasn't so sure. Maybe her head was telling her it was time to be one of the good guys for a change.

'I'm fine, why?'

'It's all over town. Another murder, at the Metropole this time. Just wanted to check in on you.'

Sarah froze. Another one? Connected to Mitchell or completely separate? Brighton didn't see a great deal of murders, certainly not this close together. She should call Tess, find out what was going on. Find out if the victim was . . .

As if she had conjured her into existence, Sarah's phone began to ring, and she knew it would be Tess.

'I'm all right, Dad, just changing,' she yelled. She grabbed the call immediately. 'Tess?' she said. 'I was just about to call you. What's going on? I just heard there's been another murder?'

Sarah's heart pounded as Tess told her how her name had cropped up in the latest murder investigation. Jesus, if they found any more evidence against her, even *she* was going to start believing she was guilty. She promised Tess she would meet her to discuss whatever this so-called evidence was, but her sister had seemed so wound up that Sarah wished she'd told her to call Frank's lawyer instead. Tess practically bit her head off when she reminded her Frank didn't want her involved. Still, she fired off a message to Gabe before texting Tess to confirm a time and place for the meeting. If she was going to have to put up with her sister in a foul mood, she might as well have some fun with it.

Chapter Twenty-Five

Brighton Palace Pier was a ten-minute walk from the station, but after being held up by Jerome she had been nearly twenty; when she got there Sarah was nowhere to be seen. Tess sighed. Once again, she felt as if she was being given the runaround, being made to feel like a bumbling TV cop who was always having her ass handed to her by the wily jewel thieves. The smell of pier food turned her stomach, and she wondered briefly when was the last time she had eaten. She'd definitely eaten yesterday, hadn't she? Her insides growled. *Where the hell was Sarah?*

She glanced aside to where a man was bundled up in a sleeping bag, newspapers sprawled out on the ground, cigarette ends littered around his makeshift camp, an open Styrofoam container next to him.

'Excuse me?' Tess called over. The man didn't look over. 'I said excuse me? Have you seen a young woman around here? Shorter than me, dark hair?'

'Sssat?' The man cupped a grubby hand to a large ear.

'A woman? Waiting for someone?' Tess checked her watch. She was right on time, there was no reason for Sarah to have come and left – unless of course she never intended to meet her in the first place. *That fucking woman.*

'Sssat?' the homeless chap shouted now. There was no point in trying to get any sense out of him. Even if he had seen Sarah, he wouldn't be much use in finding out where she was now. Tess cursed under her breath.

'No need for that language,' the man said, picking up a cigarette from the butts strewn at his feet.

'Oh, so you heard that,' Tess muttered.

'Well I ain't deaf. I seen your girl too.'

Tess started. 'When?'

'She was here sniffing around here 'bout ten minutes ago. Said you were late. Said it was bad manners to keep someone waiting.'

'Well some of us have an honest day's work to do.' Tess felt her face colour at her blunder. 'Sorry, I mean, that wasn't a dig at you – it's just the girl I was meeting. She drives me to distraction.'

'Pretty thing,' the man grunted.

'Yes, I suppose she is,' Tess admitted. 'And clever. Too clever to be making a living conning people out of their hard-earned cash.'

'Bit harsh,' the man muttered. Only it wasn't the same voice now: it was clear and young. And female.

'What the—'

The old man clambered to his feet and straightened out with the agility of someone much younger. He pulled off the grubby cap he was wearing and a cascade of dark brown hair fell to his – although now it was clearly a her – shoulders.

'You're late.' Sarah Jacobs grinned at the furious expression on Tess's face. 'Like the fella said, it's bad manners.'

'What, and you keep a vagrant costume in your back pocket now?' Tess eyed her soiled baggy clothes with distaste.

'Obviously not,' Sarah said, peeling off an ear. 'Well, Gabe did me the ears before I left. The rest is Tom's. This is where he lives – he let me borrow his stuff for a bit while he went to get lunch. It was just a bit of fun, Tess. You do remember fun, don't you? Jokes?' Her face fell and she looked disappointed that Tess wasn't roaring with laughter.

Tess wrinkled her nose. 'Smelly fun. How do you know his name is Tom?'

Sarah's disappointment changed to confusion. 'Because I asked him.'

'Of course you did.'

Sarah shrugged. 'I buy him lunch sometimes, or a hot drink or some sun cream or whatever. He's a good guy, just had a run of bad luck. And he got you talking. You said I was *purdy*.'

'Actually, you said that,' Tess replied. 'I was just being polite and agreeing with you. And, could you take that lot off now, please? I can't take you seriously looking like that, and I've got stuff to do.'

Sarah pulled a rucksack from under the sleeping bag, opened her wallet and tucked some notes underneath Tom's belongings. She produced a pack of wipes and proceeded to clean the grime from her face.

'So I heard the investigation wasn't going too well,' she said conversationally as she transformed herself back into a young woman. 'Have you figured out how your victim was stabbed yet?'

'I'm not even going to ask how you know details of this case that haven't been released to the press. Because the only obvious answer to that is that you are involved somehow.'

'The only obvious answer *you* can see,' Sarah replied. 'Which is why you came to me for help in the first place, if I remember rightly. Now you're here treating me like a suspect when all I've done is help you.'

'If you're looking for an argument, I don't have time. My DS thinks I should be arresting you and asking you these questions at the station, and to be honest if you were anyone else, I would be. So let's get this over with. The victim was Callum Rodgers.'

Sarah looked as though Tess had slapped her in the face. 'Shit.'

'Shit indeed. It gets worse. Can you tell me why there was a room in the Hilton Metropole booked in your name the night before he was killed?'

Sarah lifted her head in surprise. 'Are you still asking if I'm involved in these murders? I thought you knew me better than that by now.'

Tess sighed. 'That's kind of the point, Sarah. I don't know you at all, not really.'

'No offence taken, *partner*. I thought you at least knew me well enough to know I'm too clever to book a room at a crime scene in my own name.'

'That's what I thought,' Tess admitted. 'Which is why I'm taking a massive risk being here now. Because someone wants me to think you were involved. I need you to tell me if there's anyone you can think of who might want you in the frame for this. If I can find a viable suspect fast enough, maybe we can keep you away from the station and away from my investigation.'

Sarah raised her eyebrows. 'You know what I do for a living? I piss people off daily. If you want me to write a list of everyone I might have upset in the last twelve months, you're going to need a long sheet of paper. Maybe a roll of wallpaper or something.'

'Pissing people off is one thing, Sarah, but how many people know about your connection to Callum Rodgers and Shaun Mitchell? Because I was under the impression that it was just me.'

Sarah chewed the inside of her lip. 'Then Occam's razor would suggest . . .' she said eventually, 'that *you* killed them and you're the one framing me.'

Tess shook her head in exasperation. 'Even now you can't be serious! Even now, when you're about to become the only suspect linked to two murders—'

'Two?' Sarah snapped. 'How am I linked to Shaun Mitchell's murder?'

'Apparently someone called Sarah visited his flat the week before he was killed. That in itself wasn't enough to link you, but once they start going through the list of people staying at the hotel and find that your description matches the one the woman gave at Mitchell's flat, it's not going to take someone long. And they're going to want to know why *I* didn't make the connection sooner.'

'I'm telling you, I didn't book a room at the Hilton, and I didn't kill anyone. I don't know what's going on or who's trying to frame me . . .' She hesitated as though she was about to say something else, then pressed her lips firmly together.

'But?' Tess prompted.

'There's no but,' Sarah said, shaking her head. Whatever she'd been about to say, she'd obviously changed her mind. 'I don't have a clue what's going on, Tess, and I've told you everything I know. I swear.'

Tess didn't have to be a mind reader to suspect her half-sister was lying to her.

Chapter Twenty-Six

She ran into Jerome in the corridor of the second floor of Brighton Police Station on her way back to the murder room. He was holding two mugs of something steaming and she nodded at them, noting the one that said: *I survived another meeting that could have been an email*. It was hers – a present from Jerome for her birthday. 'Is one of those for me?'

'No,' he replied stubbornly, letting her know that all was not forgiven. 'How did your meeting go?'

'I'm not discussing that here. I'll tell you later,' she added, trying to soften her abrupt dismissal. 'Did you manage to keep Rodgers's girlfriend here?'

'She's through there.' Jerome inclined his head towards interview room three and, as she was about to make a move towards the door, he held her mug out to her. 'And this one is yours – I was just being a twat.'

'Glad to see you're back to normal.' Tess smiled. 'So what do I need to know about her?'

'Her name is Millie Diamond.' Jerome grinned and raised

his eyebrows. 'Sounds a bit pornstar, doesn't it? But she's really upset, so maybe don't mention the ridiculous name. Looks like she's been crying all morning. Very pretty, looks like money. Not like your usual "innit" and "wanna lawyer" type. She's just been waiting there for you to get back.'

'Any kind of record?'

'Nope. Squeaky clean.'

'Where was she when it happened?'

Jerome glanced down at the notes in his hands. 'She works at a recruitment consultancy in Brighton. I called them and they said she was working all morning.'

'So she's not exactly our number one suspect. Still, she might know who is.'

The young woman got to her feet as Tess and Jerome entered the room. 'I'm DI Fox. This is DS Morgan,' Tess said. 'I'm so sorry for your loss.'

Millie Diamond nodded, her eyes red-rimmed. Tess took a seat and motioned for Millie to do the same. As she sat, Tess took in the girl's appearance. Jerome was right: she was pretty. Tall and lithe, she was all arms and legs, like a ballet dancer. Her brown eyes were huge, bringing to mind a doe, her whole demeanour slight and afraid, as though the slightest noise would startle her into scuttling away. She had light brown hair pinned in a bun at the top of her head – she looked as though she should be wearing a black leotard and leggings underneath her long tan coat, instead of jeans and an expensive brown jumper. She looked up through her watery eyelashes at Jerome, and Tess saw him smile at her. *Oh Lord.*

Tess cleared her throat. 'This is a difficult question,' she said.

'But we need to ask you if you know of anyone who might have had motive to hurt Callum Rodgers?'

Millie dropped her gaze back to the table. 'No,' she whispered.

'We need to find out who did this, Millie. You can't get Callum into trouble now. I'd really appreciate it if you could tell me the truth.'

'I am,' Millie said, but the way she chewed on her bottom lip suggested she was lying.

Tess remained silent for a minute then said, 'How did Callum know Shaun Mitchell?'

Millie shrugged. 'I don't know. I'd never even heard of him until Callum said he knew the man who'd been murdered last week.'

'Did he seem upset about it? Scared?'

'Not scared, exactly, but distant. He said they hadn't seen each other for ages, that he wondered who'd done it.'

'He didn't have any ideas?'

'None. He said Shaun was a drug dealer and anyone could have got to him. I asked him how he knew someone like that, and he said he used to be a bit of a troublemaker himself when he was younger, but he'd stopped all that now. That's why he hadn't seen Shaun in so long – he moved in different circles.'

Tess nodded. So Rodgers wasn't into selling drugs any more. Then why had he been killed? 'Okay, thanks. I gather the officers have already checked your alibi for yesterday. We know you were at work, so you're not a suspect. Do you have any idea why Callum might have been at the Hilton?'

Millie looked at the table. She picked at the skin around her thumbnail and gave a sniff. 'Are you asking if he was cheating on me?'

'Was he?'

Millie shrugged. 'I'd be the last person to ask, wouldn't I? But he didn't have any reason to be booked into a hotel that I know about, so don't think it hasn't crossed my mind. I don't think I want to know. Is that pathetic?'

'No, not at all. You don't want your memories tainted; I understand. But as a woman I know that quite often we suspect things, even if we don't want to admit them.'

Millie shook her head forcefully. 'No.'

Tess tried not to sigh. She glanced at Jerome to wrap it up.

'Okay, Millie,' he said. 'We appreciate how hard this has been for you. Do you have someone at home who can sit with you today?'

Millie nodded.

'And if you remember anything at all, however small, you'll tell us, won't you?'

The young girl's eyes dropped to the table, but she nodded.

'I did see him once,' she whispered as they were about to stand. 'Going to the Bagel Man. With a girl. I shouldn't have been following him, it was stupid of me. It was probably someone from work.'

'What did she look like?'

'I just saw brown hair. She had a nice coat on – like I said, she was probably just a work colleague. I don't want to waste your time.'

Tess nodded. *Probably a work colleague.*

'And I found a message on his phone once, from a girl. Sarah J.'

Jerome glanced at Tess. 'Sarah J?'

Tears began to run down Millie's cheeks again. 'Don't tell me, will you? If he was cheating on me. I don't think I want to know now.'

Jerome glanced at Tess, but she was fighting to keep her face unreadable in front of their witness. She had no idea why Sarah might have been seeing Callum Rodgers, but it explained the hotel room. Had Sarah finally decided she wanted revenge, and managed to get close to Callum without him recognizing her? She was the master of disguise, after all. That would mean Sarah had lied to Tess again, and the idea that she had lowered her guard just for her sister to make a fool of her cut like a blade.

Fahra was waiting for Tess when she and Jerome entered the Murder Room. She was holding a stack of photographs which she kept waving like a butterfly flapping its wings.

'Guv? Is it okay if I show you something?'

'Of course it is, Fahra, what's up?'

Fahra walked over to the nearest empty desk and began fanning out the photos.

'Shaun Mitchell's neighbour from the Grove Hill flats called again. At first I thought she was just bored and wanted to be involved – you know the ones. Then she mentions talking to someone going into Mitchell's flat a few days ago, someone with the same name as his sister. She kept going "oooh, isn't it a funny coincidence, but I thought someone should know." Turns out this other Sarah went in the other day, had a bunch of keys. Blonde hair, baseball cap. Heath's gone over to pull the CCTV – he should be back any minute.'

'Brilliant, thanks, Fahra. Thank God for nosy neighbours.'

Tess felt sick. What was Sarah – if it was Sarah this time – doing going into Mitchell's flat? Did she *want* to get herself arrested? Well surely that was inevitable, now she'd been linked to Callum Rodgers. Tess was going to have to go to the chief, come clean about Sarah's early involvement in the case and let him decide if they had enough evidence to arrest her. And Tess was going to have to pray that the fact that she'd been privy to early information wouldn't damage their case too much.

'There was something else. The woman said that when this Sarah woman came out, the neighbour just happened to be passing her peephole. Bollocks if you ask me. No one just wanders past a peephole and happens to see something – you have to practically glue your eye to it. Anyway, she saw this woman come out, and she was holding something. Said it looked shiny. Maybe a ring or something similar.'

'Shit,' Tess muttered. Then, 'Who else knows about this?'

'No one.' Fahra raised her eyebrows. 'It's not your fault, you know. If SOCO have missed something, that's their lookout.'

Tess nodded absently. And if she'd allowed her sister to steal evidence and cover her tracks, whose lookout was that? Was there any way to stop this snowballing now, or had she just fucked her entire career?

Chapter Twenty-Seven

Sarah reached up to pull down the sign from above the door of the unit, revealing the chipped paint and faded logo of the ice-cream shop that was there before she discovered the empty space.

It wasn't illegal to claim to be psychic. You could charge money for psychic services, as long as you put a disclaimer in your adverts to say your work is 'for entertainment only'. Except Sarah hadn't legally rented the unit, which meant she could never stay for long.

As she bent down to shove the sign into a bag, along with everything else she'd been temporarily storing in the unit (a few props in case people wanted the full-on seaside psychic routine, including a crystal ball – Amazon, £7.99, some tarot cards from a shop in Kemptown, and a wind machine in case a ghostly breeze was required), a familiar voice made her jump.

'Why didn't you tell me you were back in touch with Callum Rodgers?'

Sarah took in a breath. 'Because I wasn't,' she replied, turning around to face Tess. Her sister looked livid. She'd seen her go through a variety of emotions in the last few weeks, most of them aimed at her. She hadn't seen her go purple before.

'Bullshit. You were seen with him.'

'By who?'

'By his girlfriend. She said he'd been seeing someone called Sarah behind her back.'

'Maybe he was.' Sarah shrugged. 'But it wasn't me.'

Tess sighed. 'I'm fed up of this whole ridiculous tango we've been doing, Sarah. I find out information – you deny it leads to you, or claim you're being framed. Like an idiot I believe you, then I find out more information that leads to you and we start again. You stole evidence from the scene. I have you on CCTV. Or were you framed for that too?'

'Excuse me?'

'You took something from the crime scene. Not to mention you took the SD card from the camera you handed over to me.'

Aw shit. For once in her life, she had nothing to say.

'We have a warrant to search Frank's house. My officers are on their way there now. Are they going to find what you took?'

Sarah reached out to put a hand on her sister's arm. Tess flinched and took a step backwards. 'Tess, come on. I can explain.'

'It's DI Fox, actually, and no, I don't think you can. You *stole evidence* from a crime scene. Do you realize I could be fired for even letting you look in there?'

'It wasn't a crime scene when I broke in there, but yeah, whatever.'

'See, this is the problem with you – you don't take anything seriously! You literally don't give a shit about anyone but yourself!' Tess threw her hands up and Sarah flinched. She wasn't done though. 'I give my life to this job! I gave up any chance at ever knowing my real father to do this job – it is *all I have* – yet the thought of me losing it is just a big joke to you, isn't it? It's okay for you – you only have yourself to answer to. You go through life making a living out of conning and deceiving people and I thought, *Do you know what, she's actually not as bad as you thought, Tess. She might just be a decent person under all those smartarse remarks and her I-don't-care attitude,* but it turns out you're exactly the criminal I had you pegged for. This is what I get for not trusting my instincts. This is what I get for giving you the benefit of the doubt just because I wanted—'

'Woah, woah, woah,' Sarah interrupted, her voice raised to match her sister's. 'Hold on one second! I didn't ask you to come and find me. You inserted yourself into my life so I could do your job for you. At no point did I say, *Please, big sis, try to make me a better person.* It's not my fault you're so desperate for a family you can't leave mine alone.'

She'd crossed a line; she knew it the minute the words were out of her mouth. Tess's face dropped. It was clear she'd not so much hit a nerve as pulled it from her chest and presented it to her on a plate. Sarah was almost relieved when the radio at her side flared up with static. She pulled it from her belt and Sarah caught the words, 'Got it. Under the bed.'

Tess looked at her in what seemed to be mocking disappointment. 'Under the bed? Really? Master criminal Sarah Jacobs?' she said, her words sharp as razor blades. 'I am arresting you on suspicion of murder. You do not have to say anything, but it may harm your defence if you do not mention when questioned something which you later rely on in court.'

Tess closed the handcuffs around Sarah's wrists, all of a sudden feeling tired. She'd slept a grand total of twelve hours in the last week – most of them on her sofa, covered in her case notes. Sarah didn't argue or make a single joke on the drive back to the station; she just stared straight ahead in silent resignation. She must have known this moment was coming. The ring she'd taken from the crime scene clearly had some relation to her; otherwise, why take it? And if she was tied to Shaun Mitchell's death, the chances were that she was tied to Callum Rodgers's as well. The only question that remained was whether she would take Tess down with her, and reveal what had happened to the third man in the group.

Only, something didn't feel right to Tess. Maybe it was just her wishful thinking that her family weren't all bad. Maybe she'd got carried away with the cheeky, fun, Artful Dodger character her little sister reminded her of, but she just couldn't bring herself to believe that Sarah was a cold-blooded murderer. And it wasn't just that they still didn't know how the killer had got away from both scenes – from an arrest point of view that simply didn't matter – but she also couldn't see Sarah being stupid – or reckless – enough to leave evidence at not only one murder, but two. Why would she book a hotel room using her own name if she'd known she was going to kill her lover there? And when was the last time a ring just conveniently fell off at a crime scene? It didn't happen in real life. If it hadn't been found by the crime scene techs, then it must have been very cleverly hidden, almost as if it wasn't intended for the police but for Sarah herself. Whoever had killed Shaun Mitchell and Callum Rodgers had wanted Sarah tied to these crimes for some reason, and the idea that she, Tess, was being played sat heavily on her as she booked Sarah into custody. The fact was, though, that her personal opinion didn't matter. Oswald had issued the arrest warrant the minute she'd told him that evidence had come to light of the woman's involvement. Evidence was key. They followed it, they logged it, they interpreted it. The one thing they couldn't do was ignore it. This was out of her control. It didn't matter that every instinct was screaming that there was still a killer on the loose; as far as the evidence was concerned they had their woman. Tess just had to hope and pray that Sarah kept her mouth shut about her motive, or they could end up being reunited after all. Behind bars.

It turned out that the holding cells at Brighton Police Station looked exactly like they did on *Prime Suspect*. Four magnolia-painted brick walls, and a slab with a cornflower-blue mattress the thickness of a KitKat, designed to make you go mad and confess to anything. Sarah called her dad when she reached the station but there was no answer, so she tried Mac instead. After an absolute bollocking, the kind she would usually expect from her father, he promised to contact Wayne Castro for her and said he'd have her out as soon as the twenty-four hours were up, as well as trying to get hold of Frank who had been missing all morning. She was still waiting, probably part of the Gestapo routine to break her down before her interview. The look on Tess's face when she arrested Sarah had told her all she needed to know. *She thinks I'm guilty. She thinks I'm a killer and she wants to see me rot in prison for the rest of my life.* That's what you got for your sister being a police officer. *Blood thicker than water my ass.* Tess was probably sweating too, wondering what Sarah might give away in her interview. Well, let her sweat.

'The ring was inside the desk,' Sarah said, sitting forwards in the Formica chair. She shifted uncomfortably and Tess thought about how out of place she looked in an interview room. Part of her wanted to put her sister in jail and forget all about her once and for all; the other part – the bigger part – wanted to give her a hug. Where was Frank? It wasn't like him not to be here, throwing his weight and influence around, moving heaven and earth for his little girl. The whole thing was making Tess more nervous than she already had been.

'I didn't know that the first time we went there, I promise. It had been hidden behind a false panel in the back of the drawer, about an inch thick. Just big enough to hide the ring and nothing else.'

'If you didn't see it the first time you were there, then how did you know about it?' Tess asked.

'Because I figured out the mystery of the marks on the door and the bin,' Sarah replied. 'I was just doodling the words *light, door, bin,* and Wes said something about it being three words. That's when I remembered an app I'd heard about, absolutely genius idea called—'

'What Three Words,' Tess finished. 'Uses three unique words

to pinpoint your exact location, so those words can be given to emergency services to locate you in an emergency. We've used it once or twice ourselves. But that still doesn't explain why you knew there was something in the desk.'

'The app I was talking about, What Three Words. You know you can reverse-type the words too, so you can type in *lights. door.bin* and get an exact location. Which I did.'

'And?'

'Gave me a random location somewhere in Scotland. Made no sense whatsoever.'

Tess sighed. 'You know I'm due retirement in twenty years. I'm hoping to find out the end of the story by then.'

'Patience, Watson,' Sarah retorted. 'So I remembered that it wasn't just a smear on the bin, it was two letters. CA. Which turns the word bin into . . .'

'Cabin.'

'Exactly! And when you type the words *lights.doors.cabin* into W3W, you get Davenport Road in Catford, Lewisham.'

'That's bloody miles away. Did you go there?'

Sarah frowned. 'Why would I go there?'

Tess stared at her sister, trying for a minute to comprehend how her mind worked. She'd just explained how she'd worked out an exact location from three random words marked by a killer, and now she was questioning why she would go to the location?

'To find out what the next clue was,' Tess explained slowly.

Sarah snorted. 'Don't be ridiculous. This isn't a scavenger hunt; it's a word game. And what's another word for Davenport?'

Tess reached for her phone.

'Don't bloody google it. I'll save you the two minutes. A Davenport is a desk.'

Tess stared at her in disbelief. 'Are you *trying* to lose me my job? Do you really expect me to go to my DCI and tell him that Shaun Mitchell's killer left you a word game daubed in horseradish, which you solved to find evidence against yourself at the crime scene? And you don't think, for a tiny second, that he's going to tell me that you're talking complete and utter bullshit? That the way you knew where to find the ring was because you were at the crime scene and left it there?'

Sarah held her sister's eye. 'I mean, when you put it like *that*, I suppose your way sounds a tad more plausible.'

'Yes, it does, doesn't it?'

'But my way is the truth,' Sarah countered. 'And I assume that still counts for something in the police force?'

'You know it does,' Tess snapped. 'When it's backed up by evidence and facts.'

'Speaking of which,' Sarah said. 'Have you had any forensics back from the rope that was around Mitchell's wrists?'

'I don't think so,' Tess said before she could stop herself. Then added, 'Not that I could tell you, given that you're under arrest.' She paused. 'Why?'

Sarah smirked. 'If I'm really a suspect, I should wait for my lawyer before I say anything else.'

Tess sighed. 'What do you want to tell me about the rope, Sarah?'

'Maybe nothing,' Sarah replied, her voice infuriatingly casual. 'Or maybe it's the key to your entire locked-room mystery.' She shrugged. 'But your DCI doesn't want my bullshit theories, remember?'

Chapter Twenty-Eight

'Danger, keep out. That's a good start,' Tess said, gesturing towards the spray-painted warning slashed red across the brick wall.

'They all write that on the walls,' Jerome said, taking Tess's hand and leading her down the rusted steel steps. 'Don't step there.'

'Jesus, I've never needed a tetanus shot after a lunch date before.' Tess leaned on the railing then, realizing her mistake, slapped her hands together to get rid of years of dust and decay.

Jerome took a cloth from his pocket and wiped down the surface of a huge steel pipe and heaved himself up. He threw the cloth at Tess, who raised her eyebrows.

'I'm okay standing, thanks.'

Her voice echoed around the walls of the empty Shoreham Cement Works. It seemed impossible now to believe that this place had ever been an industrial giant, although the 350-foot rotary kilns and the wide-mouthed pipework still gave a hint of the place's former majesty. Now everywhere was coated liberally in dust. Water leaked down the walls in a pattern of shit-coloured rust stains, and bird excrement was spattered across the floor and machinery. Warning signs hung uselessly from corroded nails, although it looked like there had been no one here to warn of danger for years. Bright sunlight streaming in through broken windows illuminated the dust spores in the air, giving the entire place a hazy, lost feeling.

'Suit yourself,' Jerome said, and Tess marvelled at how he seemed more himself here than he ever did in the station, or in a bar. He passed her today's lunch offering, a tuna mayo and salad baguette, and she reminded herself that next time she needed to bring the food.

Jerome ripped off the end of his baguette with his teeth, filling his mouth. Tess tutted at his animalistic eating style. It felt like they were an old couple sometimes, only they'd skipped the sexual attraction, the flirting and the general fun stuff and gone straight to the 'annoyed by how the other eats and not having sex' stage.

'What are your thoughts on Jacobs?' he asked, wiping his mouth on his sleeve. Tess was amazed at how quickly he was getting through his lunch when she'd barely picked at hers.

Now didn't feel like the time to admit that Sarah was a branch on her family tree.

'I don't think she's our killer,' Tess said, trying to keep her voice even. 'Mainly because the evidence against her is circumstantial at best. Someone called Sarah – or claiming to be called Sarah – visited Shaun Mitchell's flat. Her name was on the bookings register at the Hilton. That's literally it. We have no witnesses placing her at either scene at the time of the murders, currently no DNA evidence. And yes, she broke into

Shaun Mitchell's flat, but we know she's a thief. Doesn't make her a murderer.'

'Except if that ring was hers, and it has Mitchell's blood on it, that's pretty compelling.'

'Yes,' Tess mused. 'And mighty convenient, don't you think? That she should hide a ring at the first scene and use her own name to book a room at the second. When everything else seems to be so planned to perfection that we have next to no other clues. Except the two that point to Sarah. I don't know – this is different to every other case I've ever worked.'

'Plus you like her,' Jerome added. He pushed himself off the pipe and dodged Tess's swipe aimed at his arm.

'I do not like her.'

'Well, in six hours you have to charge her or release her,' Jerome reminded her. 'So you're going to have to make your mind up about your Artful Dodger pretty quickly.'

'I told you how quickly she annihilated that puzzle,' Tess said. 'Don't tell me you're not impressed by that.'

'Of course I am,' Jerome said. 'And if I was trying to win a cash prize from my *Take a Break* magazine—'

Tess snorted. 'You do not read *Take a Break*.'

Jerome shrugged. 'They have good stories. Anyway, if I wanted a puzzle solving, I'd be the first to call your trickster woman. But we want a murder solved. Two murders. So who you gonna call . . . ?'

'Ghostbusters?' Tess offered.

'Us, Tess. We are who they call. That thing they make us go through, you know, training? And those pesky guidelines like PACE? They are there for a reason. So that after we find out whodunnit we can actually guarantee a conviction. Your buddy Holmes doesn't have to worry about little details like that when she's messing around at a secure crime scene, but we do.'

'You're right.' Tess sighed. 'I know you're right. I'll speak to Oswald and tell him I don't think we have enough for a charge. Then I need to stop having my head turned and focus on the facts. On finding out who wanted these men dead. Means, motive, opportunity.'

And try to stay off the suspect list.

Chapter Twenty-Nine

Sarah Jacobs had been in custody for six minutes shy of twenty-two hours when the news broke of another murder in Brighton city centre. A shooting in the Old Ship, King's Road, making it the third murder in Brighton in less than two weeks. Despite what popular fiction would have people believe, Brighton was not the murder capital of the UK. The last week had matched the entire previous year for homicides in the BN area. Brighton had a serial killer, and unless their detainee could escape from police custody for a spot of criminal activity and then put herself back there, it wasn't Sarah.

The body was found at 3.30 p.m. A man in his fifties, shot in his bed sometime after breakfast. Around the same time, Sarah Jacobs was giving her third 'no comment' interview, Tess knew. She also knew they were running out of time with Sarah – they had less than two hours in which to charge her sister.

The ID of this victim was a mystery to her. The only two people she could think of connected to her crime fifteen years ago were dead now. Who was this going to turn out to be? Would it be linked to her again?

'Sounds like the same guy, gov,' Jerome said. He limbo'd into the passenger seat of Tess's car while balancing a Starbucks cup in each hand.

'How do you know? Report said shooting – that's a different MO,' Tess said, sliding into the driver's seat.

'Not yet. I spoke to the first officer on the scene—'

'Not Heath again? I'm beginning to wonder if he's the bloody murderer – he's our best link to all three cases.'

'No, this was a PC by the name of Kent. From the call to dispatch it sounds like they had to break into the room – it was locked from the inside.'

'It's a hotel room – they all lock on closing.'

'This one had a chain on the inside of the door.' Jerome pulled his mouth into a grimace and lifted his elbow to mimic defending himself from an oncoming blow.

'Oh for fucksake,' Tess swore. *Would this never end?* 'Who found him?'

'The duty manager. The guy missed his checkout and when they went to turn over the room the door was on the chain. The maid went to find the manager, who had the janitor bust open the door – that's when they found him lying on the bed, a shot through the head.'

'Adjoining door?'

Jerome shrugged. 'No information about the scene itself yet, but there is CCTV available from the corridor. I've asked Kent to have the manager prepare it. Scene is preserved – no one else goes in until you've taken a look. Forensics and Kay are on their way.'

'Good work.' Tess sighed, wondering what she was going to find this time. Or rather, who. One thing she was sure of – if she got there and Sarah Jacobs was on the forensic team, she might just shoot *herself* in the head in a locked room.

'Detective Inspector Tess Fox.' Tess held out her hand to the nervous-looking man who greeted them at the scene. She put him at maybe four feet eight inches, smaller than her by just under a foot, and he walked quickly, putting Tess in mind of a scurrying shrew. The brown tweed suit did nothing to dispel this rodent-like appearance, but his face was warm and open, more of a friendly cartoon rat. 'Are you the manager?'

The man nodded. 'Timothy Taylor. Although you can call me Tim. Please.' He looked as though he half expected to be arrested any second.

'Thanks, Tim. Do you have the name on the booking for me?'

'Yes, of course. It was . . .' He checked his wrist where he had written something in small letters. 'Luca Mancini.'

Luca Mancini. The name sounded familiar, but at least it wasn't Sarah Jacobs. She fired off a text to Fahra to look into it and hoped it didn't link back to her in any way.

'Quick work, thanks Tim. Now, I've had a run-down of what happened, but if you could tell me in your own words, then I'll get one of my officers to take an official statement. Sorry for all the repetition.'

Tim nodded enthusiastically. 'No problem. Yes. Right. It was about 2.30 p.m. when I was alerted to a non-checkout by the cleaning crew. It happens more than you'd think, people oversleeping, or sometimes they've gone and not officially checked out on the system, left the Do Not Disturb on the door. After twelve o'clock on checkout day, we tell the cleaner to go in anyway – that's usually enough to send the guest packing. Only this one, well, the door was on the chain so Miranda couldn't get in. She came to get me, and I went to bang on the door. Spent about five minutes trying to get the gentleman to answer but nothing. We opened the door, obviously it got stuck by the chain, but it meant I could shout inside – still no reply. That's when I went to get Andy to remove the chain.'

'Andy is maintenance?'

Tim nodded. 'Yes.'

'Okay, thanks.' Tess scribbled the details in her notebook. 'Once he'd removed the chain – what then?'

'Then I went in and saw him. It was horrible, so much blood. I never realized there could be so much blood.'

'I know, it can be a real shock. Do you need to see a paramedic?'

Tim shook his head and Tess nodded.

'Okay. So you went in first? Definitely?'

'I'm the only one who went in,' Tim confirmed. 'Andy stayed outside. I called to him to radio the desk for an ambulance. I think he assumed it was a drug overdose or something – it wouldn't be the first suicide we've had.' He lowered his voice. 'Between you and me, I think that's why he didn't come in. He's a bit on the sensitive side.'

'It's not a very nice thing to see,' Tess replied. 'You're doing brilliantly. Did you approach the man?'

'No.' Tim looked worried. 'Should I have? I thought about checking him, but he was clearly dead – there was so much blood . . .'

'No, you definitely did the right thing,' Tess assured him. So many people tried to play the hero and ended up trampling a crime scene to pieces, spreading blood everywhere and destroying evidence – she was grateful at least to have one less problem to deal with before they began. Hopefully the paramedics were as careful. 'So the ambulance came – did anyone else go in before them?'

'No,' Tim said. 'I wouldn't have let any of the staff see that. And only two of the paramedics went in first. They came out and shook their heads – there was nothing they could do.'

Thank goodness the Brighton paramedics had known what they were doing. They had probably realized instantly that the man was dead and kept staff to a minimum to preserve the crime scene.

'Thank you so much, Tim – you've been a wonderful help. I'm going to have to get you to go through all that again – if you can manage it – with an officer who will make sure we've got all the details correct. I'm going to need to speak to Miranda and Andy – do you know where they are?'

Tim swelled with pride. 'I kept them both separate,' he said. Someone had been watching his crime shows. 'Miranda is over there with the officer who first arrived. Andy went to get a cup of coffee, but I told him to come straight back.'

'Brilliant, Tim. If this doesn't work out for you, apply for the police, okay?'

The manager couldn't have looked happier if she'd pinned a badge to his chest. See, she could be good at this 'people person' stuff.

'Jerome.' Tess turned to look for Jerome, found him talking

to PC Kent. 'Could you take Tim somewhere quiet and get a full statement for me, please?'

'No problem.' Jerome looked happy to be interrupted. 'Come with me, sir.'

'PC Kent, I'm DI Tess Fox. I'm the SIO for this case.' As Tess took a breath she understood the reason Jerome was so keen to get away. The smell of stale sweat hung around the man like . . . well, like an extremely bad smell. She resolved to make this encounter short if not sweet, and hope Heath caught the next murder. 'Did you get here before or after the ambulance?'

'Practically the same time, ma'am,' he replied.

'You don't have to call me that.' Tess smiled, stepping back slightly. 'Tess is fine. Okay – so the paramedics went into the room . . . ?'

'Before me,' Kent confirmed. 'They checked for signs of life – once they had come out I secured the room, and called it in. Then I secured the corridor and made sure no one left their rooms. I took a few details from the manager, Tim Taylor – sounds like a darts player, doesn't he? – then spoke to DS Morgan, who told me to secure the CCTV, so I called down to reception who said they would get it ready.'

'And you stayed on this floor?'

'Yes ma'am, I mean, um, yes. The rooms seem mostly empty – PC Hollander over there made sure no one came up and I made sure the couple of people in the rooms didn't leave.'

'Brilliant, thank you.'

Tess had a feeling, however, that none of the crime scene preservation was going to make the slightest bit of difference to this situation. If this was the same offender as the last two, then nothing they did or didn't do was going to help.

Chapter Thirty

Luca Mancini had checked in at 4.30 p.m. He had gone down for an evening meal and had a drink in the bar, went back to his room and didn't come down again until breakfast, where the CCTV caught him going into the dining room and coming back out again by 9 a.m. The camera in the corridor showed him going back into his room at 9.06. At 9.36, a member of the cleaning crew knocked on the door and – when there was no answer – she attempted to go in and clean the room. The inside latch was on so she left.

The victim was due to check out by eleven and the room needed to be turned over for the next guest. The cleaner on the next shift attempted to access the room, but the door was still on the deadbolt. No answer from the room. She told the manager, who, after some deliberation, had a member of staff break the door lock, where they found the victim lying in bed. He'd been shot through the face once, making next-of-kin identification impossible.

The Old Ship was a five-storey hotel and their victim's room was on the fourth floor. As they walked the white corridors, Tess took in the framed pictures along the newly painted walls. It looked like some refurbishment had taken place fairly recently. On the way she'd had Jerome look up a bit about the place. It wasn't overly expensive, neither was it a cheap B&B – this was a hotel that mainly catered for tourists who wanted some Brighton charm to rub off on their holiday. The floor itself had been sealed off, but unlike Callum Rodgers's murder, this crime scene was contained to the bedroom, so Tess had taken the decision not to close any more of the hotel than necessary. She'd been to two other deaths in hotels in her time in the force, one drug overdose and one of a woman who had stabbed her husband repeatedly with a corkscrew. Both times the hotel had continued to function, with most guests blissfully unaware that one of their number wouldn't be checking themselves out that afternoon. In most cases it would be the cleaning service that alerted the management to the death of one of their guests – nothing about this case was unusual in that respect.

The door to room 422 hung open slightly, and Tess waved her warrant card at the officer stationed at the door. He stepped aside in an almost bored fashion, barely glancing at the card in her hand. Why would he – there had been a murder, he was waiting for CID, and here was someone who looked very much like a detective trying to access the room. Tess felt a flash of irritation and had to bite the inside of her lip to stop her from giving the unconcerned officer a lecture on letting just anyone waltz into a crime scene. She'd only get herself known as an asshole amongst Brighton uniform, and she already had enough of a reputation within her own unit.

The bedroom was decorated in a pleasant cornflower blue and white scheme, a large print of Brighton Pier hanging in an ornate gilt frame on an angled wall in front of the door. To the right was another door leading to the bathroom, painted in white, all very zen. The calm and serene nature of the room was only upset by the shining wet scarlet stain that obscured the top half of the large unmade double bed to the left of the door. Drops of blood speckled the white quilted headboard and dripped down, as though someone had left the lid off a milkshake before shaking it hard. Amidst this lay the slumped body of a man dressed in jeans and a navy polo shirt, a gaping black hole where his face should have been.

'Jesus Christ,' Tess muttered automatically. She stayed in the doorway, not wanting to take a single risk before forensics arrived. The paramedics didn't appear to have disturbed anything, but saying that, why would they need to? No life to preserve here – that much was clear. Averting her eyes from the gruesome sight on the bed, she pulled out her notepad and made a quick sketch of the room, noting that the blinds on the window opposite the door were pulled down three quarters and that the bathroom door was ajar. She turned slightly and snapped off a photograph of the splintered door jamb where Andy from maintenance had shouldered his way in through the chain. 'Stay out there,' she instructed Jerome. He didn't argue. Tess looked around and sighed.

'Who chains the door of a hotel room these days?' she asked.

Jerome's voice came from outside the door. 'He was afraid of something. Trying to keep someone out.'

What would Sarah say?

Don't make any assumptions.

'Or trying to keep someone in.'

Okay, Tess's voice reasoned with the other woman's. *So I'm* assuming *this guy was murdered.* She crossed the room, eyes down, careful not to miss anything underfoot, and lifted the valance that covered the bottom of the bed. No gun under there. Taking her pen, she tried not to focus on the dead man with half a head as she lifted the duvet to reveal his hands. Still no gun. She'd have SOCO do a thorough search, but she was willing to bet there was no gun in this room. And unless he shot himself in the face then got up and threw the murder weapon out of the window, she thought she was okay with her murder assumption.

What next?

You're assuming there is only one way out. Safe assumption. A check of the windows and bathroom – windows painted shut (she wasn't entirely sure about the safety regs on that one but it made things simple here) and no secret door out of the shower. That wasn't to say the killer hadn't been hiding in there until Handy Andy and Tiny Tim ran off to call the police – she'd have to check the CCTV thoroughly.

'Boss, forensics are here,' Jerome called in.

Assumption, the voice in her head chided – *you're assuming the killer isn't in the wardrobe.*

The thought ballooned in Tess's mind and she practically fell out of the room into the corridor. Jerome raised his eyebrows at her.

'What?' she asked, looking innocent. She waved a hand at the room. 'You can go in and check the wardrobe now.'

The room Tim had helpfully provided them with (most likely to get them out of sight of the other guests – nothing puts you off a continental breakfast platter for £12.95 faster than the thought of a dead body in the room above) was barely big enough to squeeze the two of them in, standing room only. This was where they were supposed to privately discuss what to do about the disaster upstairs. The walls were lined with metal racking that held an assortment of envelopes and staples, but also random items like a blow-up pineapple and a reindeer who either had a broken leg or was supposed to be peeing against a wall. A clock that had stopped, a blue plastic lunchbox with the name 'Elton' written on the side in black Sharpie, a miniature replica of a Tardis – the list Tess mentally recorded went on. It looked like the room of forgotten things from a children's book, but it'd do for now. Tess pulled out her trusty notepad, leaned back against the racking to test its weight and looked at Jerome.

'Who've you done?'

Jerome checked his own notes. 'The manager, Tim, the room service lady, cleaner, whatever it's politically correct to call them. What do we call them?'

'Miranda,' Tess replied. 'What did she say?'

'Same as Tim. She went to open the door to turn the room over and it buzzed open but the chain was on. She called into the room – nothing. It was over three hours after checkout, so she notified Tim and went on with her rounds. She wasn't present when they found the body.'

'Did this guy's room have a Do Not Disturb? There wasn't one when I went up.'

'I didn't see one either,' Jerome agreed.

'Ask Tim,' Tess requested. 'If you'd just killed a man in a hotel room, you'd want to give yourself a bit of time to escape. Seems like you'd put up a Do Not Disturb sign. Might be fingerprints. I know' – she nodded at the expression on his face – 'long shot. But we don't want to be the team that missed a set of prints because the sign got knocked off the door. Just check with him.'

'Will do.'

'Thanks. Reception?'

'I spoke to the woman on reception. It was a different guy on the desk yesterday when our victim checked in – she was calling him in to talk to us. She hadn't seen the victim so could only repeat what was on the system.'

'Okay, thanks. Anything else?'

'Yeah, well, they have full name and address details. He was staying in a double room but only his name was on the booking. The booking was made a week ago through Booking dotcom, I've made a note to trace the credit card details used. Annabel' – he said the name as though it tasted delicious and raised his eyebrows – 'was very helpful and is loading all of the CCTV onto a USB for us from the moment he checked in.'

'Where does it cover?'

'Front entrance and hallway. We should be able to see if anyone went into that room after the last guest checked out.'

'Great. With any luck we'll get a clear picture of our victim coming in, it'll help us find out if the other guests saw him talking to anyone. Perhaps "helpful Annabel" can help you with that, DS Morgan?' She smiled. 'Forensics are doing their stuff in the room now so there's not much point in all three of us hanging around here. Jerome, when you're finished with

Annabel you can come back with me and we'll take a look at the footage. I'll get Kent to stick around and speak to the other guests, see if he can't get at least one of those PCs to stay with him. And if any of you can figure out how this guy shot someone, then put the chain on the door as he left, I'll buy you dinner for a week.'

Fahra was waiting for them the minute they walked into the station.

'What have you got?' Tess asked, seeing the look on her face. *Who is this guy?*

'I ran the ID that Jerome gave me over the phone through all the databases. No criminal record.'

Tess sighed. 'It was worth a try.'

'It definitely was,' Fahra said, holding up a sheet of paper. 'Because I got something else. Luca Mancini doesn't have a criminal record, but his name did come up with regards to an active case. One of ours.'

Tess took the piece of paper. 'The Shaun Mitchell case. Damn, I knew that name sounded familiar! His references, wasn't it?'

Fahra nodded. 'Yep. And the real Luca Mancini died ten years ago.'

'Okay.' Tess looked around the corridor. 'So it's a fake name, and the only current connection we have between the two cases. Thanks Fahra, great work.'

Fahra beamed. 'I also got onto Booking dotcom.'

'You've been busy,' Tess said, impressed.

'I try. Unfortunately, they need a warrant to release the details. The good thing is that the guy I spoke to said that the information is easy enough to get once we have it.'

'Right.' Tess looked at Jerome. 'I'll give Oswald a call while you—'

'No need,' Fahra interrupted. 'Sorry, ma'am, DCI Oswald is waiting in the briefing room for you. He came across as soon as he heard about this new murder.'

'How does he look?' Tess asked.

The look on Fahra's face was unmistakable. She lowered her voice. 'Between me and you? Remember the time Janice spent a grand on that handbag then asked for the matching purse?'

'Fuck.' That had not been a good day. Tess nodded. 'Thanks. Can you do me a favour? Can you go through all the notes on these three cases and cross-reference any similarities? Anything that comes up to link the cases. I want to know everything, down to if the victims wore the same make of shoes. If we don't come up with something soon, we might all be working in hotels by the end of the month.'

Chapter Thirty-One

Dci Oswald had already cleared the briefing room in anticipation of Tess's return. When she knocked the door lightly, he grunted, 'Come in, Fox,' and she walked in to find him looking at the various notes and diagrams tacked to the walls and scrawled on whiteboards around them. 'Sit down,' he instructed.

She sat.

'This is bad, Tess.' He was shaking his head, but Tess took it as a good sign that she hadn't been relegated to DI Fox yet. He pinched the bottom of his nose between his thumb and his forefinger, his palm rubbing his mouth. It was an unconscious gesture he always made when he was stressed. He looked paler than usual and there were shadows under his eyes that she hadn't seen before. 'Three murders in less than a month. You know what that's going to mean?'

'No, sir.' This wasn't the time for smartarse quips about the female canteen budget. There was only so far you could go with Oswald, and Tess knew her limits. Right now she felt a bit sorry for him. While she was busy at crime scenes, he was shielding her from their superiors and the press. It had always seemed like glory hunting to her before, but she wouldn't want to be in his position now.

'Serial killer.' The words came out in a whisper, as though he was afraid someone might overhear. 'The press gets this and it's got serial killer headlines written all over it. They wait for a third, you know, because Google says you have to have three. Once the third is out, all hell will break loose.'

So that was what had been on his mind. No force wants a serial killer on the loose. Somehow, in the minds of the public, the idea of a serial killer was worse than the idea of three separate, unrelated murders. Even though that meant three killers. Go figure.

'Sir, I . . .'

'The fact is – the fact that I want to make clear to the press, is that we have a suspect in custody for the first two murders. But I don't want to do that if we are going to have to release her at any moment.'

Tess took a deep breath. 'I think we've got the wrong person. I think these crimes are related and I think whoever did it wanted us to think it was Sarah Jacobs.'

Oswald let out a huge sigh. 'I was afraid you were going to say that. You know how this is going to look? Like we let this happen. Like we were concentrating all our energy on this Jacobs while the real killer was free to kill again. Which is essentially true, isn't it?'

'That's unfair, sir, and you know it. While two of us were interviewing Jacobs, the rest of the team were still doing a huge amount of work in ruling out anyone the two victims might have fallen out with or upset, anyone who might have had a grudge against both of them in the past. As you can imagine, the people Mitchell and Rodgers run with – or ran with – don't tend to talk to the police.'

'Apart from the fact that these two men used to know each other at one time, do you actually have any proof their murders are connected? And this third one, how does that even fit?'

'There are links between all three cases,' Tess said.

'Links? Or consistencies? They are in different locations, different methods, the victims are different ages – all men, yes, but that isn't too concerning. What do we have that we can say this is definitely the same killer?'

'Well, apart from the drug-related offences in the past, and the fact that these two men almost certainly know each other, the time proximity of their murders, the fact that all three were murdered in somewhat "impossible" crimes. And the third victim was booked in under an alias used by Shaun Mitchell on his rental references.'

DCI Oswald raised his eyebrows. He moved to sit behind his desk and did the nose squeezing thing again. 'So nothing really concrete, then?' he said slowly. 'The third one especially – the shooting, that could be entirely separate?'

'Sir, I don't think so. The MO is the same: the room was locked from the inside.'

'Which no one has to know. Yet,' DCI Oswald replied. He was almost eager now, a tiny thread of hope getting longer. 'It was a shooting, no knife involved like the first two crimes. In fact, a completely different MO if you look at it from that angle. We have someone in custody for the first two murders, therefore, this is a different perpetrator as far as the press need to know. A spike in violent crime, yes, but not a serial killer.'

'But sir, the references . . .'

'Might not mean a thing,' Oswald said. He picked up a pen and began tapping it against his desk. 'Come on, it's a small place really. People know people, people hear names. If we treat this one as unrelated, the press might hold off on screaming serial killer long enough for us to actually charge someone.' He was talking to himself more than Tess now. 'We'll have to give it to another team though.'

And there it was. Tess had the sinking feeling that this was the whole reason she'd been brought in straight after Oswald's meeting with the powers above, that this 'sudden' decision to treat the cases as separate for the sake of the press had been less divine inspiration and more Hand of God.

'You can't just take me off the case,' she objected, knowing that her objection wasn't going to make any difference. 'I've worked my arse off since the beginning. Walker has done nothing but take the piss . . .' She stopped before her voice became whiny.

Oswald, to his credit, looked apologetic. 'You have two ongoing murder investigations, DI Fox. I'm not taking you off anything, I'm spreading the load. You and Walker can share information, and as far as the outside world is concerned, the two cases are being investigated separately. Therefore, no serial killer.'

Yeah, and if Geoff Walker gets an arrest on his case first, he'll be the first to say all three are linked. She could imagine the look on his face now as he closed her cases as well as his.

Her first lead on a murder and he swoops in to succeed where she fails. Over her dead body.

'When Walker gets here you'll need to do him a handover of everything you gathered this morning,' Oswald said. 'And I've secured you a ninety-six on your suspect.'

'Thanks,' Tess replied, pressing her tongue against her teeth so she didn't add *for nothing. I've taken your case off you, but don't worry, you have an extra few hours to question the person who you've just said you don't believe is guilty.* 'Can I go now, sir?'

'Yeah.' Oswald sighed, suddenly looking about eighty years old. When he spoke, his voice had softened. 'Look, I know Walker's a prick but he's actually a good detective. Make sure you give him everything you have on this shooting and, you never know, he might actually make himself useful. I'm still rooting for you, Tess.'

There was no way of holding her tongue this time. If she let her mouth open, then words that she couldn't take back were bound to come out. Tess stood up as quickly as she could and left without saying another thing.

Chapter Thirty-Two

'We're off the shooting,' Tess announced, checking the door to the briefing room was closed behind her. The three of them, Jerome, Fahra and PC Campbell Heath had gathered to wait for her following her meeting with Oswald.

Fahra passed her a mug. 'It's green tea,' she offered. Tess looked at her in surprise and Fahra looked embarrassed. 'I noticed you didn't usually drink your coffee, and when we were out the other day you ordered green tea. So I bought some. I hope it's the right one.'

Tess didn't know what to say. After the way she'd felt the last couple of weeks, she wanted to cry, especially right off the back of losing her case to Walker, but instead she said, with as much feeling as she could muster, so the other woman knew she really meant it, 'Thanks, Fahra. Honestly, thanks.'

'What do you mean we're off the shooting?' Jerome demanded, pulling her back to attention. 'It's one of ours. Same guy. Any idiot can see that.'

Tess shook her head. 'They don't want people to see that.

The powers that be want the public to think it's unrelated so there isn't a mass panic about a serial killer in Brighton. For what it's worth, I don't think Oswald had any more say about it than we do. It's going to Walker.'

Their faces were almost worth it. Tess knew in that instant that her team – at least this subsection of it – felt the same way about Geoff Walker as she did.

'Look.' She held up a hand as they all went to speak at once. 'I'm as pissed off about it as you, but we don't have time to stand here feeling sorry for ourselves. As soon as Walker comes through that door – and honestly I'm surprised he's not here already but I think we have the DCI to thank for that – we have to hand over everything we have on this, and I have a feeling he's not going to be particularly forthcoming about keeping us informed. My guess is that he'll keep it all in hard copy and close to his chest. So,' she turned to Fahra, 'do you think you can make copies of everything we have already? Really, really quickly?'

'I'll go like my arse is on fire.' Fahra took Tess's notebook from her outstretched hand and picked up Jerome's from the table.

Tess turned to PC Heath. 'Campbell – can you get down to the front desk and let me know when Walker arrives? Stall him if you can. I don't want him to know we're still working this case.'

Campbell nodded as if he'd just been instructed to protect the front line. 'Boss.'

Tess felt an overwhelming rush of affection for her team. She grabbed Fahra's arm as she turned to leave. 'Once word gets around we're off this case, we'll be referred back to Walker for everything. The vic will be on the way to the hospital within the next hour. Do you think you can get over there before anyone knows we're off and speak to the coroner? I want to know what personal effects the victim was booked in with. Namely his wallet.'

'No problem.' Fahra turned to leave, arms stuffed with case notes. She hesitated, turned back and leaned into Tess. 'Between you and me, ma'am, I fucking hate that prick Walker.'

Tess's mouth fell open. 'Um, right,' she stuttered. Fahra winked at her. As she walked out the door Tess called, 'And thanks again for the tea.' Fahra held up a hand as she hurried away.

'And us?' Jerome asked when they others were gone.

Tess crossed the room to the PC in the corner. 'We need to make a copy of this CCTV before we hand the USB over to Walker. It might hold the key to everything.'

The ancient PC seemed to take three times as long as usual to boot up and, just as Tess was dragging and copying the CCTV video files into another folder, her radio crackled into life.

'Boss, Walker's on his way up now.'

'Thanks, Heath,' Tess replied, watching the bar progress from 20, 30, 40 per cent. She turned to Jerome. 'Stall him.'

Jerome left the room and she watched through the clear top half of the briefing room window as he stopped Walker on his way into the office. Come on, come on, she pleaded desperately. Fifty, sixty, seventy-five . . .

She saw the top of Walker's head moving towards the door just as the bar hit 100 per cent. Hoping she wasn't corrupting the file, she yanked the stick from the machine and slipped it back inside the envelope. As Walker shoved open the door without knocking, Tess saw Fahra rushing into the open-plan office beyond.

'Geoff, *thank God* you're here,' Tess said emphatically.

Walker's eyebrows raised – that had not been the welcome he was expecting. 'I'd have been here sooner if your team weren't so keen for a chat. Oswald not told you the good news?'

'News?' Tess looked innocently vacant.

Walker's eyes glinted at the thought of being the first to break it to her. 'I'm taking the shooting off your hands. I hear you're a bit busy – still haven't charged anyone for the other murders.'

The door behind Walker eased open and Fahra's arm slid through with a pile of papers. She pushed them lightly onto the table and stuck a thumb up at Tess.

'Oh, *that* news.' Tess grinned. 'Didn't Oswald tell you? It was my idea for you to take that case. I heard on the grapevine that the victim was a male sex worker and thought you might already know him. Here.' She pushed past him and grabbed the file and shoved it at him. 'The hard work's already been done for you. Now you get to sit at your desk and figure out how all the pieces fit together. Don't worry, I know you're only used to ten-piece jigsaws but I'm sure you'll be fine.'

Walker pulled his face into a smirk. It was even less attractive than usual. 'Here, maybe when I've finished solving this one, I could come and help you with yours. There's no shame in asking for a bit of assistance.'

Tess glanced through the window, where she could see Jerome and Campbell waiting for her, imagined Fahra rushing to the hospital to arrive at the same time as the body. 'Don't you worry,' she said, moving past him to leave. 'I've got all the help I need.'

Chapter Thirty-Three

When Fahra slipped back into the office nearly two hours later, she gave Tess a nod and walked straight through into the briefing room. Tess saw Walker's head snap up from where he'd been poring over the pages of notes she'd handed him and gave him a small smile as she followed her DS.

'What did you get?'

Fahra frowned. 'No ID on the body or with any of the evidence checked in by SOCO.'

Tess sighed. 'Okay, thanks for trying.'

'I did more than that.' Fahra smiled, and handed her a piece of paper. 'I went by forensics on my way back up here and they asked me to bring you this. They obviously hadn't got the memo about Walker being lead on the shooting yet.'

'And you didn't enlighten them?' Tess grinned, looking down at the sheet of paper in her hand. 'Fingerprints! Fucking hell, that was quick work for them. Fahra, you sta—' The praise died on her lips when she saw who the prints had been matched to.

'There must be a mistake . . .'

Fahra shook her head. 'No mistake. Do you know him? Apparently he's kind of a big deal here in Brighton. In property. But forensics were saying he's linked to organized crime – they've just never been able to prove it. All fits, I guess.'

But Tess wasn't listening. Her chest was heaving. She didn't know if she was going to be sick or collapse.

Fahra saw what was happening and grabbed hold of her as her legs gave out from underneath her. 'Jerome!' Fahra screamed.

Tess thought she saw a shadow dart across the room, maybe Jerome but everything was blurred; she needed to close her eyes, to try and get a grip. It couldn't be. This wasn't happening. The man lying dead in the Old Ship couldn't be who forensics said he was. Her father couldn't be dead. But there it was in black and white. Their third victim was Frank Jacobs.

'Are you going to tell me what that was all about?' Jerome asked, his voice gentle.

When Tess had found her feet again, she had managed to stumble to the toilets, mumbling something about a lack of food, and that she'd be fine. She'd sat on the toilet sobbing as quietly as possible for half an hour, washed her face and emerged to see Jerome waiting for her, a lukewarm cup of green tea in his hand. He'd taken her into a vacant interview room where they now sat, Tess staring at the wall.

'I don't think I can.' Her voice was no more than a croak. It was true – who could she speak to about this? She had no one she could tell, no one who would understand the fucked-up relationship between her and Frank Jacobs, no one to give her a hug and console her. No one she could admit to that she had wanted Frank's love and admiration more than anything, and it broke her heart to know that she'd worked hard all her life only to find her biological father actually so ashamed of her that he couldn't stand to look at her.

'You can give it a go,' Jerome encouraged. 'There's nothing you could tell me that would shock me. I've been a police officer a long time and—'

'Frank Jacobs was my father,' Tess said, cutting him off.

Jerome's eyes widened so comically that Tess would have laughed if her face hadn't hurt so much from crying. 'What the fuck, Tess? Frank Jacobs the property guy? But he's—'

'A criminal,' Tess finished. 'Allegedly. But he is. And he's also the victim in our shooting case this afternoon.'

Jerome exhaled slowly. 'God, Tess, I'm so sorry. This must be . . . I mean it sounds . . .'

'Complicated?'

'Yes, complicated. Did the two of you have a relationship?'

Tess shook her head. That much was the truth. She couldn't tell Jerome the whole truth though, could she? How she'd started working for Frank's crew until things had turned just about as sour as they could go. She decided on a sanitized version, the version she wished had happened anyway.

'When my dad – my mum's husband I mean – when he died, Mum told me that Frank was my real dad. I went to see him, when I first found out. He told me I was welcome in his family, looked pretty delighted to have another daughter. Then I told him I was training to be a police officer.' A lie, of course, but a necessary one. Tess had made the decision to join the police only after she had stabbed a man to death, but there were some things Jerome didn't need to know.

Jerome pulled a face reminiscent of the time he'd accidentally drunk Tess's green tea instead of his strong black coffee. 'How did that go?'

'Oh, brilliant. He couldn't have been prouder. He was particularly looking forward to when I'd have to arrest him. Not that that's a problem any more, I guess.' Her eyes filled with tears again.

'Wait, so Sarah Jacobs, downstairs in the cells . . .'

'Is my half-sister. You should be a detective, Morgan.'

'Oh shit.'

Tess sighed and pushed herself up from the table. 'Oh shit indeed. And I'd better go and tell her that our father is dead.'

Chapter Thirty-Four

Tess had no more time to waste. The team were all briefed on Frank's murder and she trusted them all to get on with their respective jobs. But the longer she put this off, the harder it was going to be. Who was she trying to kid? The longer she put this off, the more likely it was that Walker would find out the victim's identity, and she needed to be the one to break the news to Sarah.

It felt like an eternity before a figure appeared at the glass pane in the door. The door swung inwards and Sarah was led in by a female officer who looked as if she had the ghost of a smile on her face. Sarah was being her usual charming self, no doubt. Tess felt a pang of regret at the blank, indifferent look on her face when she saw her at the table. Sarah sat down opposite her.

'What is it?' she said immediately. 'Why isn't my lawyer here? Why haven't you let me go? It's been over twenty-four hours – what's going on?'

'We were granted an extension,' Tess practically whispered.

'Castro knows. He agreed to let me speak to you. I take it he knows who I am?'

'He's my dad's lawyer, he knows everything about us. Ish. Don't worry – he won't drop you in it. But you've got to let me out of here. I'm no use to you in here, Tess. You know I didn't kill Mitchell and Rodgers. You're just pissed off that I didn't tell you the whole truth about the ring.'

'Sarah.' Tess didn't know how to say it. This was excruciating. 'Sarah, this isn't about the case. It's about Dad.'

Sarah looked confused. 'Have you arrested him? Wait, did you just call him Dad? What the hell is going on here?'

'There was a shooting at the Old Ship Hotel today. The man who was shot died instantly. It was Frank. I'm so sorry, Sarah. Dad's dead.'

She heard the words, but they didn't make any sense. Dead? Her father wasn't dead. Even the idea was so fucking ridiculous she almost laughed. Did she know who their dad even was? Frank Jacobs did not get shot in a hotel room like some scummy two-bit criminal. He was one of the best grifters the country had ever seen. He was cleverer than the whole Sussex Police Force put together. How could he be dead when all these idiots around her were still alive?

'Sarah, did you hear me? I'm so sorry.'

Sarah exhaled. 'You're going to look really stupid when you realize what a mistake you've made. Obviously you've got the wrong person. What would Dad even be doing at a hotel two minutes from his own home? It's not like he's having an affair.'

'I'm sorry . . .'

'Stop saying that! Stop apologizing to me, and go and find whoever your dead guy's poor family really is. And find out why he used Dad's name on his hotel booking if you can manage it.'

'It wasn't Frank's name on the booking, Sarah. We had to use his fingerprints. I can't believe it either. I know he hated me but—'

Sarah looked up sharply. 'Hate you? Dad doesn't hate you, Tess – he's proud of you. If anything he hates himself, for not being the father you needed him to be. You remind him that there was a good part of him once.'

Tess sat back in her chair and inhaled sharply. 'I thought he was ashamed of me. I don't know what to say.' Sarah saw tears begin to form in her sister's eyes.

'You really believe it's him, don't you?' Sarah asked. 'You think he's really gone?'

Tess nodded, the tears beginning to spill over her cheeks again. She was grateful Oswald had allowed her to have this discussion without the tapes present – she'd argued that it wasn't a formal interview and that even Sarah deserved some privacy to learn about the death of her father. The truth was that, for once, Tess felt more aligned with this woman than anyone else in the world.

'Can I call Mac? He'll have to tell Wes and Gabe. That's it. We don't have anyone else.' Sarah could barely get the words out; she was struggling to think, to breathe. Her dad? Gone? It wasn't possible, and yet – would Tess have told her if she wasn't certain? Or could this all be a trick to try and catch her out? She'd been going crazy in this cell for over a day now, 'no comment' the only words Wayne Castro had allowed her to repeat. Now she was saying that while Sarah had been sitting here, staring at the cracks in the ceiling, her dad was dying?

'There's no one else,' she repeated, the sudden realization that her life was, and always had been, as lonely as Tess's. 'It was just us.'

Chapter Thirty-Five

Tess escorted Sarah to the toilets and stood outside to give her some privacy while she composed herself. Now that Sarah had been entirely ruled out from the latest shooting, Tess could go ahead and suggest they forgo the extension and release her without charge. But as long as Oswald was still trying to pretend there wasn't a connection between this and the previous two murders, that probably wasn't going to work. Still, she needed to get Sarah out of here so she could be with her family at the worst time of her life.

Five minutes later Sarah emerged, her face wet and shiny with tears. She looked resolute. 'I need you to promise to find whoever did this to our . . .' She looked around, remembering they could potentially be overheard in the corridor. 'My dad. And I need to know if it's connected to what happened to those two guys, and to what we—'

Tess interrupted before Sarah could say something incriminating for them both. She took her arm and led her quickly back into the custody suite, where they wouldn't be overheard. 'We will get to the bottom of this, I promise.'

'Then let me go,' Sarah replied, putting her head into her hands, her elbows resting on the table. 'Drop this pretence that I had something to do with all this and I can help you. Please Tess, work with me on this.'

'I am, I promise. I've already told my DCI that I don't think you're involved. He's secured us an extension on your questioning, but it's all political – he just doesn't want the public to think the murders are connected. You're stuck in here as a smokescreen so the people of Brighton don't start shouting "serial killer".'

Sarah sighed and looked up. 'I'm sorry, Tess – you know that?' Her voice was full of regret. She glanced at the clock on the wall and an awful feeling crept over Tess.

'Sorry for what?' she asked, a warning tone in her voice. 'Sarah?'

'I'm sorry that we're on the wrong sides. Sorry that your life is always going to be bound by these stupid rules and procedures. I'm sorry that neither Dad nor I could be the people you want us to be. I don't want to get you into any trouble or lose you your job, but I'm not part of your world and I can't sit in here while the person who killed my dad is out there, just so your adoring public can be kept in the dark. Do you understand?'

'I don't think I do,' Tess said slowly. Her eyes locked onto her sister's, whose were full of fear and anger. Regret and raw pain. And at that moment, as the fire alarm began to echo through the room, she understood perfectly what Sarah was about to do.

Chapter Thirty-Six

'Please tell me this isn't your doing,' Tess said as the fire alarm began to shriek through the building.

'I'm really sorry,' Sarah said, as she smacked Tess hard in the side of the head, knocking her to the floor.

Sarah was no boxer. Tess would come round in less than a minute, she well knew, so she had to move quickly. Pulling off her sister's jacket and snatching her warrant card from her handbag, she slipped out of the door of the custody room and glanced at the exit where a crowd was already gathering.

A hand grabbed her arm. 'This way,' Mac hissed, and dragged her down a long empty corridor. There was a fire exit at the end, one officer standing in front of it.

Sarah flashed Tess's card at him and shouted, 'DI Fox, move!' Luckily he didn't seem to know what DI Fox looked like and he stepped hastily aside. As the door closed behind her, she thought she heard the sound of Tess shouting, but it might have been her imagination.

The car was running and in gear as they approached, Wes

in the front seat. Mac slid into the passenger seat as Sarah launched herself into the back. 'Go.' She slammed the car door behind her, and Wes didn't hesitate. She lay across the back seat as he accelerated off, leaving the police station and Tess in the distance.

When they were safely away, she shifted herself into a sitting position and Mac twisted to look at her.

'Tell me what you said on the phone was a lie,' he demanded.

'What?' Wes asked. 'What is it?'

'It's Dad,' Sarah said, her eyes fixed on Mac's. 'Tess just told me that he's dead. Is it true? Has anyone spoken to him today?'

Mac shook his head. 'I haven't been able to get hold of him.' His voice was little more than a croak. 'I saw the commotion in town and knew there had been another murder. I've been calling him constantly . . .'

Sarah could see the pain in his eyes and felt terrible for ever thinking that Mac might be the one who planted evidence in Shaun Mitchell's flat. Dad was his oldest friend; it was Mac who had taken him under his wing, taught Frank everything he knew. Mac was his mentor and the closest thing he had to a brother. Although technically she didn't know if that was true: he might have a real brother for all she knew – Dad hadn't spoken to his parents since before she was born and he never spoke about them, however much she asked. Now she'd never get a chance to ask him.

Wes slowed down. 'What? No, I just saw him yesterday. He can't be . . . what do you mean?'

'I'm so sorry, Wes.' The tears spilled down her cheeks and she choked back a sob. 'Someone shot him. That's all I know.

I should have found out more but I needed to get out of there. I wanted to make sure you were both okay.'

'The most important thing is that you're where you belong,' Mac said, and she could see the cogs turning. 'We have to find out who did this, of course, but mainly why. And make sure you're safe. It could be any of us next.'

'What are you thinking?'

'We've got no evidence the safe house is compromised; I think we should stick to the plan and bug out there. Then we can start trying our contacts, see who knows what . . .'

'Here's the thing,' Sarah said. 'I've got some "coming clean" of my own to do. I need to tell you about the other two murders.'

'The other two? You think they're related to what happened to Dad?' Wes asked.

Sarah was less shocked at hearing him call Frank dad than she had been at Tess but it still made her breath catch in her throat. She bit the inside of her lip to stop her crying. *You are never going to see him again. He's gone.*

'I know they are,' she said, when she could trust her voice. 'And it's funny what a day in a police cell will do for you. They should put the detectives in there, might make them work faster. Because I know who killed them, and how.'

Tess sucked in a breath and opened her eyes. Her head felt as if she'd had it tightened in a vice, and saliva filled her mouth – she was going to be sick. Throwing out a hand she tumbled sideways, her wrist twisting underneath her weight.

A sickening crack came from her own bones. Pain shot through her entire arm, refocusing her mind from vomiting to screaming. She looked around, the sound of the fire alarm still shrieking inside her head. Sarah was gone.

'Fuck!' Tess cursed, pulling herself up against the table with her good hand. Her right wrist was pulsing with pain but she didn't have time to think about that now. She steadied herself and staggered outside to where officers were moving prisoners outside in cuffs. 'Stop her!' she shouted at no one in particular. 'Shit!'

Through the front doors of the police reception, she just made out a car spinning off at high speed. They'd obviously been waiting at the fire exit. Tess grasped for her radio. 'Jerome?'

'I'm outside, boss. You okay?'

'No, I'm not fucking okay,' Tess practically shouted. 'It's Sarah – she's escaped. Get every available person you can and search the area. If we don't find her, I'm fucked.'

Chapter Thirty-Seven

Once they were out of the city centre at last, Sarah fell into an exhausted sleep. She woke to see motorway surrounded by shades of green stretching out as far as she could see. They weren't far now from the Kent Downs, where Frank's safe house was located. That they had escaped from police custody and were nearly securely tucked away where she couldn't be found felt like performing a miracle, the same kind of rush she got when she was in the throes of a con. Would she get that feeling again, without her dad? Or would it all fall apart now? The memory of the last time she had been driven to their hideaway slammed into her like a freight train through her exhausted fog. Her dad driving, eleven-year-old her in the passenger seat, excited about their adventure holiday. It had been another few years before she'd come to realize that it hadn't been a holiday at all; that her dad had been running away from something – although exactly what, she had never found out.

'Sometimes all you need is to get away for a couple of weeks,' he'd told her as they pulled up outside the old run-down cottage and dragged their scant belongings from the car. 'This is the perfect place to escape. Only you, me and Uncle Mac know it exists.' Tears filled her eyes as she realized that the cottage was all hers now – she and Frank would never escape here again.

The cottage looked in a far worse state of disrepair than she remembered it. Flakes of paint were peeling off the outside walls and the garden had run wild, ivy obscuring almost the entire right wall. Through an eleven-year old's eyes, she had thought it looked mysterious and exotic, whereas now it looked sad and forgotten. It felt as though the house was in mourning for the man who had made it a sanctuary.

'It's a fixer-upper,' Wes commented, and Sarah felt an irrational stab of annoyance. Okay, she'd been thinking the same only seconds ago but that was different.

'It's beautiful,' Sarah snapped, and Mac gave her a fleeting glance.

'You okay, kid?' he asked as she unloaded the bug-out bags that Mac and Wes had thrown in the car before coming to spring her from the police station. She gritted her teeth and nodded. She would not let herself start to cry. If she started, she wouldn't stop.

'Fine. Work first.'

She thought of Tess, and the huge search that would be under way at this very moment – no doubt led by a furious DI Fox – to hang Sarah and her crew, tar and feather them. Still, Sarah would have been no good to her dad waiting it out in prison – she'd been given no choice but to escape.

Wes and Sarah followed Mac through the front door into a musty-smelling hallway. While Mac fumbled with the fuse box, trying to turn the electricity back on, Wes carried their bags into the sitting room, a cloud of dust puffing up from the chair he threw his rucksack onto.

'It's bloody freezing in here,' he grumbled.

'Well, what are you doing in there? Through here,' Mac instructed. They exchanged confused looks and followed him into a large old-fashioned kitchen, complete with original Aga and copper pans hanging from the ceiling. It would be cosy and quaint if it didn't smell so old.

But Mac didn't stop in the kitchen. He had a bunch of keys in his hand and began to unlock a pantry door. When it swung open it was full of tinned food, bags of pasta and tubs of something indiscernible. Mac pulled at the sparsest shelving unit and it swung forwards to reveal another door, this one locked with a combination. Behind that was a staircase. Mac took a deep breath and disappeared down. Sarah shrugged at Wes and followed.

'Shit,' Sarah whispered at the bottom of the stairs. 'Mac, what is this?'

It was like walking into a TARDIS. The room ran the entire length of the cottage, with doors indicating that more was yet to come. In the far corner was a sleek sofa and chair arranged around a huge flat-screen TV mounted on the wall. There was a brand-new kitchen to her right, a coffee maker still in the box on the counter. Bookshelves along the wall directly in front of her were lined with all her favourite books, ones she thought were still in boxes in her dad's house. In the middle of the room was a vast oak table and six chairs.

'Your dad wanted you to have somewhere to come if the worst happened,' Mac replied. 'I'd say the worst *has* happened, wouldn't you? Come on, I'll show you your rooms.'

'Our rooms?' Sarah repeated stupidly. 'Aren't they upstairs?'

Mac laughed. 'Upstairs is just a smokescreen these days. There's a ramp in the barn that leads to an underground garage of sorts, only big enough for one car on a turntable. When I've moved it in and locked the front up, the entire police force could descend on this place and they'd walk straight over us. It's all soundproofed down here; we could have one of those raves and no one would be any the wiser in the kitchen.'

'When did he . . . actually, never mind that – *how* did he do all this? It would have taken contractors, tons of them. I'm surprised he would entrust that to anyone.'

'He got out-of-towners in, said it was a surprise for his son when he came back from uni. His own little flat to live in. He did a lot of it himself. You can't see it from the road so it's unlikely anyone would have noticed the work being done. He was careful, your dad.'

Not careful enough to stay alive, Sarah thought bitterly.

'Let's see this room then.'

Her room was simple but stylish: a queen-size bed, some wardrobes, her own TV and a drink preparation area. It looked like a modern hotel room, except for the bookshelf in the corner filled with a collection of crime novels.

'Well done, Dad,' Sarah breathed.

'Not bad, eh?'

'Why didn't he tell me about this place?' she demanded. Mac shrugged. 'He was probably going to, when you needed it. I daresay he imagined unveiling it to you himself.' His voice cracked and he cleared his throat. 'Chuck your stuff in – I'll go and sort out the car and lock up the front. Then we need to talk.'

Chapter Thirty-Eight

'So I'm not suspended?' Tess asked for a second time. Her head still ached slightly and she wanted to make sure she'd heard him correctly. Oswald sighed impatiently and began moving things around on his desk. Shit, he was getting irritated.

'We don't suspend people for being punched in the head, DI Fox.' He looked up at her. 'Unless you want to be suspended? Are you playing some kind of rule-annihilation bingo that I have no idea about?'

'No, sir,' Tess muttered.

'Right then.' Oswald stood up. 'I don't like being here. I don't like this little fake office they have given me and I don't like having to come in on my day off. We have three possible cars seen leaving John Street by the camera on the corner of Edwards. I've BOLO'd every force in Sussex. Question – do you think Sarah Jacobs killed any of the three dead men? Even one of them, perhaps?'

'No, sir,' Tess answered. 'Not even one.'

'Right.' Oswald looked disappointed but nodded. 'So, as

important as it is to find her and reassure the public that we don't just let murder suspects wander out of here, you still have a killer to catch. Maybe two, if the body in the Old Ship is unrelated.' He held up a hand. 'Which you think unlikely, I know. If you feel up to getting straight back to it, Fox, I've got to go and draft a press release about this entire mess. On my day off. If you want to go home and recover—'

'No, I'm fine, honestly. I'm fine. There's still a lot of forensics from the second crime scene to wade through. I'm hoping the murder weapon turns out to be the same one used on Shaun Mitchell.'

'I'm hoping it's got the owner's name engraved on it, but barring that, a nice fresh set of prints will do. Right, let me know if anything press-worthy turns up.'

Feeling like she'd dodged a speeding bullet, Tess made her way to the murder room where her team were gathered. Six concerned faces looked up at her when she walked in.

'You okay, guv?' Heath asked.

'A little sore, but fine, thank you.'

'Not fired?' Jerome lifted an eyebrow.

'Not fired,' she confirmed. Everyone sighed – was that in relief? They all *looked* pleased. Fahra grinned and stretched her hand out for a high-five, which Tess returned with a laugh.

'So I gather you've all been working while I've been getting a bollocking?'

Jerome handed her a sheet of paper. 'We've already searched the home of every known ally of Sarah and Frank Jacobs. The problem is that although we knew of Frank, he was always particularly cagey about who he worked with, and he owned property all over.'

'Right, well, I'm just going to say it. I don't think Sarah Jacobs killed any of these men, and Oswald agrees. So he's happy for uniform to keep up the search for her and her gang while we get back to finding out who is actually responsible for the murders. Any forensics back on Callum Rodgers? Any idea when the PM is scheduled for?'

'He's booked in tomorrow at twelve. I know, don't look at me like that – Kay is away giving some lecture on blunt force trauma.'

'I got some information on the butterfly found in Shaun Mitchell's throat,' Harris, a DC borrowed from Brighton spoke up. 'It was an *Adelpha californica*, otherwise known as a California sister. Native to California, also found in Oregon, Nevada – extreme northwestern USA. Not found in the UK.'

'Okay, I'm guessing it didn't just take a wrong turn. Are we looking at some kind of *Silence of the Lambs* nut-job?'

'That was moths, but the symbolism is the same. Maybe this is a message about change. Perhaps Mitchell was looking to get out of the criminal life.'

'Or maybe he swallowed the butterfly to catch a fly.' Tess was on her feet, pacing. 'I don't know why he swallowed a fly, perhaps he'll die.' Her irritation was starting to show. No two pieces of evidence seemed to work together. And she'd heard enough of the word 'sister' to last her a lifetime. Unless . . . was that what Mitchell's killer was getting at? Trying to point to her sister once again?

'If he was looking to get out of the criminal life, he was going a funny way about it,' Jerome said, interrupting her thoughts. 'According to three of his known associates, he was in debt, big time. He's implicated in three violent assaults and owed money to more than one drug dealer.'

'Well, that sounds like a good way to get yourself killed,' Tess said, allowing herself to hope that this was still a battle between members of the criminal underworld, praying that the fact that it was a 'sister' butterfly was a coincidence. 'But no one's talking?'

'Not even between themselves. No one has a clue who's responsible. Rodgers hadn't even been involved in organized crime for years, as far as I can tell.'

'Ma'am,' Fahra interrupted, gesturing to her screen. 'You might want to see this.'

'What am I looking at?' Tess bent over to read what looked to be a booking confirmation.

'I sent the warrant to Booking dotcom just before the alarm went off, to get the payment details for both hotel rooms: the one in the Hilton under Sarah Jacobs, and the one in the Old Ship under Luca Mancini – Frank's room. Both paid for by credit card in the name of—'

'Millie Diamond,' Tess finished. 'Come on, Jerome, looks like we need to pay a visit to our grieving girlfriend.'

Chapter Thirty-Nine

The house Tess and Jerome pulled up outside on Rodean Vale was a modern white building with a perfect sea view. Tess had done some searching on the way and found it had last been sold for £650,000 to a Mr and Mrs Diamond. Tess assumed they were Millie's parents. As they ascended the steps to the expensive-looking front door, Jerome gave a low whistle.

'Mr and Mrs Diamond have got some cash,' he remarked as Tess rang the doorbell.

'And potentially a psychopathic daughter who can turn invisible slash walk through walls,' Tess added under her breath.

After a few minutes the front door was opened by a tall, thin woman with dark hair pulled into a messy ponytail. She was dressed in a paint-splattered overshirt and had a brush in one hand. She looked very much like she could be Millie Diamond's mother.

'Mrs Diamond?' Tess asked, glancing over the woman's

shoulder into the white-walled, wooden-floored hallway beyond.

'Yes. Can I help you?'

'DI Fox, DS Morgan. We were wondering if we could speak to your daughter – Millie, is it?'

The woman gave a concerned frown. 'Emily. She's not due home for another . . . wait, what time is it?'

Tess glanced at her watch. 'Five seventeen.'

'She should be back in ten, maybe fifteen minutes. What's this about? Is she in trouble?'

'We're not quite sure,' Tess said. 'We'd just like to ask her some questions. Can we come in and wait?'

'Of course.' The woman moved aside to let them pass. 'Go through to the kitchen if you like. I'll just pop through to the studio and take this off.' She gestured to the overshirt. 'Please, have a seat.'

They followed her through to a large open-plan kitchen-diner, all white marble surfaces and chrome appliances. Mrs Diamond waved at two stools up against the breakfast bar. 'I won't be a second.'

'You think she's going to warn the girl?' Jerome asked as the woman went through the patio doors towards what looked like a summerhouse in the back garden.

'I don't think so,' Tess replied. 'I might be wrong but she didn't look to be lying. I don't think she has a clue what this is about.'

'Poor woman.'

Mrs Diamond reappeared after a couple of minutes, her overshirt gone to reveal a long-sleeved navy T-shirt and jeans.

'There, sorry about that. If I'm not careful I can get paint everywhere and John goes mad.'

'John is your husband?'

Mrs Diamond nodded. 'My name's Patricia. This is all quite strange, I must say. Can't you tell me anything? Should I be worried?'

'Hasn't Emily mentioned her boyfriend, Mrs Diamond? He was killed a couple of days ago at the Hilton Metropole. He was stabbed.'

Patricia went white. 'I saw that on the news, of course, but Emily didn't say – I mean, I didn't even know she had a boy-friend.'

Tess and Jerome exchanged a look. Tess thought of how distraught Millie had been the last time they had seen her. How had she managed to keep that from her own mother? 'Hasn't she been upset at all? Didn't she mention coming into the police station to give a statement?'

Before Patricia could answer, there was the swish and thud of the front door opening. 'That's her now,' Patricia said.

Tess and Jerome both stood up, ready in case Millie turned to flee as soon as she saw them again.

'Emmy? I'm through here,' Patricia called. 'There are some—' Tess cut her off with a frantic shake of the head and the woman's eyes widened in fear. She seemed only now to grasp the gravity of the situation.

'I hope the end of that sentence is snacks.' Millie's face dropped when she saw them all standing in the kitchen. 'Oh, sorry, I didn't realize you had guests.'

'These aren't guests, Emily – they're police officers. They've come to speak to you about your boyfriend apparently?'

Millie looked confused, and Tess knew exactly why. Because the woman standing in front of them wasn't the person who claimed to be Callum Rodgers's girlfriend. Tess had never seen this person before in her life.

'So you're saying this woman gave you my name and my address?'

Once the initial shock had worn off and Emily Diamond had realized she wasn't under arrest, her mother had put the kettle on and started fishing out pastries and biscuits as if she was hosting a tea party. Tess got the impression this was how they dealt with 'normal' guests in this house. Emily's hand still shook slightly as she lifted the cup of mint tea to her lips, though. She was shorter than the fake Millie Diamond, and slightly plumper. Her hair was pulled into a ponytail, but it was the same colour, and her eyes were the same rich brown, only a regular size. Tess remembered the large watery eyes of the fake Millie – the one thing it would be hard to disguise.

'This is the information we have on her.' Tess passed her a sheet of paper and the real Emily Diamond scanned it quickly. 'It's not much because she was never a suspect – she came in of her own accord to make a witness statement.'

'This is all correct,' Emily confirmed. 'Well, I mean it's not correct because she's not me, but she's got everything about me right. That's my date of birth, that's where I work. This is so weird.'

'And are these your credit card details?' Tess handed

her the printout of the email DS Nasir had received from Booking dotcom.

Emily reached into her bag and took out her purse. 'Yes – oh God, she's stolen my card details?' The young girl looked as though she was going to burst into tears. Her mother reached over and placed a hand on hers.

'Don't worry about that, I'll call them straight away and cancel the card—'

'We'd rather you didn't, actually,' Tess said apologetically. Patricia looked confused. 'If you cancel the card, you'll only alert her to the fact that she's been found out. It's much better for our investigation for us to monitor the activity – we might be able to use it to catch this girl. We'll make sure the credit card company knows what's going on – they have special fraud teams who can help us. You won't be charged for anything.'

Patricia nodded. 'Anything we can do to help.'

'Thank you. I understand how much of a shock this is for you both, but we're going to have to ask you a lot more questions.'

'You said she came in to give a witness statement about her boyfriend being stabbed. Is that the guy in the hotel the other day? Do you think she did it?'

'Like we said before, she was just helping us as a witness.' Tess tried to keep her voice neutral; she didn't want to scare the poor girl any more than necessary. 'She had an alibi, we called Range Recruitment and they confirmed it, but obviously . . .'

'That was my alibi,' Emily finished. 'I mean, it was me at work that day. Which means she doesn't have one.'

'Exactly,' Tess agreed. 'Which is concerning, obviously. And you're certain you don't know Callum Rodgers?'

Tess slid the picture of Rodgers across the table again. Emily shook her head. 'I really don't recognize him at all.'

Tess was certain she was telling the truth.

'The passport our Millie Diamond used is almost definitely fake,' Jerome told them now. 'But it's a good fake. Our team is in the process of tracking where it might have come from. She probably wouldn't be able to fly with it, but it would work for most other things: bank accounts, driver's licence – things where people barely give it a second glance even though they should. We're trying to find out if she used it anywhere else to obtain by deception. She looks enough like you that even the desk clerk at the police station didn't give it a second thought when this woman used it as ID because she was only a witness.'

'God, this is so horrible,' Emily said, putting her head in her hands. 'I feel like my whole life has been stolen.'

'Don't worry,' Tess assured her. 'We will find out who this woman really is. We're going to get her.'

Chapter Forty

'There he is.' Tess pointed at the screen as a man entered the top of the corridor. 'Right, go back twenty-four hours. Remember the CCTV from Mitchell's flat? The outage was twenty-four hours before he died.'

Jerome pulled the time counter slowly backwards, watching Frank going out for breakfast that morning, coming in the previous evening, going out for his evening meal, then checking in. When the footage showed the room being made up the previous day, Jerome stopped it and fast-forwarded to the moment Frank Jacobs re-entered the room for the final time.

'Okay, so we know there's no one in there waiting for him.' Tess nodded at Jerome to restart the footage. Frank's hotel room was halfway down the corridor, fully visible to the camera but not close enough to see inside when he opened it. The next person to approach was housekeeping, the cleaner making her way through each room in the corridor. When she got to Frank's room she tried to push open the door, but was stopped by the chain. She tried again then moved on to the next room.

'So the chain is already on and there's no answer from Frank. Is he already dead? What's the time stamp?'

'Nine twenty. We don't have access to the post-mortem yet, no time of death.'

Jerome forwarded through the CCTV, but from the moment the cleaner left until the afternoon cleaner knocked, Frank's door was undisturbed. Nobody in, nobody out. They watched housekeeping leave a second time, then fifteen minutes later the manager, Tim, and the maintenance man, Andy, appeared to force the door open.

Tess sat back in her chair and sighed. 'So they didn't get in through the door. The window opens from the top in but there's no way of climbing through. There's no connecting door or vent and the gun is nowhere in the room so it can't have been suicide.'

'There is one good thing though, boss.' Jerome grinned.

'I literally can't see anything good about this case.'

'I can. It's Walker's now.'

Tess smiled. 'Well, there is that. I bet he's doing his nut. Might go and take him a coffee, make some smartarse jokes about the invisible man.'

The door to the briefing room opened and Tess closed the CCTV quickly. The last thing she wanted was for Walker to find out they were still investigating Frank's murder.

'Oh good, it's just you,' Tess said, watching Fahra appear around the door frame. 'Come in. How's the real Emily Diamond?'

'She's been here all morning, ma'am,' Fahra replied. 'She's given us lists of basically everyone she knows, as well as Facebook, Instagram and Snapchat friends. I've shown her the pictures we have of our suspect and she said she vaguely recognizes her. She thinks she saw her being dropped off at the end of her street a few times in a red car.'

'Rodgers's car?'

'Probably. If she was using Diamond's address, then he was bound to drop her at home on occasion.'

'According to his work colleague, he told her that Diamond's parents were strictly religious – one of the only things about her life that doesn't match up to the real Diamond. Of course she couldn't take him home to meet them and she had to give him a reason.'

'But his parents met her?'

Fahra nodded. 'Once. By accident, it sounds. They said she was sweet, very charming. His friends barely knew anything about her; said she didn't go out with them and they didn't get the impression it was much more than friends with benefits.'

'Rodgers's social media?'

Jerome gave a wry smile. 'This is where it gets interesting. She barely features in any of the photos – four to be exact – and the ones she was in, her face is obscured by her hair, or she was pulling a face. He wasn't exactly the world's biggest social media user himself, to be fair.'

'Print them all off, anyway. Did they "check in" anywhere? Geotags on the photos? I want a complete profile of their movements so we can try and catch this girl on CCTV at some point. Perhaps then we can follow her back to where she really lives.'

'Do we have any pictures of her at all?'

'Only from the CCTV in the reception. It's not a bad picture though, to be fair.' He passed over another piece of paper, which Tess tacked up on the board next to her.

'Hold on a minute.' Fahra leaned in closer. She tapped the picture. 'I know her.'

'She's been into the station,' Tess said, packing up her things to head out. She would call Heath on the way, see if he'd found anything more concrete on their mystery woman. 'I thought you were out on enquiries though.'

'No, not from there. I know her from somewhere else.' Fahra snapped her fingers. 'That's it! I know who she is.'

Chapter Forty-One

The three of them sat around the oak dining table: Mac, Wes and Sarah. Mac had been out and moved the car into the secret garage and locked up the house, so that to anyone looking, the cottage would appear completely empty. Now he placed a bottle of whisky on the table and handed them each a glass. Wordlessly he poured them each a shot and picked up his glass. Sarah and Wes did the same.

'To Frank,' he said, holding the glass up in front of him.

'To Frank,' Wes echoed.

'To Dad,' Sarah murmured. They each clinked the glasses together and knocked back the amber liquid. Sarah shuddered as the whisky burned the back of her throat.

'Now,' Mac said when their ritual was done, 'it's time you told us what you know.'

Sarah nodded and took a deep breath and proceeded to tell them everything. How she had tried to put the dead men, Mitchell, Rodgers and their associate Darren Lane out of their horrific business by conning them out of ten grand, fifteen years earlier. Mac inhaled sharply when he heard the name, but said nothing, just listened as she recounted the details. That she had arranged to meet them at the Three Flamingos to close the deal, even though Tess had begged her not to go. How quickly it had become clear that they had known she was trying to con them, and how they would have probably killed her, or worse, had Tess not plunged a dart into Darren Lane's neck and managed to drag her sister out of an unbolted fire escape before the other two had returned to discover they were gone. Tess had managed to hit an artery and Lane bled out before his so-called friends had bothered to get him help. In actual fact, Tess and Sarah realized they must have fled the scene without even calling 999, because the news had reported that he hadn't been found for an excruciating week when he was reported missing by his on-off girlfriend. And now the two men were dead, with links to her turning up at the crime scenes.

'Jesus,' Wes breathed when she'd finished her story. 'Tess killed him?'

'To save my life,' Sarah said. 'She did what she had to do. If she hadn't, I'd be the one dead.'

'I get that,' Wes said. 'I was just thinking how hard that must be for her to live with. She's such a good person.'

Sarah didn't like the implication that she wasn't a good person because she'd found Lane's death much easier to live with than Tess, given the things he'd whispered that he was going to do to her once she was hooked on the drugs they sold. Even if she'd escaped without Tess's help, Lane would have been free to do whatever he liked to the next woman he deemed to have crossed him. Tess had probably saved more than one life that night, in a way that the law often couldn't.

'That's why she left.' Sarah nodded. 'She said she couldn't ever be in the position where she might have to kill a man to save one of our lives again. She left because of me, and I let Dad think it was because she hated what he was. She said she was joining the police to try and help victims like the ones Mitchell and Lane took advantage of. Help them the right way.'

Mac reached out to put an arm on her shoulder. 'Your dad loved you more than anything. Even if he knew the truth, he would blame himself that you'd put yourself in danger to prove something to him, or that he hadn't been keeping a close enough eye on you.'

Sarah sniffed and gave him a small, grateful smile. 'I still can't believe . . .'

'I know,' Mac whispered. 'I know, sweetheart.'

They sat in silence until Wes cleared his throat awkwardly.

'So the men who were killed in Brighton last week . . . ?'

'. . . were the other two men in the Three Flamingos that night,' Sarah confirmed.

Wes frowned. 'It sounds like they were bad men, Sarah. I'm just surprised they weren't killed sooner. I doubt it's anything to do with what happened to you.'

'So did I,' Sarah agreed. 'Until I found my ring hidden at the scene, crusty blood and all.'

Mac's mouth fell open slightly. 'You found what?'

'I know. And it made me wonder, if they were trying to frame me, then why hide it so well that the police never even found it? But there's more. Someone visited the crime scene before Shaun Mitchell was murdered and they gave my name. And they left behind a flier for the Three Flamingos . . . and a dart.'

Wes screwed up his attractive face. 'Not *the* dart?'

'I doubt it,' Sarah said. 'But it's not impossible, I suppose. Depending on how close the killer was to Darren Lane and the original crime scene.'

'But you said you knew who killed those men,' Wes said.

'I think I do.' Sarah pulled a sheet of paper from a pad. 'I just don't know who they actually are.' She drew a rectangle on the pad, sketched in a space for the balcony, desk, door and window. 'This is Shaun Mitchell's flat. Out here . . .' Sarah coloured the space outside the front door. '. . . was covered by CCTV in the twenty-four hours after he was killed. My source tells me the CCTV was checked for looping – they couldn't find any.'

'Your source?' Mac asked, raising his eyebrows.

'I've been working with Tess,' Sarah said, her tone suggesting she didn't want a debate about the wisdom of joining forces with a police officer. She looked at Wes, who merely raised his hands. He wasn't about to argue with her. He was always on her side, and they didn't have to worry about what Frank would say about this now. 'So, we can't guarantee no one got *in* because there was CCTV interference twenty-four hours before – but we know that no one got out.'

'No one got out *that way*,' Wes corrected.

'True,' Sarah acquiesced. 'So let's look at the other ways out. The balcony being the obvious one. There's no CCTV to prove they didn't climb off the balcony – although by that time Mitchell was on the pavement and literally dozens of witnesses were gathered looking up. Let's pretend for a second that they could have avoided being seen – where do they go? The flat next door was locked up, with no sign of breaking and entering; the other side is an elderly lady who is unlikely to have let in a killer covered in blood and hidden them in her home. Even if she *had*, say under duress, there was no evidence of that happening and she has remained remarkably calm about it ever since. So I'm going to rule out the balcony for now. So on to the vent.'

Sarah made a cross on the far wall of the flat.

'Unless our killer was a child, it is really unlikely they would fit through this vent. I'm ruling it out as an escape tunnel. What options does that leave us with?'

Wes had been watching, deep in thought. He held up his fingers. 'One: that the killer was still in there when the police arrived.'

'Good.' Sarah nodded. 'That was my first thought. The flat was apparently searched thoroughly but we know how much that means. Is it possible that the killer could have been disguised as a police officer, ready for a team to come in? Could they have slipped out and simply walked away?'

'That must be it,' said Mac, leaning back in his chair. 'That's what we'd do.'

'It is,' Sarah agreed. 'Which is why I was a bit gutted when I worked out that they were much cleverer than that. I went over that CCTV a dozen times – not one officer comes out who didn't go in. Not one person leaves that flat who is afterwards unaccounted for. Even in the hours after the flat was searched – I checked that in case they had found a way to hide from the searchers. There is literally only one option left.'

'Which is?'

Sarah pointed to a spot outside of the flat and made a huge X. Wes and Mac looked even more confused.

'The killer was never in that flat.'

Chapter Forty-Two

Everyone around the table stared expectantly at Fahra.

'What did you say?' Tess asked, unable to believe what she was hearing.

'I know who she is,' Fahra repeated.

Could they be as lucky as to discover Fahra just knew this woman from school or something?

'I interviewed her after Mitchell's body was found. She was the first on the scene – she found the body. The Frenchwoman, remember, sobbing in the corner of the tent. She had dark red hair then, though.'

'No.' Tess shook her head. 'You're mistaken. Our interviewee is Callum Rodgers's girlfriend – or at least she claims to be. She also claimed to be called Millie Diamond, and gave us fake references. But she's definitely English.'

'Sorry, ma'am, but that's her all right. She was standing by the ambulance, being checked out, when we arrived. She was pretty shaken up, covered in blood. Said she'd been waiting for a bus when he'd landed right next to her – she'd gone to check a pulse and realized his throat had been slit. She started screaming and someone called an ambulance. She was in shock but I definitely remember her face.'

'So she's first on the scene at one murder, then the victim's girlfriend at another? She's giving false identification and changing her nationality? We need to find her.' Tess swore under her breath. 'She's involved, without a doubt.'

'But how?' Jerome asked. 'How did she throw him off a balcony then get down the stairs in seconds without being spotted as the first person at his side? Unless she jumped after him and landed on her feet.'

'I'm not saying she killed him, necessarily, but she knows something. For now, circulate this around the entire team. I want to know if anyone else has seen her. Pull out her first statement and the details she gave. I want to know who this woman really is. Good work, Fahra.'

'Thanks, ma'am.' Fahra hesitated. 'This is one of the weirdest cases we've ever had and you're doing a great job, you know that?' She suddenly looked embarrassed, as though she regretted speaking.

Tess didn't know what to say. She felt her cheeks burn and managed to stutter a thank you before turning away, praying she didn't start to cry. She cleared her throat. 'I'm going to review the interviews with our other Emily Diamond. Um, keep up the good work, guys.'

She sensed all eyes on her back as she left the room as quickly as she could.

She was still reading through all the extra information that had been gathered on the woman posing as Emily Diamond when there was a knock at the door and a PC poked her head through. 'Two notes for you. Toxicology on Shaun Mitchell – he had been using some pretty heavy drugs before he died.'

'Expected.' Tess nodded, reaching over to take the report. 'What else?'

'Fingerprint analysis from Callum Rodgers's bedroom. The only prints in the room were his. Except for one single print, on the bottom of the bedpost. Want to see the results?'

'You got a match? Stop dicking around and give it here.' Tess took the paper from the PC. 'Oh. You have got to be kidding me.'

'Thought you'd be interested in that.'

Tess stared at the report. The name on the top was Sarah Jacobs.

Chapter Forty-Three

'That's genius,' Wes breathed when Sarah had outlined her theory. 'You think she could have pulled this off?'

'I have no idea who she is,' Sarah admitted. 'So I have no idea if she could have pulled it off. But for me it's the only way it all fits in. The rope around his wrists, the cut to his throat, the butterfly in the mouth. I don't know yet what it all means, but as for the *how* . . . I think that's what she did.'

'So what do we do now?'

Sarah took a deep breath. She knew that they weren't going to like her idea, given that they had just pulled off a daring heist to get her out of custody. 'I think we should take this information to the police, let them deal with it. Well, Tess at least.'

Mac looked disgusted. He shook his head and jabbed a finger at her. 'You're not leaving this place. There's a reason it's called a safe house. Because you're safe here. Frank's number one rule: no police. If this person really wanted to frame you, they might try to hurt you instead.'

'So what, I *live* here now? In an underground bunker? They won't just give up and get bored of looking for me – I'm a murder suspect, and as far as we know I'm the only one they have.'

'And you're going to walk up to the police station and tell them that you know how those men were killed, but you didn't do it, you promise? Come on, Sarah – Frank would be turning in his grave.'

'What exactly do you think I should do, Mac? What would my dad want me to do – wait here for someone else to sort this?'

'That's exactly what he'd want you to do.'

'Yeah, well, I didn't listen to him when he was alive, so I'm guessing he would expect me to ignore him now too. And I really want you to be with me, not against me.'

Mac looked at the floor. 'I'd never be against you,' he said, his voice quiet. 'But I wouldn't be your dad's best friend if I didn't try and convince you to stay put until they have another suspect.'

Her heart swelled with sadness and affection. Mac was the closest thing she had to a father now and it hurt her to argue with him, to question him.

'I've got to do *something*, Mac.'

He took a deep breath in through his nose, held it for a few seconds then exhaled, as if coming to a difficult decision.

'Okay. If you can't do as you're told' – he almost looked proud of her when he said it – 'then we'll catch this woman ourselves. Let us help you. What do you say?'

If they could pull it off, it would take the kind of multi-levelled con that Sarah had never imagined having to do without her father's advice. She had to be the ringer now, and she would need some help. Someone with the con in her blood, the same way it was in Sarah's and had been in Frank's.

'We need my sister. I'm not doing this without her.'

Chapter Forty-Four

Tess had been sitting in silence, staring at the photograph in front of her for so long that the sensor-controlled lights in the office had all gone off around her. This woman, their fake Diamond, so to speak – had she really killed Shaun Mitchell, Callum Rodgers and Frank Jacobs? No one was going to believe this woman was a cold-blooded killer just by looking at her, and Tess knew that if she was going to make a case against Millie Diamond, or Emilie Jasper, the red-headed French witness, or whichever gemstone she was calling herself these days, it needed to be watertight. And none of this was. They still weren't even sure how she'd committed the murders and disappeared in a puff of smoke, leaving no trace of her behind. Unless they could show the how, the where, and importantly the why, catching this woman was the least of their worries. She would never be convicted.

Tess thought back to the Millie Diamond who had come into the station and insisted on talking to the lead detective on the case. Why had she done that? It was an enormous risk, that someone would recognize her from the first murder scene, that she would slip up, give the game away. She must have been full of confidence – or desperate to see Tess face to face, for some reason. It wasn't unusual for killers to insert themselves into the investigation somehow, Tess knew that. If you asked Ian Huntley, he'd practically been leading the investigation into his victim's disappearance. This felt different though. Millie Diamond had come into the station with a purpose. *She came in to implicate Sarah*, Tess thought. *That was the only information that we got out of her interview. That Callum Rodgers was having an affair with someone called Sarah.*

Okay, so let's say she could rest on the assumption that the first two murders were committed to implicate Sarah. For what reason Tess didn't know, but where her half-sister was concerned, it wasn't difficult to imagine her pissing someone off so much that they wanted to commit two murders to send her to prison. The question still remained: why kill her third victim while Sarah was in custody? And why kill Frank, the one person Tess could never be convinced that Sarah would want dead?

Tess was alone in the murder room and barely registered it when the door opened and the lights flickered on. She didn't look up until Jerome was by her side.

'If you've come to tell me there's been another murder, you can get lost,' she murmured.

'Not yet,' Jerome replied. 'But Fahra found something in the friends and family statements. One of Rodgers's mates remembered dropping Millie on Grove Hill.'

Tess's heart took a jump. 'Outside Shaun Mitchell's flat?'

Jerome shook his head. 'As if it was ever going to be that easy. Said he dropped her at the end of the street.'

'Right, get someone down there, start knocking on doors and showing her picture around. I want her found.'

'And Sarah Jacobs, boss? How is she fitting into all this?'

'She's everywhere and bloody nowhere, Jerome, that's how. Are we any closer to actually finding her?'

'Nothing yet, boss.'

Tess sighed. 'Okay, thanks. Just keep me informed.'

As he left the room, Tess stared up at the five pictures on the wall. Three victims, two suspects. One was a picture of the real Sarah Jacobs, her half-sister. The other picture was of a woman who had been arrested for pickpocketing two years ago; who had been fingerprinted and given her name as Sarah Jacobs. It was the same woman they knew now as Millie Diamond, but of course even that wasn't her real name.

'Are you in it together?' she asked the pictures softly. 'Are you running circles around me, little sister? Or is the fake Diamond getting the better of us both? And if so, what next? What is her endgame? Does she disappear into the night, leaving your life ruined and my case unsolved? Or is she going to tell everyone what we did to Darren Lane all those years ago? Is this her revenge?'

Tess was astounded the idea hadn't occurred to her before. She'd been so intent on making sure no one connected the first two murders to Darren Lane that she hadn't thought to look into his family tree herself. Their mystery woman was around Sarah's age – old enough to have been in her teens when Tess killed Lane. Was she his sister, perhaps? Girlfriend even? Okay, fifteen years seemed a long time to wait for revenge, but she had clearly taken her time planning this one. Perhaps she blamed Callum and Shaun for leaving their friend to die; perhaps she had got the truth out of them about who really killed him, and this was her twisted game, her way of avenging Darren. And if that was true, then maybe catching her was the worst possible thing they could do.

Tess's phone rang in her pocket. 'DI Fox,' she answered.

'I need to see you.'

Tess recognized the voice instantly. Sarah. 'Excellent, where are you? I'll send a squad car to pick you up.'

'I'm pretty sure I know who killed Shaun Mitchell and probably Callum Rodgers too. Except I don't know who she really is – or why she did it.'

'So do I. What else have you got?'

There was silence on the line, then Tess heard Sarah let out a breath. 'Wow, I underestimated you. Do you know how?'

'Not exactly . . .'

'Who is she?'

'I don't exactly know that either, although I have a theory,' Tess said. 'Do you?'

'Not yet,' Sarah admitted. 'But I intend to find out – and why she was trying to frame me. Does your theory include that?'

'Yes, and it doesn't end well for either of us. Are you calling to hand yourself in? Because the only way I can make sure you're not framed for any more murders at the moment is if you're in custody.'

'Not exactly. I'm calling for a favour. I need to know exactly how Dad died. All your evidence.'

'You're on the run, Sarah. You want to just walk into the police station and take a look at the files?'

'Obviously not. I want you to bring them to me.'

'And tell me exactly why I shouldn't turn up with a team of police officers and arrest you after you punched me in the head and nearly lost me my job?'

'Sisters fight all the time?'

'Try again.'

Sarah sighed. 'Because you know I didn't do this, Tess. Even if you believe I killed Mitchell and Rodgers, you know I didn't kill my dad. And I can tell you how this woman did it – perhaps together we can figure out who she really is.'

'And how do you know I'm not going to turn up with my team and arrest you anyway?'

There was a pause at the other end of the line and Tess thought for a second that Sarah had hung up on her.

'I don't,' Sarah replied, and for the first time ever Tess heard a quiver in her voice. 'I guess I've just got to trust that you want to get the person who actually did. I guess I've got to believe in someone. I can't do this on my own.'

Now it was Tess's turn to hesitate. She'd made stupid decision after stupid decision where her sister was concerned; was she about to do the same again? She let out a sigh.

'You going to punch me again?'

'Probably not.'

Tess didn't know whether to smile or scream. 'Where do you want me to meet you?'

Chapter Forty-Five

From her seat at the back of the café, Sarah could still feel the breeze coming in from the sea and smell the salt in the air, a welcome experience compared to being in a police cell or an underground room. It felt good to be back in Brighton, and out of the depressing safe house that had only served to remind her that her father wasn't there.

She only realized when she saw Tess coming in that she'd subconsciously chosen the seat that made her the easiest to arrest. There was no way to escape if her sister led a team in after her. It had been a test. If Tess came for her, she wouldn't fight. She didn't have anything left to fight for. Or perhaps she did. This was her way of finding out, she supposed. She had chosen the location of their meeting with deliberate care. The seafront café was the place Tess had told her half-sister that she wanted nothing more to do with their life. This was the last place they had seen one another, before Tess had crossed the line to the other side of the law. Would the same happen again this time?

Tess walked in. She scanned the café, not immediately

recognizing the brassy blonde wig, the huge sunglasses and the bright red lipstick Sarah was wearing. Eventually her eyebrows rose and she made her way to Sarah's booth. Alone, so far.

'I like the new look,' she commented, sliding into the seat opposite Sarah.

'Cavalry outside?' Sarah asked.

'They should be,' Tess replied. 'If I had half a brain in my head, I'd have the entire Sussex Police outside. Do you have any idea how much trouble I'm in for letting you get away?'

'I'm genuinely sorry for that,' Sarah said, her hand on her heart. She wasn't. It had to be done, so she'd done it. Once upon a time, Tess would have understood.

'I'm almost certain you're not the least bit sorry, but I didn't come here to be charmed or conned. I came because I happen to believe that – on this occasion – you're innocent. And I want to find the person genuinely responsible for what happened to Frank.' Her voice broke slightly.

Sarah reached out, placing a hand over her sister's. 'I'm sorry you never got to know him properly, Tess. I'm so sorry that you'll never know that he was loyal, and loving and caring and kind, and most of all I'm sorry that it's my fault you left us.'

Tess let out a small sob as tears began to stream down her cheeks. Sarah sat in silence, her emotional quota all but drained. She didn't really know what to do in the face of this. Should she get up and hug her sister? Eeesh.

Tess was quicker to react. She grabbed a handful of napkins from the table in front of her and mopped up her tears, trying to muffle her sniffs. When she had composed herself enough, she waved a hand at Sarah. 'Tell me why you wanted me here.'

Sarah opened her mouth to try and say something consoling.

Then she closed it again. She knew her limits. Instead she pulled out the drawings she had done in the bunker for Mac and Wes. 'Do you know who we're looking for?'

'I have some questions for the woman on the scene of the first murder. She came into the station as Callum Rodgers's girlfriend and implicated you in his murder. Then one of my officers recognized her as the woman who called 999 at Shaun Mitchell's murder.'

'Is she related to Darren Lane?' Sarah asked.

'Impressive,' Tess said. 'That's the conclusion I came to eventually. She finds out we were responsible for his murder, but she can't prove it so many years later. So she kills the other people she deems equally responsible and frames us. Well, you. Rodgers and Mitchell never knew I was even there, so I can't imagine anyone else does.'

'So it's a coincidence that your first cast is someone you . . .' Sarah made a thrusting motion towards her neck and Tess winced.

'Well, that does trouble me a little, sure.'

'And it still doesn't explain how she got hold of my ring.'

'She's a thief, Sarah. A con artist. Did Dad employ any cleaners in the last few years? Electricians? Sex workers?'

Sarah pulled a disgusted face. 'All right, Jesus, spare me the visuals. Possibly. Well, it has to be something like that. Because the alternative is that . . .'

'One of your crew was helping her.'

'We're not a crew,' Sarah snapped. 'Which you know very well. We're a family. A *family*.'

'Okay.' Tess held up her hands. She reached into her bag and pulled out a photo, sliding it across the table. 'This is Millie Diamond, otherwise known to us as Emilie Jasper.'

Sarah studied it carefully, the long dark hair, the huge, doe-shaped eyes, a small delicate nose. She wanted to remember this woman if she ever saw her again, whether it was as a bartender, a cleaning lady, or a zookeeper.

'The only print found in Rodgers's bedroom linked in our database to a Sarah Jacobs. When I looked at the file, it was her picture I found. The very same woman who claimed to be Callum Rodgers's girlfriend, and who first reported Shaun Mitchell's murder.'

'Suicide,' Sarah corrected.

Tess frowned. 'Suicide? Are you saying he cut his own throat, then fell off the balcony?'

'No,' Sarah said slowly. She watched her half-sister's face. Was she going to believe her? 'I'm saying she waited until she knew he would be off his face on drugs, then watched until he swung off the balcony using a piece of rope. The drainpipe she'd cut most of the way through snapped under the weight of his body and hey presto.'

Tess's eyes widened. Sarah smiled as she watched the penny drop.

'That's genius,' she breathed. 'She cut his throat and shoved the butterfly in his mouth as he lay dying in front of her.'

'Retractable knife on a wrist cuff most likely,' Sarah confirmed.

'Then she used the rope to bind his hands so she didn't have to get rid of it or explain it.'

'How did she know he was going to jump?'

Sarah fell silent. 'I've got an idea, something I've been read-ing up on. Wes is checking it out for me. It sounds a tad radical without the proof.'

'Because the rest of this is run-of-the-mill,' Tess said, her voice deadpan.

'Fair enough. I'm still going to wait to hear what Wes finds. But I think we can be sure that it was her that cut the drainpipe, knowing that when he put his weight on the rope it would snap. And she set up the message to me and planted the ring ahead of time too.' Sarah looked at the photo again. 'When was this arrest?'

'It was two years ago, here in Brighton,' Tess replied. 'She was arrested for picking pockets – the one and only time. She gave her name as Sarah Jacobs.'

'I thought you said my prints weren't in the system. Why didn't this come up when you arrested me?'

'Because none of the other details on the file matched you. Different photograph, different date of birth, different prints, different last known address. She wasn't claiming to be you, daughter of Frank Jacobs, when she got arrested, just to have the same name. She just wanted your name in this investiga-tion, for some reason, however briefly. The prints would be compared to yours and you'd be off the hook. It's like she just wanted to make sure your name came up.'

'If she's related to Lane,' Sarah mused, 'then what took her so long to decide to get her revenge? Even two years ago was still thirteen years after he died.'

'Good question,' Tess said. 'And if she doesn't know about me, then is it just a coincidence that she happens to take her revenge in the same month that I become acting DI?'

They fell silent for a moment. Their theory fitted in so many ways, but fell short of having all the answers.

'Are you going to tell me how she killed Callum Rodgers?' Tess asked eventually.

'I am.' Sarah cleared her throat. 'She poisoned him.'

Tess raised her eyebrows in shock. 'What are you talking about? Rodgers was found with a stab wound.'

'Have you had the PM report?' Sarah took a sip of her coffee and motioned for the waitress. 'Hey Jess, can I get one of your crepes?'

'Peanut butter?'

'Sure. You could chuck some strawberries on if you're feeling generous.'

'Always.'

Sarah turned back to Tess. 'Well? Have you?'

Tess shook her head. 'We're expecting it back any day now.'

'Well, when you do, I'm telling you that there's no way Callum Rodgers died from that stab wound. It wasn't deep enough. So my theory is that there was some kind of poison on the knife.'

'How do you know the wound wasn't deep enough to die from?' Tess questioned, but she knew Sarah was right. She'd noticed it immediately: there was too little blood. The wound looked deep but she'd seen stab wounds before – people had survived deeper, especially given how quickly he'd been found.

'Because he'd never have been able to walk into that lift if it was.'

Tess took a minute to let her words sink in. Her mind was working so fast, her mouth was struggling to keep up. 'Because he'd already been stabbed when he got into the lift.'

'Thanks, Jess.' Sarah took the plate handed to her and shovelled a forkful into her mouth. 'God, that's good. He sure as hell wasn't stabbed when he was in there. He was alone for about six seconds – the killer would have had three, maybe four, to get in, stab him and get out. And don't you think he'd have put up a fight if someone lowered themselves in through a lift shaft anyhow?'

'Someone would have noticed if he had been stabbed. And why wouldn't he alert the front desk? Get help? Why just walk into a lift to die?'

Sarah pointed her fork at Tess. 'Because he was in love with the person who stabbed him.'

Tess took a deep breath. 'So the fake Millie Diamond stabs him somewhere outside the hotel, and Rodgers thinks he can make it back to his room and sort himself out, gets into the lift and dies from the poison on the knife?' she asked.

'Exactly,' Sarah confirmed, as though Tess had just said something entirely reasonable.

'That actually fits with the CCTV,' Tess acquiesced. 'The way he's walking, it looks uncomfortable, like he's in pain. And he never takes his arm away from his stomach. But it's batshit crazy. And the blood on the door—'

'Was from him walking in – not the killer walking out,' Sarah finished.

'Okay, let's say I accept that he was stabbed before he went in, and the poison on the knife, but there's one thing you haven't explained. How did she get the knife in the lift shaft? I know she's good, but I doubt she could have walked in and dropped it down there in the middle of the investigation. We checked all the cameras from the minute he walked in until we arrived. The woman pretending to be Millie Diamond isn't on a single one.'

Sarah swallowed – in four bites, she annihilated her crepe. 'Exactly. You checked every moment *after* Rodgers walked in. What about before?'

'You think *he* followed *her* in there?'

'That's precisely what I think. I think she walked into that hotel with the knife after stabbing him. She got a lift down to the staff floor where there's an emergency hatch. She ditched the knife and went back up to the ground floor. Meanwhile, Callum Rodgers is getting into the *other* lift to go up to his room, where he thinks Millie is. She gets out on the ground floor and leaves the hotel while Callum Rodgers is dying in the lift.'

'Fuck.'

'Indeed. So now what?' Sarah asked, debating whether to order another crepe.

'Now?' Tess asked.

'Yeah – you want me to come in here and solve two murders and expect nothing in return?'

'In return, I'm not arresting you.'

'Not arresting me for murders you know I didn't commit. You're giving too much, Tess – how will I ever thank you?'

Tess sighed. 'Fine, what exactly are you expecting?'

'Two things,' Sarah said, holding up two fingers. 'I want to know exactly how our father died, which means I need to see the scene. And I want you to rejoin the family.'

Chapter Forty-Six

*R*ejoin the family.

'You have got to be kidding.'

Tess's first instinct was to get up and leave. She'd imagined having this conversation in her head so many times over the last fifteen years, rejoining the family she had cut herself off from, having people to rely on, to love. They all ended the same way. Her job was just too important to her. Except saying that out loud, to Sarah, with her expectant eyes . . . it wasn't as easy as telling her subconscious. She sighed.

'We've had this discussion before, Sarah. I'm a police officer. I can't just spend weekends pulling off bank heists as my downtime. I made a choice.'

'And your job is your choice? Over us? You said yourself, you are hanging in there by a thread! If they find out who your dad was then they'll kick you out anyway. Leave now, before you're pushed. Please?' Sarah's voice cracked, and all of a sudden she looked just like a kid sister again.

Tess shook her head, not knowing what to say. Before

she could figure it out, Sarah seemed to catch herself being vulnerable and held up a hand. 'You know what? Forget it. You've made your point a thousand times. But hear me out. How about you join us temporarily? We want to catch this woman as much as you do. More. If she killed Dad . . .'

'We?' Tess's heart began to thump. 'Mac knows about what happened?'

Sarah turned her gaze away. 'Mac and Wes know everything.'

'By which I presume you mean *everything*?' Her chest felt heavy. This was the beginning of the end of everything. Just like Millie Diamond, or whatever her name is had wanted, she presumed. The old saying came back to her: *three can keep a secret if two of them are dead*. She and Sarah had both had a vested interest in keeping the secret to themselves, but this was about to become uncontrollable. If they arrested Diamond, she would undoubtedly give the reason she had committed two murders. And if they didn't catch her, Tess was beholden to a crew of grifters who all knew she was a killer.

'I couldn't keep it from them any longer,' Sarah said. 'They won't tell anyone, Tess – they aren't about to implicate either of us.'

'Until they get arrested for something and realize they have leverage on a DI. Jesus, Sarah, how could you be so stupid?'

'They wouldn't do that. You're one of us.'

Tess put her face in her hands and resisted the urge to scream. How many times before Sarah realized that she wasn't one of them, and she never could be?

'Okay,' she said, taking a deep breath. 'They know now, and there's nothing I can do about that. Say I agree to work with you on this – and I haven't yet. What did you have in mind?'

'I need to see where Dad . . . where it happened,' Sarah said. 'Gabe will suit me up. I won't even be recognizable to you, let alone any of your colleagues. You will sign me in as the duty manager of the hotel and if questioned you'll say I'm confirming the location of several items in the room.'

Tess sighed. None of this was what she had expected. From the moment she had stepped into the tent at the first murder and seen the victim, this whole case had been spiralling out of her control, threatening to take her career down with it. She felt as though she didn't know which way was up any more. 'I can't get you in there.'

'Why not?'

'Even if I could walk you in there, I'm not on Frank's case any more. My DCI doesn't think it's related to the first two and at this present moment in time I can't prove it is.'

Sarah gestured for the bill. 'Well, we're still going. You think the uniforms on the door know that you're not the SIO any more? Nobody tells them anything.'

'Uniforms?' Tess laughed. 'SIO? Careful, you're starting to sound like one of us.'

'But I'm right.'

Tess shook her head. 'You'll get ten minutes tops. And I'll be watching you like a hawk the whole time. If you touch anything, I'll have you arrested. Again.'

'And that worked out for you so well last time,' Sarah couldn't help herself from saying.

'Stop being a smartass. Meet me at the car park off Queen's by the community kitchen in two hours. There are things I need to brief my team on here. This woman could be in another country by now.'

'She isn't,' Sarah said.

'What makes you so sure?'

'Because she wants me between the eyes. I know she killed Mitchell and Rodgers. I think she killed Dad as well and I intend to prove it. She wants to frame me for these murders and she wants me to know it was her. This isn't over.'

'I'd say that's a hell of a grudge for a person to have,' Tess said. 'But having met you, it isn't exactly surprising.'

Sarah grimaced. 'Why make friends, when you can make playmates?'

Chapter Forty-Seven

The afternoon had morphed into beautiful sunshine as Sarah made the drive to see the place where her father had been killed. She felt a swell of sadness in her throat so sudden she thought she might choke on it. She was an orphan now, the only thing that remained of two beautiful, creative, adventurous souls. She missed her mum, of course she did, but her memories of her mum were so vague, whereas the loss of her dad had cut so deeply into everything she knew that she thought at times that it might sever her from reality entirely. In the darkness of the night, in the slamming of a door, leaving her completely and fully alone. She pinched her wrist so tightly it left two crescent-shaped fingernail marks on her skin. *Work first.* The sunshine felt like a reminder that she was doing the right thing, that this was the way it should be. Dad would have wanted this to be a time of action, not grief. That would come, and Sarah knew it would come hard.

She pulled up in the car park at the top of Queen's, where Tess was waiting for her in an unmarked police car. Just looking at it made her itch. She could have walked to the seafront from here and saved herself the allergic reaction to police.

'Can we not go in mine?' Sarah called out through the open window. Tess raised her eyebrows. 'Don't you ever feel like turning up anywhere in style? Comfort even?'

Tess held open the passenger door and nodded her head in.

'Fine,' Sarah said. 'If anything happens to my car . . .'

'You can file a report.' Was her sister smirking?

'You want a cigarette first?' Sarah held out the packet, expecting her to say no. Tess took one and the lighter and lit it, leaning against the car.

'This is pretty weird for me,' Sarah said, joining her.

'I know. It's the first time I've been back since I found out it was Dad. Are you sure you want to do this? I can just draw you a diagram.'

'No.' Sarah shook her head. 'I want to see it for myself. Just in case.'

Tess gave her a sideways look but didn't comment.

'You know, just in case you've missed . . .' Sarah started.

'Yeah, I get it,' Tess said. There was that smirk again. 'Come on, let's get going. I'm on a murder investigation.'

As they drove the short distance, Sarah said, 'You know I called my cat Tess after you left.'

'A cat? Really? I'm touched. Where is she now?'

'She got hit by a car.'

Tess snorted. 'You don't do this much, do you?'

'Do what?'

'You know.' She waved a hand. 'Talk to people.'

'I don't have many illegitimate sisters to converse with on the way to crime scenes, no,' Sarah replied. 'It's mostly just me and . . .' She stopped when she realized what she'd been about to say. *Just me and Dad.* They fell into an uncomfortable silence.

The corridor leading to Frank's hotel room was taped off, but apart from that there was barely any sign there had been a murder in the hotel at all. Business as usual – in a place like Brighton, closing any hotel for too long was impossible. No doubt the police were under pressure from all sides to get the place back up and running.

'No need to sign in or suit up,' Tess said, a note of relief in her voice. 'SOCO are all done. The room will be cleaned and opened as soon as possible. Usually it would be done by now, but Walker has told the manager he doesn't want cleaning to start in the room itself before he's figured out how it was done.'

'Well, I bet none of the guests were queueing up to stay in the room where a man was shot through a locked door.'

'You'd be surprised.' Tess grimaced. 'You get those Jonathan Creek types, you know, those geeks obsessed with—'

'Hold fire.' Sarah held up a hand. 'Careful you don't insult the hired help.'

'I'm surprised, with your love of detective fiction, that you didn't think about training as a police officer.'

Sarah let out a chuckle. 'Yeah, sure. I could have brought Dad in for Show and Tell at the Academy.'

'It's not called an . . . you know what? Never mind. We'd better go in.'

'Wait.' Sarah placed her hand over Tess's as she readied herself to enter the room. 'I'm ready to know some of the details. No theories, just facts. What happened here?'

'Look, you don't have to do this,' Tess said, gently squeezing

Sarah's arm. 'We'll figure this out eventually – we already know who we're looking for.'

'And you'll be able to convict her, will you? If you can't tell the jury how she actually killed him? No, you won't. I am doing this, okay? No offence, but Dad wouldn't trust the police to find out what happened if it was me lying in that morgue, and I'm not going to let him down.'

'Do you realize that by saying "no offence" it doesn't actually make the things you're saying less offensive?'

Sarah shrugged.

'Fine,' Tess snapped. She ran through the facts of the case they had so far.

Sarah took in all the information, nodding every now and then.

'No adjoining room, obviously?'

'Do you think you'd be here if there was? No balcony, or vent big enough to fit through. The window opens top-in to stop small children falling out – not impossible to climb through, and if it was a middle-of-the-night murder, I'd be looking at that as a point of entry. But it was daylight and the room faces the seafront.'

'She thought of everything,' Sarah murmured.

'What do you mean by that?'

'Assuming she booked the room – which I think she did – she made sure that it could be seen from the outside. Plenty of these rooms have walls that face less public places, she could have asked for one. And there are rooms here with adjoining doors. She wanted us to know it was impossible for her to get in and out – just like the others.'

'Okay, noted. Are you ready to go in?'

Sarah nodded. 'There's something I need to see.'

They stepped into the room. The smell of blood and something sharp and citrusy hit them as soon as the door opened. Sarah saw what she was looking for the minute she entered and knew how her father was killed. She couldn't avoid looking at the bloom of rust-coloured blood that covered the pillows, *her father's blood*, and turned instinctively to run, her fight-or-flight instinct compelling her to *get away. Get out of this room*. But she forced herself to root her feet to the spot and take a deep breath. This would be the hardest thing she would ever have to do. Once it was done . . . nothing else would compare.

'Are you okay?' Tess asked, and for a split-second Sarah thought she might hug her. She wasn't sure if she was relieved or disappointed when Tess didn't move – she didn't think she'd ever needed a hug more or wanted one less.

'I'm fine,' she managed to say. 'I've seen enough.'

'What?' Tess looked confused. 'Have you figured it out?'

A quick nod, not trusting herself to open her mouth to speak. Warm bile was mounting in her throat and saliva filled her mouth. 'The picture.'

As they walked in, there was a double bed to the left, flanked either side by tables, a bathroom door to the right, window on the wall to the left of the bed. The wardrobe was set back in an alcove just behind the bed and the wall opposite was angled slightly. A print of the Brighton Palace Pier hung on the angled wall.

Tess frowned and stepped over to the print in its large gilt frame. Too large, too ornate for a standard print that could be found in practically every hotel in Brighton.

'There might be a piece of thread – quite strong, maybe like fisherman's line on the bottom,' Sarah said. Tess was already snapping on a pair of latex gloves and running her finger around the frame. In a second, she located the string dangling from the bottom and the sisters locked eyes. 'There's probably something sharp on the bottom of the frame, so be careful,' Sarah warned. Tess lifted it from the wall and laid it on the bed.

'Where would you usually see a heavy gilded frame like this?' Sarah asked.

'I don't know,' Tess said. 'A mirror maybe?'

'Exactly.' Sarah gestured for her to touch the picture. 'It's not behind glass. It's covered in a film, like a screen protector, to look like glass. Watch.'

Sarah peeled back the print, knowing what she would find but half expecting to be wrong. It made sense from what she'd seen, and it was the only way her dad could have been killed, but it was just so elaborate, so clever, and so *unnecessary*. If she'd wanted to kill Dad she could have done it at his house – Sarah had no doubt she knew where they lived, and she'd wager the mystery woman knew a lot more about them than that. But why all this show-boating?

Tess took in a small breath as it all became clear. The moment the curtain was pulled back and the wizard was just a regular man. Except in this case, she was a woman. And a cold-blooded killer.

Sarah lifted the front of the frame away from the false back that had been installed, taking the print with it and revealing the mirror beneath. It didn't look like a long-term solution but it had done the job of making it harder to figure out what had happened.

'So she covered the mirror. That doesn't tell us how she got in or out. Or why she covered it.'

'Try looking at it this way.' Sarah took Tess's elbow and steered her towards the door. She left Tess outside and she could hear Sarah on the inside putting the chain on. 'Just a second. Wait there . . . okay, open the door.'

The buzzer sounded and the door opened two inches before jamming against the chain. 'Now what?' Tess sighed.

'Look through the gap.'

Her eye to the gap, Tess groaned.

'What can you see?'

'The bed.'

'Bingo.' Sarah closed the door and reopened it fully. The mirror was back up on the angled wall opposite the door, offering a perfect view of the bed from behind the mostly closed door.

'So they didn't have to be in the room.'

'Nope. Laser spot on the gun, chain lengthened by an inch, enough to fit the gun through – the room was set up perfectly.'

'If she didn't come in, how did she cover the mirror afterwards?'

Sarah pulled the mirror down again. 'Same way Banksy shredded his own painting after someone paid millions for it. Inside the frame.' She wiggled the front of the frame and gave it a tug. Nestled into the top and bottom were a pair of rollers.

'She ran the wire along the wall to somewhere she could grab it from outside,' Sarah explained. 'She shoots Dad, then pulls the fishing wire so the print rolls down to cover the mirror. A little wiggle and this tiny razor cuts the wire off at the bottom so she can dispose of the excess.'

'CCTV shows that no one entered the corridor from the time the maid checked the room until the duty manager opened the door four hours later and . . . wait, it was the maid, wasn't it?'

Sarah smiled and nodded. 'You said the only people to approach the door that morning were the cleaners. Plural. Except if someone is due to check out that day, the morning cleaner wouldn't have tried to get into the room – they would wait until after checkout time. That's why your room is never cleaned on the morning of departure – no point in doing it twice. But the cleaner is the only person who had a valid reason for trying to open the door, and the only person who would be ignored by anyone who saw them. If you look at the camera, she probably blocks the door with her body as she opens it – that'll be to jam the gun in. Lines up the sight in the mirror, takes her shot.'

'And Frank didn't move, get up, object, because?'

'Because she didn't just pose as cleaning staff, she posed as serving staff as well. In the restaurant that morning, she served him his coffee. It would have taken two seconds; she takes off a jacket while none of the other staff are watching and walks over to the table. She pours him some coffee and leaves the restaurant without anyone even noticing her.'

'Something to make him sleep.'

'He feels groggy, goes to lie down. She leaves it a predetermined amount of time and then bang.'

'Well, it all adds up very neatly.' Tess sighed. She rubbed her hand over her face.

'Does it bugger,' Sarah muttered.

'What? What doesn't add up?'

Sarah's eyes grow wide. 'None of it adds up! You see you're looking at it as if there's a body here and the killer was here and this piece goes here and don't we have a nice little jigsaw! But you didn't know our dad. You're missing the piece that explains why one of the cleverest men you'll ever meet went into a hotel to meet someone he suspected to be a killer and yet barely checked the room over, felt groggy after breakfast but didn't just leave the hotel and get a taxi home – went and lay down on the bed exactly like she planned? If you knew Dad at all, you'd know the jigsaw is barely started.'

'Okay.' Tess nodded. 'Granted, there are still some things we need to figure out. But now we have more to go on. I'll get CCTV stills of the maid, see if we can confirm it's our Millie Diamond. If we can definitely connect this to the other two murders, then we'll be ready with charges when we finally catch up with her.'

'I'm going to speak to Mac, see what I can find out about why Dad was so bloody stupid. I'll look through his phone too.'

'We have his phone,' Tess reminded her. 'Forensics collected it.'

'You have *a* phone.' Sarah raised her eyebrows. 'Don't forget who your victim was. I'll let you know if I find anything.'

'Make sure you do. And stay undercover – you are still a fugitive who escaped custody. If I get caught with you, my career is over.'

'And you're presumably working as hard as you can to get that charge dropped, of course?'

'Of course. But until that happens, keep your head down and out of sight.'

'Whatever you say, boss.' Sarah saluted, and Tess knew there was no chance of her listening to a word she said.

Chapter Forty-Eight

The silence was almost worse than a bollocking.

DCI Oswald's entire head had gone a shade of pink that Tess had never seen on him before. He seemed to take several attempts to speak, change his mind, only to repeat the process again a minute or so later. Tess was getting concerned that he might be having some kind of heart attack when he finally spoke, his voice low and measured.

'Is. This. Some. Sort. Of. Piss. Take?'

She cringed. She'd known Sarah's theories wouldn't go down well with the team – least of all Oswald – but she hadn't expected quite this level of vehemence. He picked up a stapler from his desk then placed it back down again four inches to the right of where it had been. Tess got the distinct impression he was trying to keep his hands busy to stop himself strangling her.

'Am I supposed to go to the chief superintendent and tell him that this woman killed the victim after he was already dead? And that she poisoned her other victim, who then chased after her into a hotel without anyone noticing he'd been stabbed?'

'Do you really think I would be presenting these theories if I could see any other way these murders could have taken place?' Tess said, annoyed at herself for the note of pleading in her voice. She had planned to come in here and present Sarah's theories in a no-nonsense, no-bullshit way, leaving Oswald no choice but to slap her on the back and hand her the promotion. She wasn't a mind reader but that didn't seem to be the way this was going. 'I've spoken to Kay,' she continued. 'She's saying that all the physical evidence fits what I've told you now. I don't believe it's any coincidence that this woman was at the scene of all three murders, and actually neither would you if she was a man.'

DCI Oswald looked as though he was about to argue. Instead he held his breath and Tess could sense him counting to ten. When he was done, he nodded once, perhaps considering his 'everyday sexism' leaflet again. He studied Tess intently, and it occurred to her he might be wondering if she was about to shout 'gotcha'. Eventually he said, 'Okay, let's assume that you're right, and this "Millie Diamond" is some sort of super intelligent female assassin. How do we plan on finding her?'

Tess took a deep breath. If he'd been angry at her first suggestion, then God knows what he was going to think of this one.

'There might be someone who can help.'

Oswald sighed. 'Please tell me you're not talking about Jacobs.'

'I am, sir. I think this woman wants us to see a connection between Sarah Jacobs and these murders.'

'And Sarah Jacobs is still currently at large?'

'Yes, sir.'

'So the suspect who escaped from you, and is currently on the run, is the person who told you how the crime was committed? And your response is to dismiss her as a suspect? And you don't think the person with such an intimate knowledge of the workings of a crime such as this would be the actual fucking murderer?'

Her face burned scarlet. 'Actually, sir, no, I don't.'

If possible, Oswald looked even more incredulous.

'I see exactly where you're coming from,' she rushed on. 'But in this case I genuinely believe that Sarah Jacobs had nothing to do with these crimes. And I suppose you're going to either have to trust me or remove me from the case, because I don't think we can get to the bottom of this without her help.' She winced, hoping that last bit wasn't overkill.

He looked for a second as though the preference was to fire her, not only from the case but from the entire department – the country, if he could get away with it. Then, with a sigh of pure resignation, his shoulders sagged. 'I want to make it clear that I'm not stupid, Tess. I think you continued to work the Old Ship case despite being told that another DI was taking over, and you took a big risk letting Jacobs in on aspects of the investigation that she shouldn't be aware of. But the fact is, this isn't a pissing contest, and I don't give a shit who finds out who did this as long as someone does. So you'd better tell me how you think we're going to catch this woman and pray you're right about Sarah Jacobs. Because if we find out she was involved in these killings and you've allowed her to trample all over our crime scene, this will be the first and last murder case you ever work on.'

Tess returned to her desk, heart still pounding. She knew that with another DCI that conversation could have gone very differently. But Oswald seemed to have faith in her – a faith she was no longer sure was warranted. At the start of this case, she would have sworn an oath that she deserved the promotion she so badly wanted. Now she wasn't so certain.

'Do we have any more information from the hotel?' she asked Jerome, trying not to fall any further into despair. She had to keep going; she had to see this through.

Jerome shuffled through the papers on his desk and pushed a folder towards her. 'We sent someone down there to recover the mirror and the frame. It's been checked for prints but they found nothing. The mechanism that had been hidden inside the frame was a complex piece of kit, so I've got someone trying to find out if there's anyone in Brighton who could have put that together. I've got one of the interns going through a list of every booking the hotel had taken for the last two months, to try and spot anything that looks out of place – she had access to that room at some point, and she knew the layout of the rooms, the uniforms of the breakfast and cleaning staff and how to make that mirror blend in enough with the décor that it wasn't spotted instantly. Our guess is she must have spent some time there. The next step would be CCTV, but that's going to take extra time and resources.' He lifted an eyebrow at Tess, who nodded.

'Understood. I'll speak to Oswald and see what we can do. The Rodgers forensics?'

'No prints on the knife; we've sent the swabs to tox for screening in light of the poisoning theory. We found Diamond on the CCTV a few minutes before Rodgers arrives at the hotel. She was wearing gloves. Her hair is over her face but he's reasonably certain it's her. The height and build matches. Not that it's any help – it wouldn't stand up in court.'

'Has he found her leaving?'

Jerome shook his head. 'That's the thing – she doesn't leave through the front. We can't find her leaving the hotel at all.'

Tess sighed. 'It doesn't matter. Good work, thanks for that. Let me know if anything turns up.'

'We'll get her, boss.' Jerome grinned. 'Like you said, no one is so good that they never make mistakes.'

Chapter Forty-Nine

Sarah didn't get it. Her dad never made mistakes, yet he'd made every mistake in the book the day he'd died. Drinking the hotel coffee, going for a nap when he'd felt drowsy instead of calling her or Mac to pick him up. It was practically suicide. But her dad hadn't been suicidal. So who had he thought he was meeting in that hotel? Someone he was sleeping with?

The sea air was bracing. It whipped spray up into her face and forced her to hold on to the rocks beneath with damp fingertips. Few things could clear out her mind like staring off the edge of the land into the vastness of the ocean beyond. Every time Sarah came to the marina and climbed over the barriers, there was a part of her that wanted to fling herself forwards – not into the grey water just below that looked cold and uninviting, crashing into the rocks and churning up white foam, but into the blue of the water far away from shore, push one arm in front of the other and keep swimming until she hit her desert island. Maybe today was the day – after all, what was there here for her now? Her dad was gone. She didn't know who she was without him.

Her tears mingled with the salty spray of the sea on her face and she didn't bother to wipe them away. Her dad always said that emotions didn't get you anywhere in their game. She'd spent so long shoving feelings to one side in favour of action that she barely recognized the horrific stone in her chest as grief. It was a weight, dragging her down, and she wondered – if she let it pull her too far – if she'd ever be able to get back up.

'Your dad used to like it here.'

She'd been expecting this voice over her shoulder. Sarah didn't need to turn around. She didn't want him to see her crying. She didn't want to see if he was crying too.

She heard him pulling himself over the barriers and felt his presence next to her. Without thinking too much about it, she laid her head against his shoulder and he snaked his arm around her. They sat for a while in comfortable silence, both of them contemplating a life without the man who made them who they were.

It was Mac who spoke first. 'There's something you should know. Something your dad wanted you to know, when the time was right. I think it's right now.'

Her body stiffened. Sarah knew instinctively that whatever he was about to tell her would change things, perhaps change the way she felt about her dad forever, and suddenly she didn't want to know.

'Your dad loved your mother very much.' His voice cracked slightly, hesitant now. 'You and your mum were his world.'

'How did you meet Dad?' Sarah asked, suddenly desperate to delay whatever Mac was about to say. She felt him shake his head.

'I'll tell you about it another day. It's not something I'm proud of, but it's not something I can regret either. It brought all three of you into my life, and I'll never regret that but . . . not today. Today we need to talk about your mum.'

Her mum. A woman she barely knew and yet she had shaped her life in so many ways, mostly by her absence.

'What was she like?'

'She was wonderful. Beautiful.' Sarah wasn't sure she'd ever heard Mac's voice fill with so much love. 'She was the kind of woman who made you feel like the clouds would clear and the rain would stop just by them being near. She had a way of knowing how to read people and she was obsessed with learning about the way our minds worked. And she loved your dad so much. Being around her, being around the two of them together was like looking directly at the sun. Dangerous, but you couldn't look away.'

'Dad loved her so much.'

'He did. Almost as much as he loved you.'

The tears started again, silently pouring down her cheeks, then faster, harder, until it was hard to breathe. Mac just held on to her without saying anything, waiting for her to pour her grief out onto the rocks below.

'He told me all about her, how it was when they first met. Young, teenage love, despite the disapproval of both families. Probably more intense because of it. Your grandfather would never have let him out of the house if he'd known where he was going, and who with. And her family – well, it didn't do for travelling folk to fall for town people. Dwellers, they called them. But they fell for one another hard. Your mum begged Frank to join them on the traveller way, but he was determined to get a good job and build a life for them both. He knew that if he ran away with the fair, that's all they would ever be. He didn't realize at the time that's all *she* ever wanted to be. She loved the travelling life – moving around was in her blood.

'She was furious that he wouldn't go. They fought like never before – of course he didn't know then what the implications of that fight would be. When she left with the fair that year, she said she'd never come back. Frank waited all year, and when the fair returned, your mother wasn't on it. He asked everyone he could find, but they claimed they had never even known her.'

Sarah knew all of this. Dad had told her the story of their years apart when Tess had shown up.

'But she did come back,' Sarah said.

'Two years later she showed up on his doorstep in the middle of the night. Only she wasn't the same, your dad said. There was a piece of her missing, like a little light inside her had gone out. He had a good job by then, he was training to be a lawyer. Like his father.'

Sarah almost slipped forwards at the force of the shock. 'Grandad was a lawyer?'

'He was a prosecutor, by the time I met him,' Mac said. His voice cracked a little. 'One of the best I've ever met, right up until the day he retired. Anyway, your dad felt like his entire world began again the day Lily Dowse reappeared. He found them a flat, they were married within two years. And in time she bounced back to being the same bright girl he'd fallen in love with on the fair all those years ago. She never told him what happened to her in those two years she was away from him – she just told him that her family had taken her far away so she didn't go back to him. He didn't find out until the week before he died. Three days before Mitchell was killed.'

There was so much Sarah wanted to ask, about her mother, her grandfather the *prosecutor*, who Mac spoke about as if he liked, respected even, and about her dad – before she had been born he had wanted a real job? – but she didn't dare say anything. Because this was it. This was where she found out what her dad had been keeping from her, possibly the reason he had died. This was where she discovered what had led him to making his fatal mistake.

'It was her family who kept her away,' Mac said at last. 'If only he'd just agreed to go with her – or if only they had never had that fight, Sarah. Because what she didn't tell him that night is that she wanted him to go with her so badly because she was pregnant. They took the baby away from her and raised her as one of her aunt's children, so Frank never even knew. Not until she turned up at his house all these years later.'

'Who turned up?' Sarah whispered, but all of a sudden she knew exactly who. She had seen that woman with the huge brown eyes; eyes so familiar because they belonged to her own mother.

'Julia. Your big sister.'

Chapter Fifty

Tess and Sarah stood together in silence as the viewing platform began to rise, both contemplating the gravity of what Mac had revealed. As the futuristic glass pod made its slow ascent, they gazed out over the Brighton skyline, the whole of the south coast and Sussex beyond, laid out before them like a patchwork quilt. Sarah pressed her hand against the glass and rested her forehead briefly against it. She'd been up in the viewing pod of the i360 a few dozen times since it opened; there was something about the feeling of leaving the world behind as you rose above it that was almost spiritual. She knew that plenty of Brighton folk thought it an eyesore, a blight on the Brighton coastline, with its silver tower shooting up out of the sand and the spaceship-like pod that carried tourists high above the beach, but Sarah found herself on it whenever she really needed to concentrate on something – like she was removing herself from the world by being so high above it.

'You want a drink?' Tess asked, gesturing to the bar that curved around the middle of the pod.

'Sure,' Sarah said. 'Why don't you get us something with a percentage.'

For once Tess didn't object, and Sarah went back to watching the people below, scurrying around like ants, going about their daily lives, not even contemplating that they could be being watched from on high. *She's down there somewhere*, Sarah thought. *My sister is down there. The woman who killed my dad.*

Mac hadn't been able to tell her much more – her dad had thrown the woman out, called her a liar. He'd accused her of all sorts, of being a stooge for the police or a con artist, then told her to leave. Mac said it was shock but, if she knew her father, it was pain. Pain that his beloved Lily had kept such a secret from him. It was Julia who Mac had met with in the café the day he'd been seen by Sarah and Tess. She'd begged him to talk to Frank, to make him see sense. Mac believed that she really was Lily's daughter, but had told her that he wouldn't go against Frank's wishes and he wouldn't risk their relationship to try to convince him to meet her. *Give him time,* Mac had told Julia. *Give him time and he'll come around.* Now he was dead.

Tess returned to her side, a bottle of champagne in her right hand and two glasses in her left. 'I know we're not exactly celebrating but . . .'

'Break it open,' Sarah said.

'So, your sister,' Tess said, trying to digest the information she had just heard. 'My half-sister. Jesus.'

'I found out where she got the butterflies from,' Sarah said. 'I know a guy – looks like a bit of a lunatic but he's an expert on butterflies. The "sister" butterfly isn't native to the UK.'

The vast silver viewing platform came to a stop at its final height of 450 feet and several people around them gasped.

'Pretty specialist, obviously,' Sarah continued. 'My guy contacted every seller. They sent it six weeks ago. I got an address.'

Tess's eyes widened. 'Why didn't you say?' She pulled out her phone but there was no signal. 'What is it?'

'There's no point,' Sarah replied. 'We went round there. Millie, Emilie, Julia – whatever her real name is – has long gone, if she was ever there. She's not stupid. She's bloody clever, in fact. Cleverer than me.'

'Don't say that,' Tess said, looking as dejected as Sarah felt. 'You figured it all out. How she did it.'

'Mac thinks it was an accident, you know,' Sarah said. 'Not the murder, obviously, she planned that pretty well. But he still thinks she couldn't have meant to kill Dad. I think he just doesn't want to believe that he knew all along that she was here and didn't tell us. That's who he was meeting that day we had lunch. She was right there next to him and he let her go.'

'So who does he think was her intended victim?'

Sarah watched as a couple of brave – or foolish – children ventured out into the freezing cold surf below. She couldn't hear them but she could imagine their shrieks as the water enveloped their feet and they hurried back onto the beach.

'One of Dad's old rivals, Harry Derwent, contacted him saying he'd been called by a woman claiming he'd won a free night's stay at the Old Ship. He knew it was a con and suspected us – we've had a sort of beef with Harry for years; nothing serious, but enough to make Harry think we were trying to corner him. Dad told him to accept the woman's offer and Dad would go in his place. Mac thinks he suspected it was Julia at this point and wanted to confront her. Mac doesn't think she even knew they had switched – he thinks she still thought it was Harry in that bed.'

'She must have known – when she drugged him. She would have seen that it was your dad.'

'Three other people staying in the hotel complained of feeling drowsy and went back to bed after breakfast. One missed checkout. We think she drugged the coffee while it was still in the kitchen. There's so many things I won't know until I find her.'

'We might never find her, not if she doesn't want to be found.'

Sarah took a sip of her wine. The i360 began its slow descent, back to earth, back to an investigation where they had no idea how to find the killer they were looking for. Unless . . .

'She wants to be found,' Sarah said. 'But not by you – by me. Look at it. She's obviously been watching us for a while. She was arrested nearly two years ago and gave my name when her prints were taken. She'd been dating Rodgers on and off for a year and collecting information on the real Emily Diamond for at least that long. Then, when she's ready, she goes to see my dad – perhaps she's hoping she never has to put her plan into place. If she can convince him to take her in, to make her part of the family, then she wins without ever having to kill anyone. It was when Frank rejected her that people started dying.'

'So what?' Tess replied. 'What difference does any of that make?'

'It might make all the difference,' Sarah said. 'If she's spent two years planning to get my family's attention, she's hardly going to quit now she has it, is she?'

Tess went to speak but Sarah held up a hand.

'Wait, don't ask me any more. I think I have an idea, but I need to talk to the family. You coming?'

Chapter Fifty-One

The ceiling of the secret room thrummed from the vibrations of a band upstairs in the bar of the Black Dove, playing on, oblivious to the gathering downstairs. Five individuals glared at each other around a table, the door locked behind them, each one wondering what the hell they were doing there.

'I've had my team searching every variation of Julia's name we can think of and nothing,' Tess said. 'She probably has fifteen other identities we haven't discovered yet.'

'Julia is the name Lily gave her,' Mac insisted. 'It was why I knew she was telling the truth when she turned up here. Lily once told us her great-grandmother was French, her name was Julia.'

'And dad still didn't believe her?'

'He said she was a con artist, she would have done her research. But she knew stuff. Other stuff.'

'What other stuff?' Sarah snapped.

'And speaking of knowing stuff,' Tess interrupted. 'How exactly did Julia know that Mitchell was going to jump off his balcony at that exact time, on that exact day?'

Sarah glanced at Mac. 'I've got a theory,' she said, avoiding Tess's eye. 'But I'm still looking into it. It's a bit unusual – which is obviously my thing – and if I'm right then she's more dangerous than we first thought.'

But Sarah didn't look scared; if anything, she looked impressed by the ingenuity of their perp. Tess wasn't impressed. She was more stressed out and concerned than ever. She'd agreed to work with Sarah and her family because they had information that would help her find this woman, but maybe now it was time to put the power back where it belonged. With the authorities. If only this crossroads were that simple.

'Look, Sarah,' Tess said, not knowing how to approach the idea of letting her team in. She just needed to say it. God she was being a coward. 'I think it's time to pass back to CID now. Wait—' She held up a hand as Sarah started to cut in. 'I'm not saying I don't appreciate what you've done, because I do, I promise. I wouldn't have figured out half of what's gone on here without you. But you're grieving—'

'And you're not, I suppose?' Sarah snapped. 'Because you don't care about Dad? Because he wasn't your idea of the perfect father?'

Tess stepped backwards, as though she'd been physically pushed, her leg banging against the wood of the table behind her. 'Ow, shit! That is completely unfair. My feelings about Frank might not be as straightforward as yours but . . .' She looked around at the group, suddenly aware that the two of them had an audience. 'I'm not doing this here. Not now. If you hadn't lied to me . . .'

'You arrested me!'

'You *stole evidence* from a crime scene!'

'So did you!'

'I'd place a bet that this is why the pair of you aren't exactly Sherlock and Watson,' Wes broke in. 'This isn't getting us anywhere. This woman could be halfway to Bahrain by now and you're squabbling over who has more right to be annoyed at whom.'

Sarah sighed. 'He's right. Look, you came into our world for help, Tess. You stepped through the looking glass the minute you sought me out, and everything's been back to front ever since. Now I don't know where this is going to end, but it's not going to end at all if we count on your way. You know what they say: to catch a grifter, you have to think like a grifter, act like a grifter. You have to be two steps ahead of them – four if you can. You just can't do that if you're waiting for evidence and arrest warrants. Like Wes says, she could literally be on her way out of the country as we speak and you will never find her again. But if you join us, we can get her together. We're a team, and once you're in we don't let you fall. You know it's true.'

Tess chewed the inside of her lip and took a deep breath in. She'd spent so long denying this side of her family, and now here she was anyway. Almost one of the gang. She glanced at Mac who was standing slightly in front of Wes and Gabe, the group always ready to protect one another, and felt a pang of longing. *Isn't this what she'd always wanted? A family?* She let out the breath. What were her instincts telling her?

'My instincts are telling me . . . that if I'd trusted you in the first place instead of trying to deny that we could ever be . . .'

'Friends?' Wes suggested.

'Sisters,' Tess corrected. 'Then our father might still be alive.

If you can forgive me for that, I'd like to hear what ideas you have for catching this woman.'

'I'm glad you feel like that. Because I've already put the word out. I've given Julia's photo to anyone she might come in contact with. The message is clear: the family is looking to expand, and we need an illusionist. Interviews are being held tomorrow at the old Republic offices.'

The plan was simple. Frank's identity hadn't been released to the public yet, and Sarah had spread the word around the Brighton criminal community that they were looking for an illusionist – hopefully the opportunity to either kill them or join them would be too good for her sister to resist. When Julia turned up at the meeting, all Sarah had to do was get her to confess to killing her father, sit back and wait for her invite to join MI5.

'This is a bad idea,' Mac said. He held his hands up at her expression. 'I'm just saying. We don't get involved with the police – it's one of our rules.'

'She's not just "the police", Mac – she's my half-sister. And Frank's daughter. And I happen to trust her.' Sarah looked around at the other two. 'What do you two say?'

'She's also in the room,' Tess said.

Wes shrugged. 'I'm not really here to make decisions.'

'Well, the person who made our decisions isn't here any more,' Sarah said, her voice a little sharper than she intended. 'Because of this woman, this Julia, who thinks she can out-smart us. And I don't know about you lot, but I want her caught. I want some justice.'

'We don't need the police to catch her,' Gabe said, avoiding her eye. 'We can catch her ourselves.'

'And how many people does she kill in the meantime? How many deaths on our conscience?'

'It's not on my conscience,' Mac said. 'It's not my job to catch killers.' He turned to Tess. 'Take the information we've given you back to your team and do your job.'

Tess felt as though she'd been slapped in the face. She should have known she couldn't just be part of the team. She would never be accepted.

'I wish we had,' she said, her voice cracking. 'I wish I'd done my job. I wish I'd caught her sooner and then maybe Dad would still be here.'

'So what, we're working with the police now? Your father would turn in his grave.'

'He can spin cartwheels in it for all I fucking care,' Sarah snapped, losing patience. Part of her was still so angry with her dad, and yet here he was, running the show from beyond the grave. 'If he'd wanted the deciding vote, he shouldn't have been stupid enough to walk into her trap. He practically committed suicide. And it's not working *with* the police – it's having the police work for us. We draw her in, they arrest her. You know they won't catch her without us, and I don't think we could catch her without them, or not as quickly. If anyone has a better plan, I'm happy to hear it. If not, this is what we're doing.' She turned to Tess. 'I don't blame you for what happened, Tess – none of us do. This woman has been clever, maybe she's the cleverest person I've come across. Hell, if she hadn't tried to have me arrested, I might have been offering her a job.'

Tess almost smiled at that. 'Instead, you're joining forces with the enemy.'

Sarah shrugged. 'Yeah, well – play your cards right and I might be offering you a job instead.'

Tess snorted. 'Over my dead body.'

'Both of our dead bodies, if Julia catches us before we catch her.'

Chapter Fifty-Two

'Don't do this,' Jerome said, as Tess shoved case files into her handbag. She ignored him. He motioned to outside the incident room, where Fahra and Campbell waited patiently to be allowed in, probably wondering what the hell was going on now. 'I know this is complicated for you but you have a good team here. A *loyal* team. They've worked hard for you, Tess – don't reward them for their loyalty by shutting them out.'

Tess stopped what she was doing, stood up straight and looked at her DS. Jerome had been her only friend, her only confidant while she'd lived out her self-imposed exile. And he was right: her team had been loyal, even when she'd asked them to go against Oswald's instructions and work on Frank's murder behind Walker's back.

'I'm not shutting them out,' she said, going back to collecting the things she needed. 'I'm just following a lead.'

'By yourself. Without telling your team – or your boss – what you're doing.'

'Just who is in charge here, DS Morgan?' Tess snapped.

Jerome's eyes widened. Tess sighed. 'I'm sorry. This is all pretty stressful for me. But you're right, the team have shown up for me when I needed them.' She didn't have to do this all Sarah's way. She was a police officer, and a good one, with a loyal team. She couldn't shut them out when the endgame was upon them. She sighed.

'Call them in.'

She told the team some of the truth. Enough to get them onside, and to get clearance from Oswald for the operation. The woman they had formerly known as Millie Diamond was the main suspect in the deaths of Shaun Mitchell and Callum Rodgers. Tess had purposely left Frank Jacobs off the list; otherwise she'd be contending with Geoff Walker trying to get in on her operation. She'd already heard that he had bitten off more than he could chew trying to uncover Frank's illegal enterprise, and not being able to get hold of Sarah was driving him crazy. So she'd told DCI Oswald and her team that she had reason to believe, from a Covert Human Intelligence Source, that Diamond – or whatever her real name was – would be at the old Republic building, and she had obtained a warrant for her arrest. Now it was just down to her team to await her instructions to move in on the building. They didn't need to know that she was working with Sarah's team and that it was them inside, nor that Sarah herself was there. She was still wanted for her violent escape from custody and had promised to make herself scarce as soon as Tess's team moved in. It was easier for everyone that way.

'This is the woman we are looking for,' Tess reminded them, holding up the picture of Julia from when she had been arrested, posing as Sarah over the back of the car seat, her large doe eyes still her most striking feature. The Republic building loomed over them. 'She has potentially murdered three men and should be considered dangerous and really fucking clever.'

'What's she doing here?' Fahra asked, wrinkling up her nose in distaste at the towering building, left neglected and derelict. Windows had been smashed and hastily covered over with loose boards that clattered in the wind, and plastic bags were stuffed into the cracks concealing inside from out. Tess could see Fahra itching from the dust, even from outside in the car. They watched another man approach the building and be buzzed in, the third in the half an hour since they'd arrived. Tess was impressed at how many people actually wanted to be part of Sarah's crew. She could put a stop to a whole lot of organized crime in Brighton if she sealed off the building right now. But she had even bigger fish to fry today.

As if reading her mind, Fahra asked, 'And why are so many people going in and out? Is it something illegal?'

'I think it's supposed to be some sort of job interview,' Tess said. She didn't dare glance at Jerome in case she gave something away. They were stationed on the corner of the street, watching the front and left-hand side of the building. Campbell and a borrowed DC were watching the back and right side. When Julia was in the building, they just had to wait for Sarah's signal that she was in a room on one of the higher floors. Somewhere even she couldn't disappear from.

'Look, I think that's her!' Fahra pointed to the end of the street, where a woman was walking towards the building, peering over her glasses at the numbers on the warehouse fronts. Her long dark hair was pulled up into a sleek ponytail that bounced slightly as she walked. Black-rimmed glasses only served to accentuate her huge eyes, the fringe that grazed the top of them being the only difference in her appearance from the last time Tess had seen her. She had been a red-head the first time, in the street outside Shaun Mitchell's flat. She wore a tight skirt and heels but still walked briskly towards the entrance of the building.

'I reckon we can take her now, boss,' Jerome remarked. 'She might be able to walk quickly in those things, but she can't outrun me.'

'Stick to the plan,' Tess said. She knew that she'd never hear the end of it if she didn't let Sarah have her time with Julia. Her half-sister had some questions for the woman – as did she.

'But guv—' Jerome started.

Tess glared at him. 'I *said* we stick to the plan.'

'Okay,' Sarah said, taking the man's ID and glancing back at him. 'Elias Rance? That your real name?'

'Nope.' Rance looked back at her with small, untrustworthy eyes. Even if they were taking people on, it certainly wouldn't be this guy. The most important weapon a con artist had in his or her arsenal was to look like you were the only person in the room who *could* be trusted. Sarah glanced over at Wes, who was watching a small man with impossibly large ears execute the cup and balls trick. Cute, if they were looking for a children's entertainer.

We're not actually looking for someone, she reminded herself. *We're not replacing Dad.*

Sarah had never realized until this morning how many

shysters and tricksters there were living in and around Brighton. It had been a useful exercise just in that respect, and she'd seen some pretty nifty illusions that morning, including a variation on the Elmsley count that she'd never seen done so expertly before, and a deadly silent riffle pass that even she found hard to replicate. But so far, no Julia.

'Right.' Sarah sat down and gestured for Rance to sit across from her. 'What do you do?'

'I steal things,' Rance replied. *No shit Sherlock.* 'Wallets and stuff.'

'Okay, well our advert said we're looking for an illusionist,' Sarah said, glancing at the door. One of the conditions of including Tess and her team in the plan was that no microphones would be turned on unless Julia showed up – Sarah wasn't about to piss off every petty thief in the area – but she was still half expecting Sussex Police to run in any second and bust the lot of them. 'We have plenty of pickpockets, sorry.'

'You don't understand,' Rance replied. 'I steal things just by looking at you.' He steepled his fingers and made a face like he was mildly constipated. 'There, I just stole your phone.'

Sarah reached into her pocket, pulled out her phone and placed it on the table in front of him. 'This phone?'

Rance frowned and dipped his hand into his own pocket. He pulled out a small calling card and held it up. It read *Thanks for trying out. Better luck next time!* Elias let out a moan.

Sarah smiled. 'Thanks for your time.'

'Wait! How did you . . . ?'

Sarah nodded towards the door and Rance got up to leave with a scowl. She sighed, rubbing a hand over her eyes. This was hopeless. Julia wasn't coming. Best-case scenario was a morning wasted; worst case was that she'd figured out they were on to her and she was on a plane to Venezuela. She made a 'wrap it up' signal to Wes just as her phone buzzed. It was Mac. He had taken a vantage point in one of the empty offices upstairs with a complete view of the street.

She's here.

Chapter Fifty-Three

Sarah took a deep breath and steeled herself for the knock at the door. When it came she positioned herself in front of the window – her signal to Tess that Julia was in there with her – and called, 'Come in.' The eagle had landed, and all that.

Julia's mugshot had certainly not done her justice. In real life she was petite but lithe, athletic-looking like Sarah. Her creamy skin was flawless, red lips standing out against their pale canvas. Long, sleek dark hair was pulled back from her face into a ponytail and, even shaded behind her glasses, she had the widest eyes Sarah had ever seen on a human. It was a testament to her skills as an illusionist that she could still change her appearance with such an arresting characteristic. The whole point of deception was not to be remembered. Sarah didn't think she'd ever forget Julia's face now she'd seen it in person, undisguised.

'Who are you?' Sarah asked, trying to keep her voice casual, bored even. She had played this game so many times, taken on so many personas and told so many lies, but it had never felt like this. There had never been so much at stake. She tried to stop her eyes drifting to the top drawer of the desk, where she had placed her insurance policy. A revolver her father had given her, that she'd sworn she would never use. She hoped she wouldn't have to break that promise today.

They had chosen the room upstairs purely for Julia. While the rest of the candidates had been interviewed on the ground floor in what used to be the reception, Julia was to be escorted upstairs, to the sixth floor and a room which had nothing but a set of fitted shelves and a desk so thick with dust it looked like a tablecloth was laid over it. She wasn't escaping from this room. There was nowhere to disappear to.

Tess and her team were stationed outside the building, waiting for her signal. Tess was getting around Sarah's involvement by using her as a Confidential Informant, and Sarah had never felt dirtier. If Julia turned up and was arrested, that made Sarah a grass, and she knew her father would never have agreed to that. If word leaked that Sarah and her crew had set Julia up to be arrested, they would be ruined. *What the fuck was she doing?*

But then again, they were dealing with a dangerous woman. Murder was not a game of cards. This had to be done. Sarah had to know for sure that Julia had killed three people, but most of all she had to know why.

'Ruby Salter,' Julia lied, holding out a hand. Sarah didn't take it. She smiled. 'I heard you were looking for someone with a very specific skillset.'

'I don't think you're it,' Sarah said dismissively. 'Sorry. I'm sure you'd make a very good magician's assistant though.'

Julia laughed. It was throaty and a little disarming. Sarah

was expecting she'd have a 'tinkled like broken glass' kind of laugh. Dad always said she read too much.

'You want me to at least show you something? Or have you decided to judge a book by its cover? I'd have thought you'd be better than that.'

She was right. Sarah did know better than to judge someone's worth, intelligence, or innocence, by how they looked, and yet she still couldn't bring herself to believe that she was staring at a cold-blooded killer. What had this woman been through that had taken her so far away from what Sarah was? Or perhaps Julia was just more like Frank Jacobs than Sarah had ever been. Perhaps she never would have questioned him, forced him to think about morals in the marks they hit. Who would Frank have been if Julia had been the daughter who stayed? Was this really the dark version of her own self staring her in the face?

'Touché,' Sarah said eventually. 'Go on then.'

'Why don't you check your pockets? You had a wallet in there, right?'

Sarah sighed. It was disappointing, really, that the woman that killed her father would turn out to be a second-rate pickpocket. She lifted her wallet out of her pocket and placed it on the table. 'You mean I *have* a wallet in there.'

'Aw, shucks.' Julia grinned. 'So I guess I have one of those cute calling cards in mine.' She turned her pockets inside out and feigned shock when they were empty. 'No, wait! Where *could* it be?'

She motioned to Sarah's wallet with her eyes. When Sarah didn't react, she repeated the gesture, more animated. 'This is where you open the wallet,' she whispered.

Sarah flipped open her wallet. A rectangular white card stared up at her from one of the card slots. She smiled wryly. 'Okay, very neat. You have my attention.' She indicated the seat in front of the desk. 'Have a seat and tell me about yourself, *Ruby*.'

She didn't react to the sarcasm as Sarah said her name.

'I grew up with travellers,' Julia said, sitting down as instructed. Sarah crossed the room and sat down opposite her, glancing again at the drawer where the gun was hidden. 'I was raised by my great-aunt after my mother ran off with a townie.'

Sarah barely managed to veil her surprise. She nodded. 'Go on.'

'I left the fair when I was sixteen. Lived from place to place, just floating around, picking pockets and making street hustles until I was taken on by a magician. No lie,' she said quickly, as she saw Sarah's eyebrows rise. 'You were right when you said I'd make a good magician's assistant. I was. Good, I mean. I was small enough and thin enough to twist myself into his contraptions without getting stuck or getting my head lopped off. And I'm fast.'

'So why did you leave?'

'I wanted to find my family.'

Her words landed exactly where she aimed them, and for the first time it really hit Sarah that she was sitting opposite her sister. *Her flesh and blood.* Ever since Tess had abandoned her, all she had wanted was a sibling, someone to talk to about the crazy life she lived. If her dad hadn't turned Julia away, how different things could have been. He would be alive, for a start. And she wouldn't be alone. But she wouldn't have Tess back either.

And just how Frank could have denied that Julia was his daughter when she turned up on his doorstep was beyond Sarah. She was a beautiful mix of both her parents, with the bohemian beauty that Sarah had seen in pictures of her mother, and her father's strength and wits. Sarah wondered what Julia thought of her, a pale imitation of both mother and father when Julia was clearly the real deal. Sarah could never have pulled off what Julia had with these murders. Despite learning a hundred illusions and street hustles at Frank's knee, Sarah had never worked with a real stage magician, or had to fend for herself the way Julia had. She had barely left Brighton, while Julia must have travelled all over the country. Was Sarah a disappointment as a sister?

'Your family?'

'Yes. But by the time I found them, my mother was gone. But I knew I still had a sister.'

'Lucky you. You realize that having a family in this game just hinders you? Most of us are alone, we only have each other.' Sarah fought to keep her voice even as she said those words. She'd learned that truth the hard way.

'I know.'

Sarah wondered for a moment if the pain she could see in Julia's eyes was real. But she listened to her tell her story.

'It doesn't matter. My dad didn't want anything to do with me. He said he didn't believe I was his daughter, but I think he just didn't want to admit his wife had lied to him, kept me a secret all these years.'

'I'm sure she had her reasons,' Sarah murmured, but it was a question she'd been asking ever since Mac had told her the story. Okay, so Lily had been young when Julia was born, and she understood that her traveller family had made the choice for her. But what about after Sarah was born? Julia would have been three, her father training to be a lawyer – they weren't kids any more. Why did Lily never look for her daughter? Even when she knew she was dying, she didn't tell their father the truth. Sarah didn't understand it.

She cleared her throat. 'What makes you want to work with us?'

'Because you're the best.' Admiration filled Julia's voice. 'Harrow – that's the magician I worked with when I ran away from my aunt – he took a liking to me, taught me everything he knew about illusion. He was into mentalism, like I'd heard my mum was. I spent hours studying it. Then my uncle found out I was working with Harrow and came to get me, so I ran away again. I fell in with a group of grifters and that's when I learned all they knew about short cons. But everyone knows, if you really want to know the best tricks, you learn from Frank Jacobs. He never lets anyone in, keeps his family close. So when I heard he was looking for someone . . . it's all I ever wanted. A family, like yours.'

So she didn't know that it was Frank who died in that hotel room. It had been an accident after all, just as Mac had suspected. Julia honestly thought she was applying to work for her father. Sarah wondered what she expected to happen when Frank saw her – he'd slammed the door on her once; what made her think he wouldn't react the exact same way the second time?

'Wait, your mum was a mentalist?'

Julia nodded. 'That's what she did in the fair. Before she ran away to go back to my father. Mind reading, hypnotism, that was her act. She was a "psychic".' Julia inverted her fingers around the word 'psychic'.

'I didn't know that,' Sarah murmured.

'Why would you?' Julia asked. An amused smile crossed her face. 'She was *my* mother.'

'So you want to work with Frank Jacobs?' Sarah said, suddenly angry that this woman knew more about her mum than she did. 'Well, there's something you should know.' Her voice was harsh, her words clipped. 'I'm surprised you don't know already but it'll be common enough knowledge before long. Frank Jacobs is dead. Gone.' The words hurt to say them out loud again. 'He was shot in a hotel room. We think by one of our rivals who set him up to be there. That's why we have space on our crew. We're looking for a replacement for my dad.'

Julia froze. She looked like she was going to scream; her face was ashen and her mouth opened slightly, her breathing coming fast and sharp. *Oh God,* Sarah thought. *I hope she doesn't throw up.*

'Hey, are you okay? You need me to call someone? I have a guy downstairs; he can take you—'

'No,' Julia gasped. 'I'm fine. I just . . .' She gripped the edge of the desk. 'I'm sorry,' she said, her words coming out in a rush. 'This is a terrible mistake. I'm not the person you're looking for.'

Sarah opened the drawer, lifted out the gun and placed it on the table, pointing towards the other woman. She laid her hand on top of it and looked from the deadly weapon to her sister. 'I think you're *exactly* who we're looking for. Sit down please, Julia.'

Julia did as she was told and, keeping her eyes on the gun,

lowered herself slowly into the chair in front of Sarah. Sarah leaned forwards and pressed the button on the microphone taped to the underside of the table. Tess should now be able to hear everything they were saying.

'So you know who I am,' Julia said, giving a small nod. She seemed more composed, now that all the cards were on the table. 'How much more do you know?'

'Everything. That's what you wanted, wasn't it? You wanted me to figure it all out. The butterfly was called the "sister", for God's sake. The ring in the desk? Booking the hotel room in my name? Tell me, were you trying to get me sent down for murder, or was that just a side benefit? Did you want to take my place in the family altogether?'

'Don't be stupid,' Julia said. 'You know there was never any real evidence against you – no forensics, nothing that any decent lawyer, especially your fancy Castro, wouldn't rip to pieces. I just wanted your attention.'

'Oh, you got that all right,' Sarah said. 'I was arrested for murder. And how, pray tell, were you expecting me to figure out the trail of clues you left for me? If you hadn't noticed, I'm not on Sussex Major Investigation Team.'

Julia snorted. 'Could've fooled me.'

'All right,' Sarah conceded. 'But that was a fluke, a coincidence. Who were you expecting to work out your little riddles if I hadn't had access to the crime scene?'

'I figured you'd find your way onto the scene one way or another. But if you hadn't, no big deal.' She shrugged. 'The ring and all that was just an extra little flourish. Anyway, I was fairly sure Tess would think of you when she saw that scene. Not to mention I put up no less than nine signs and posters on the drive to the scene that had some variation of *Find Sarah,* or *Jacobs can help.* She was primed to the hilt to call you. The only three books on Shaun Mitchell's shelves were *The Puzzle Cube* by Sarah Clarke, a *Slow Cooker Cookbook* by Sarah Jacobs and *Solve the Equation, Save the World* by Charles Jacobs. I literally fed you to her.'

'Jesus Christ.'

'Julia Jacobs, actually. Although I grew up with Mum's name. I've been integrating myself into your world for the last two years, waiting to introduce myself to Frank and become part of the family. He knew, you know. He knew that everything I was saying was true. He knew I was his daughter, his flesh and blood. And he was too afraid to let me in. Afraid of what *you* might think, *what you might find out.* So I used everything I'd seen, everything I'd discovered, to take your revenge for you, to show him what I could do.'

Sarah's eyes flickered to the corner of the desk where the tape recorder was hidden. Shit, she had to steer Julia away from the topic of revenge. All she needed was to get her to admit she killed three men, then Tess could get in here and take over before she spilled their darkest secret.

'So you killed those men? And Dad?'

'Frank was an accident,' Julia said, her eyes shining with tears. 'But the other two were for you. It was all for you.'

Chapter Fifty-Four

'For me?' Sarah almost glanced at where the microphone was transmitting her every word, but forced herself to keep her eyes on Julia. If this was Julia's attempt to fit her up and take Sarah down with her, she could think again.

'I wanted your attention. To prove I was good enough for your family. *My family.* I fed Tess the information she needed to the people she used to find you. I'd seen you mapping out the melon drop three times at the same time of day. I just had someone tell Tess that if she went to North Street at that time, she'd find you sooner or later. I didn't know she was going to pull her own little charade on you, however. Julia raised her eyebrows. 'Do you still think any of what happened to you was a coincidence?'

Sarah sat back in her chair, momentarily stunned at the arrogance of this woman. 'Are you trying to tell me that my meeting with Tess was your doing? What if I hadn't even seen her little performance?'

Julia smiled. 'When you put out the call to set this little trap, you said you were looking for an illusionist. You were wrong. I'm much more than that, Sarah. And clearly you have no idea who you're dealing with yet.' She made a move to reach inside her leather jacket and Sarah froze, forgetting completely about the gun on the table. Julia lifted her hands in the air and with one finger opened her jacket.

'Just my mobile.' She lifted it out and placed it on the table. 'Did you ever break concentration on a con before, Sarah?'

Sarah frowned. 'I don't know what you're talking about.'

Julia pressed something on her mobile phone and a song from *The Greatest Showman* began to play. Something jumped inside Sarah's head. 'It's called "The Other Side",' Julia informed her. When she spoke next her voice transformed completely, she sounded younger. *'I can never find it when I need it. You'd think I'd learn and put it in the other side, or inside my jacket or something.'*

The words sounded so familiar, yet Sarah couldn't place them. Then . . .

Sarah snapped her fingers. 'You were in the doorway when I was waiting for Friedman. On the melon drop con, where I ran into Tess that first time . . .'

Julia smiled. 'The other side? Inside my jacket? And where were you looking, when DI Fox's partner went to pull his phone out of his jacket? Maybe . . . at the *other side* of the street, at the man with his hand *inside his jacket*?'

Sarah pictured the scene that day on North Street. Why had she looked across the street at the moment she had seen Tess? Was it because of a few words muttered at the right moment? And if it was, then she had been right about her insane theory . . .

'You convinced Shaun Mitchell to jump.'

'That was even easier.' Julia pulled a face. 'What a fucking idiot he was. Drugged up so much of the time that he didn't know what was real and what wasn't. But what he did know was that there were people after him most of the time.'

'So you planted a speaker in the vent of his flat. Wes found it yesterday. That's what the CCTV outage was for. Out of interest, what did you play?'

Julia swiped through her phone again. The sound of banging filled the room, a hammering on the door. Voices were yelling at Shaun to come out. Then a long high beep and a lower, softer voice. *The only way out is to climb over the balcony. Use the drainpipe. You can't get away from them. It's the only way . . .* and more of the beep, then voices and banging again.

Sarah shook her head. 'I can't believe that stuff really works. I had my suspicions that you'd used some auditory hallucination to get him to jump but jeesh.'

'It doesn't work on its own. Not without months of priming to those beeps feeding the suggestions, and fuelling the paranoia that someone was after him. He was all in – you saw that he'd boarded up the door, he was so certain someone was going to try to get in. I was taught by the best.'

'I've never believed in that mentalism bullshit,' Sarah said.

Julia spread her hands. 'And yet here I am, and here you are.'

'No thanks to you. I was arrested for murder, remember? I should be in prison.'

'But they couldn't keep you in there. Can't you see? We're the same, you and me. We're soulmates.'

'Except I never killed a person in my life.'

Julia raised her eyebrows, as though she was about to contest Sarah's words, but she didn't. 'Those men deserved to die. They tried to kill you.'

'And how exactly did you know about that? No one knew about what happened to me.'

'The whole family knew all along. Frank made them keep quiet about it. Mac told me – don't get mad at him; I spiked his drink and used some of my best interrogation tactics. I could teach you mentalism, you know – it's so useful. He said he'd had to convince Frank not to kill them. That's why he was so careful to protect you, spying on your boyfriends and so on. I thought you'd both be pleased they were dead.'

Oh, this just got better and better.

'You are a fucking psychopath,' Sarah spat. 'I don't hate anyone enough to have them killed. Except maybe you.'

Julia flinched, as though Sarah's words had made physical contact.

'I just wanted you to think I was clever,' she said. 'I just thought—'

'You thought that framing me for murder was a good way to engineer a family reunion?'

'I told you I never wanted you to be arrested! I just wanted to get your attention. Those men were fair game. I thought you'd see what I did and we'd turn a corner as a family. How was I supposed to know that stupid cow would arrest you?'

Tess won't like that, Sarah thought. She wondered if DI Fox's face was burning red. At least Julia hadn't mentioned the family connection. Sarah needed to get this wrapped up before she said too much and lost Tess her job.

'How did you get my ring, anyway?' Sarah asked, leading the subject away from Tess.

'Mac. I told him it was our mother's, and that I wanted to get the same one made for myself. He believed me. Said Frank must have believed me too because it was obvious I was Lily's daughter just looking at me. I said that if I told Frank that Mum had left the same ring with me as she gave to you then he couldn't deny it any more. He had no idea Mum had never even seen that ring. From your old boyfriend, was it?'

'Well, now we don't have a mum or a dad.' Her throat tightened at the words. 'What? Didn't you know? Mum died too. Cancer. When I was three.'

Julia looked confused, shook her head. 'Did Frank tell you that? It's not true.'

'Afraid so,' Sarah replied. 'Just you and me now, *sis*.'

Julia let the words sink in, then stood up, as though hearing of her mother's death had given her new strength. Perhaps it was because she knew she truly had nothing to lose any more. She had no one left.

'Fine, so you've got me,' she said. 'What do we do now? You going to snake on me? Are you an informant now, Sarah?'

It was a question she'd asked herself a dozen times, but coming from her, the woman who'd killed her dad, the words hit a nerve, making something inside her snap. She reached under the table and yanked the wire from the microphone, cutting the feed. Tess would be in there as soon as she worked out the mic wasn't working. She only had a couple of minutes, but two minutes was long enough.

'Don't talk to me like that, like you know me. You *don't* know me. You don't know anything about me.'

Julia's eyes flashed, and in that instant she looked just like Frank. 'That's where you're wrong, dear sister. I know more about you than any of your so-called family. We're blood, and we're more alike than you realize.'

'You think you know me so well?' Sarah stood up sharply, the chair spinning to one side and in seconds she was standing behind her, the gun jammed into her neck. 'Fine. You've got ten seconds to say something that will stop me pulling this trigger and making it look like self-defence.'

Sarah was expecting her to go with the family angle – 'all they have left is each other' crap. Perhaps she would tell her she loved her. If she really was anything like Sarah, she'd challenge her to do it and hope she chickened out. Maybe Tess and her team would burst through the door and Sarah would be arrested for real. At this exact point in time, after everything she'd lost, she didn't care.

But Sarah had forgotten that her sister was *much* cleverer than her.

'Who do you think taught me how to influence people's minds, predict their choices?' Julia asked. Mac's words ran through Sarah's mind. *Your mother had a way of knowing how to handle people, how to get them to do exactly what she wanted and make them think it was their idea. She was obsessed with learning about people, about the way our minds worked.*

Julia smiled. 'Dad might have been the master con artist, but Mum was the mentalist. She taught me everything. *Our mother isn't dead.* And I know where she is.'

Chapter Fifty-Five

The line went dead and Tess looked at Jerome in disbelief. 'Has it gone completely?' she demanded. 'Did it lose signal? What happened?'

The red light appeared, and the unit began to beep.

'The connection's been cut,' Jerome said, opening the car door. 'Something's wrong.'

'Let's move in,' Tess said, climbing out of the passenger side. She took off her radio. 'Campbell, come in? Have you seen anything your side? We've lost connection.'

'No one in or out here, guv,' came the reply. 'We've had eyes on the entrance the whole time.'

As they ran towards the building they saw Wes emerge, pulling a small wheeled trolley behind him.

'What's going on up there?' Tess demanded. 'We lost signal.'

Wes looked confused. 'No idea. I was downstairs pretending to audition wannabe magicians and conjurers. Sarah is upstairs on her own with Julia.' His eyebrows rose in concern. 'You lost communication? So she's up there with a murderer and no one can hear what's going on?'

Tess pushed past him into the building and her team followed. Her heart pounded in time with her footsteps as they slammed against the stairs, each slap echoing up the empty stairwell.

'What floor are they on, guv?' Jerome asked, as he moved to run ahead.

'Six,' Mac's voice came from behind them. 'And for fucksake hurry up.'

The door to the office crashed open and Tess appeared in the doorway. 'What happened?' she asked, scanning the empty room.

Sarah gripped the edge of the table, pulling herself up. The side of her head was pounding, and she was certain it was already beginning to bruise.

'She attacked me,' Sarah said. 'I must have blacked out for a minute. Did you catch her?'

'Catch her? I didn't even see her. She never came past us.' She glanced at Jerome. 'Did she?'

'She must have done,' Sarah snapped. 'The only other way out is the window.'

DS Morgan crossed the room and peered out of the window. 'It's a sixty-foot drop. No balcony in sight. There's no way she could have got out through there.'

'Maybe someone caught her.'

Jerome threw Sarah a scowl. She got the impression they weren't going to be best friends.

'Jerome, get down there – take Fahra,' Tess demanded. 'We'll search the other offices. Better call it in – we have a homicide suspect on the run – get as many people as you can on it. Jerome, I want you to co-ordinate the search, check every garden, empty houses, the lot. Get a team in this office block and secure the perimeter – if she's in there I want her trapped.'

Jerome nodded. 'Yes, boss.'

'Then, get a statement drafted for the press. We want people looking for this woman. Arrange a briefing. I'm going to have to call Oswald.'

Jerome nodded and turned to race off down the corridor – Sarah resisted the urge to shout *there's a good boy* to his retreating back.

When he'd gone, Tess turned to Sarah. Her face was unusually blank – Sarah had expected her to be furious.

'I guess she's had enough time?' Tess asked.

Sarah blinked. 'Enough time for what?'

'To get away,' Tess said. Sarah took a step back. 'She couldn't have been comfortable folded up into that tiny case,' Tess continued. 'The kind of trick only a magician's assistant can pull off. I hope you didn't make Wes pull her down six flights of stairs in that thing.'

Sarah's tongue felt as though it was stuck to the roof of her mouth. For perhaps the first time in her life, she was speechless.

'You knew?' Sarah finally managed to get her words out. 'I don't understand?'

'Come on, Sarah. To con a grifter, you always have to be two steps ahead – four if you can. It's in my blood as well, remember?'

Seeing her confusion, Tess held up an earpiece. 'I bugged the room. While everyone else was listening to your wire, which conveniently cut out just before she attacked you – I heard the rest of what happened.'

Sarah leaned back against the stone wall, her heart pounding. 'You mean you knew she was in that case the whole time? Why would you let Wes just wheel her out?'

Tess was silent for some time. She was staring at something in her hand, and Sarah realized it was her warrant card. Eventually she spoke.

'It's like Mac said. If I'd caught her sooner, our dad would still be alive.'

Sarah started to speak but Tess held up her hand. 'Don't. I know you don't blame me but that doesn't stop me blaming myself. I never got to know Frank because of my own stubbornness and unwillingness to accept who he was. You haven't known your mum all these years through no fault of your own, and I think you deserve answers. I had a split-second to decide, and I went with my instinct. If she kills someone else because of that . . .'

'I don't think she will,' Sarah said. 'She said she killed Mitchell and Rodgers to prove her loyalty to us. I believed her.'

'And about your mum being alive? You believe that too?'

Sarah shrugged. Her eyes showed her pain. 'I don't know. I don't know why Dad would lie to me, but if there's the smallest chance she's telling the truth, then I have to find her.'

Tess pulled her half-sister into her arms and Sarah allowed herself to be hugged. It felt so natural, her big sister. Eventually Tess pulled back and held her at arm's length.

'So what happens when you find your mum? You just hand Julia over to us, simple as that?'

Sarah nodded. 'She killed our dad. Whether she meant

342

to or not, I can't forgive that. I know she's got to face the consequences.'

'I hope that's true, Sarah. Because I haven't let her get away for good – I've bought you some time to find your mum. Julia killed three people and she has to be held accountable for what she's done. Sooner rather than later.'

'I know,' Sarah said firmly. 'I know, Tess. I want her to be held accountable too. I promise.'

But even as she said the words, she was wondering if it would be that easy. Wondering if one day she'd have to make the choice between her sisters, and when the time came, if she was going to make the right one.

Acknowledgements

This book has been a long time coming, and so it is inevitable that there will be people I should thank along the way whose names have long gone from memory, but I'll do my best.

First, as always in the ten years I have been under her wing, my thanks go to my agent, Laetitia Rutherford. When I approached her with an idea that wasn't the psychological thriller that I was contracted to write, but instead a self-indulgent, super fun locked-room Jonathan Creek meets Hustle idea, I more than half expected her to tell me to find another agent. Instead, her enthusiasm and love for the project spurred me on, even when I felt I might have bitten off more than I could chew. You have inspired me, edited me, championed me and no doubt apologised for me, thank you. To Ciara McEllin, whose emails are fifty percent payments and fifty percent tax forms, thanks for keeping me fed and legal.   And to Rachel Richardson, for bringing my books to a wider audience.

To the team at HQ, first of course the delightful Cicely Aspinall with her infectious smile and boundless enthusiasm for not just *Three Card Murder* but the entire world of Sarah, Tess and their friends. And if it takes a village, etc, at HQ we have a city. Thanks go to Seema Mitra, Kirsty Capes, Becci Mansell and Kate Oakley for keeping me on schedule, filling my social calendar and producing the work of art that is the cover of this book. My thanks to Katie Lumsden for an excellent proofread.

Thanks go to The Woman Behind The Bar in the Black Dove, Brighton, who gave me a history lesson (and a ghost story!) about their 'secret' room. To Ceri Flavell who put up with much talk of this book, and loaned me the books that Sarah made her living from (which I realise I never returned). To all the YouTubers whose content enabled me to learn the three card monte (don't ask me to do it, my chubby fingers are not cut out for street magic).

To the bloggers and magazine feature writers who make cover reveals, publication days and blog tours both magical and terrifying. I can't possibly name you all but you honestly make this job worth it. Special thanks to Nina Pottell and Teresa Nikolic (who reminds me when my publication days are).

Writing can be a lonely old job, but luckily I write crime, and therefore have the constant support and procrastination of a very special group of people. Particular thanks to Lucy Dawson, Susi Holliday and Kat Diamond who are always there in a crisis and sometimes also when I'm trying to work/ clean my house/sleep. May I forever wake up to your incessant ramblings. And it doesn't come more supportive than my own personal cheerleaders, Jo Jones, Sarah Bevan and Lorna Hounsell. I could go on listing people who have supported me, I've known nothing but support from family and friends my entire publishing journey – in fact a lot of people believed in me before I did – but the music is playing me off and the curtains are dropping. To my mum and dad – I love you so much, you are wonderful and you did a great job on me.

Lastly, of course, thank you to Ash, who I can confirm does know the names of at least three of my books, and does a better job of putting up with me than anyone else would have. To Connor and Finn, without you my house would be cleaner, my fridge fuller but my heart emptier. Love you all.

And to the people who bought and read this book, if you've got this far, THANK YOU BOTH.